PRAISE FOR *OUR* 1

"In this spirited coming-of-age ....,
renders Josh and his fellow middle-school misfits as they seek
understanding and acceptance in a world that wishes only to trap
them into a stifling conformity. *Our Bodies Electric* is poignant and
comic, and Vernon's linking Walt Whitman's celebration of indi-
viduality to the characters adds to the novel's pleasures."

—Ron Rash, author of *The Caretaker, Serena,* and *In the Valley*

"Take one strong-willed and curious kid and set him spinning
through a tumultuous adolescence in small-town South Carolina.
Mix in sea turtles, Walt Whitman, surly waitresses, a snake charm-
er, and more than a few scorching summer days, et voila! You've
got the unforgettable, enjoyable, and heartfelt *Our Bodies Electric.*
The specificity of Josh and his friends—and their hijinks—on
Pawleys Island are a lot of fun, but it's also a special treat to see
Vernon speak about one young person's journey and recognize
something universal: the challenges and hard-fought rewards of
figuring out who you want to be in the world."

—Emily Nemens, author of *The Cactus League*

"I haven't heard music so sweet and heartfelt since I first read
Lewis Nordan. Imagine a novel that sings like a love-drunk cross
between *The Perks of Being a Wallflower* and *The Breakfast Club.*
Now imagine it set in the sweltering heat of lowcountry South
Carolina. Now imagine it told in the spirit of Walt Whitman.
Now imagine that book in your hands."

—Mark Powell, author of *Hurricane Season* and *The Late Rebellion*

"In this debut novel, Zack Vernon renders the awkward, glorious
gauntlet of adolescence with wild tenderness. We come alongside Josh in his wrestle with a rigid theology, his flutterings of
first love, and his passage through coming-of-age rites inflected

by the offbeat, small-town culture of Pawleys Island, South Carolina. In one chapter, we're cracking up over the shenanigans of young teens; in the next, we're delighting in the realization that the body 'was not a font of shame, nor was it a frail mechanism made of meat. It was a sparkling funhouse.' More than anything, this book is about the miracle of the body beloved."

—Jessie Van Eerdan, author of *Call It Horses*

"In Zack Vernon's *Our Bodies Electric*, young protagonist Josh navigates the relentless world of ever-watchful parents and oddball friends, forever obsessed and enamored by the endless beauties of All Things Female. Josh is curious, intelligent, and intent on doing what's right. How could so many plans go wrong? This is one heart-rending, comedic coming-of-age novel."

—George Singleton, author of *The Curious Lives of Nonprofit Martyrs*

"*Our Bodies Electric* tickled my funny bone and my heart. Every page flickers with profound sincerity and indelible strangeness. I want to hug Josh and Chloe—and Zackary Vernon for writing such a beautiful story about the splendor and sadness of growing up. I only wish this book would've existed during my adolescence."

—Caleb Johnson, author of *Treeborne*

"Zackary Vernon's debut novel, *Our Bodies Electric*, is not only excruciatingly funny, but also a powerfully imaginative tour-de-force of endearing teenager Josh's attempts to come to grips with the tyranny and impulses of his body—in face of his mother's edict: 'A mind full of sex is like a mind full of maggots.' Indeed, Vernon's sentences crackle with electricity; and, often, the emotional and sexual voltage is simply too much for Josh—who swelters in every valence of that word in the South Carolina Lowcountry that Vernon knows so well and dishes up so memorably. It's like a jolt from a 220 line—Walt Whitman hovering wryly in benediction over every syllable." "

—Joseph Bathanti, author of *The Act of Contrition*

OUR BODIES ELECTRIC

Zackary Vernon

Fitzroy Books

Published by Fitzroy Books
An imprint of
Regal House Publishing, LLC
Raleigh, NC 27605
All rights reserved

https://fitzroybooks.com
Printed in the United States of America

ISBN -13 (paperback): 9781646034574
ISBN -13 (epub): 9781646034581
Library of Congress Control Number: 2023943402

Cover images and design by © C. B. Royal

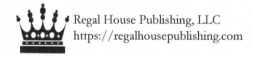

Regal House Publishing, LLC
https://regalhousepublishing.com

The following is a work of fiction created by the author. All names, individuals, characters, places, items, brands, events, etc. were either the product of the author or were used fictitiously. Any name, place, event, person, brand, or item, current or past, is entirely coincidental.

Printed in the United States of America

For my high school English teacher, Mary Ginny DuBose, who gave us Whitman and taught the outcasts of Pawleys Island to celebrate ourselves.

1

THE PARADE ELECTRIC

The old gray maestro sets his beard South, the leader of this open-
ranked parade.
He tramps along, his only signs a black cloak, rakish hat, sound
shoes, and baton fresh cut from the forest.

Sound forth the reveille. Peal the familiar cry once more.
Come up the bugles, you the fifers; and what of you drummers?
Bang the gong, and set the children to dancing.

A crowd, feet pounding, heeds the call, cutlasses lashing and
pennants aflutter.
Bayonets glint in the sun, rifles and cannons crack and thud.
Hurrahs, huzzahs, and welcome-clapping hands.
Shouldering their duds, the people come forth, join up, and fetch
more as they go.

A boy leaves off loafing and makes his egress from the home of
his youth.
Feeling pangs of music in mad-sweet bursts as they fill him full,
he assumes his place among the crowd.
For this cabaret, no solemn cortege, is for the boy, his feet of the
waves and hair the sky.
In the turning sun, the boy is a-sparkle, no longer merely made of
meat and dust.

The old man eyes him, seeing through broadcloth and gingham.
Taking him by the hand, the man proclaims,
    Long enough have you waded in the shallows;
    leap forth and a bold swimmer you will be;
    know wickedness and virtue, and be fond of each.

Untold gibbering congeries sweep in on the boy, a
   flashing phantasmagoria.
All about him, the timpani roar, the brass boils, and snare drums
   pepper a beat.
The labial sound spreads as a cantatrice sings from the madding
   crowd, setting all flesh to quiver.

A new rhythm from the drummers is fitted for the boy, and the old
   graybeard trills a joyful madness,
A soiree to corroborate the spirit of this silly child, to promulge his
   body among the high steppers.
From Paumanok to Pawleys Island, and from Mannahatta to
   Myrtle Beach, on they go, spinning to fulfill his foray.
From top to toe, the boy sings.

Breach born, backwards, and yet he now marches on,
   incandescent in the light of day.
He rises in the parade, as if from mud, to nibble the sacred cheese
   of life,
To grow his bones and place upon them a worthy rind,
To do his meed of good for the greater brood of man and fowl and
   beast.

As the sun wheels overhead and his flesh-machine runs smoothly
   on, apparitions appear beside him.
The maestro commands the crowd and possesses the boy,
   screaming the world go hang.
Tattooing the road with their bewildered dance, godless gods all,
   they march forever onward in the parade electric.

SIXTH GRADE

2

THE QUICKENING

Josh was home alone with his father, who was pushing a lawnmower across the backyard. The grass grew almost knee high. Josh watched him pull wildly on the starter cord. The mower kept cranking and then sputtering out like an emphysemic's rattling cough. He pulled again: crank, cough, silence. He kicked the mower and said, "Shit."

Josh was supposed to be watering his mother's flower garden on the back patio. This was the summer before sixth grade, and his mother was trying to teach him about responsibility. "High time you grow up," she kept saying.

As he filled a watering can, he examined the dirt at the foundation of the house where a broken spigot continually dripped. An earthworm emerged, and Josh picked it up and let it dangle and twist. He then placed it gently in a nest of mud.

"Josh," his dad said. "We have to take this mower to the shop. Come help me lift it into the truck."

Josh lingered, staring at the writhing earthworm. Out of the corner of his eye, he saw a roly-poly meandering along the dirt just outside of the nest. He picked it up and, without thinking, popped it in his mouth and swallowed.

"Josh," his father yelled.

"Coming."

&

They left Pawleys Island and drove past Georgetown and way out into the country. After the blacktop gave way to gravel, they turned into a narrow driveway next to a hand-painted sign that read *Charlie's Small Engine Repair*. The roadside was choked with kudzu as far as the eye could see.

Charlie stood in the yard outside of an old trailer, baby blue except for the rust spots. The yard was full of dead lawnmowers, and there was a soggy mattress on the ground that looked like it had once been on fire.

Josh and his father sat in the truck with the windows down, watching two barking Dobermans dash out from under the trailer until their chains snapped them back.

"Shut up, Hooter; shut up, Cooter," Charlie yelled. "What say?" he asked, as Josh and his father got out of the truck and met him in the muddy yard. The air was wafting the smell of rotten eggs from the paper mill down in Georgetown.

Charlie wore frayed jean shorts and nothing else. His stomach hung low over the shorts like a tight sack of flour, and his belly button stuck out bigger than a golf ball.

"Charlie, the mower's acting up again."

"Well," Charlie said. "We'll get her looked at."

Josh could not stop staring at his belly button.

"Thing is," his father said, "I need it back by tomorrow. My wife's having her church ladies over for dinner, and she'll kill me if the grass isn't cut. The neighbors are mad too. Somebody's already called the HOA."

Charlie looked down at Josh. "What the hell are you staring at?"

"Whoa," his father said, stepping forward. "There's no need to curse in front of the kid."

"He looks old enough to handle it."

"He acts younger than his age sometimes."

"Well, tell him to stop looking at me like a freak."

Josh turned away. He was staring now at the giant Confederate flag that Charlie had mounted on the porch of the trailer.

"There's something off about that boy," Charlie said. "Kindly gives me the heebie-jeebies."

"Yeah, he does that," his father said, grabbing Josh by the shoulder. "It's not polite to stare, son."

Josh nodded, and the two men went back to talking about the lawnmower. Within a few moments, Josh's eyes were again locked on the belly button. He was trying to determine if there was a single wrinkle in that tight ball of flesh.

Charlie stopped talking and looked back at Josh, who didn't even realize the men's conversation had halted.

"He's goddamned doing it again," Charlie said. He bent down, and Josh started, stumbling backward when the eye-level belly button was replaced by Charlie's face a few inches from his own.

"What are you looking at?"

Josh glanced up at his father who just shrugged.

"What?" Charlie asked again.

"I've never," Josh said, "seen an outie before."

Charlie straightened up and laughed, running his hand over his belly. "Well, that's queer as hell, kid. But I guess this ole belly button is a sight. Sometimes I forget about it."

"How'd it get like that?"

Charlie thought for a second and said, "One day I was at the beach, and my girlfriend wanted me to blow up one of those big floaty rafts. She'd just bought it at the gas station. The thing was green and had an alligator's head at one end, kinda like a pillow. I was there blowing and blowing, and I was so out of breath at one point that I told her I needed a break. Well, she got this sad look on her face, very disappointed like. So I kept on blowing. When the raft was full and getting right taut, I blew one final time, real hard. I strained and emptied all the air from my lungs. Then I heard a tee-tiny pop like opening a Coke. I thought at first the raft had busted. But then I looked down, and my belly button was exactly how you see it today."

Charlie winked at Josh's father.

"Is that true?" Josh asked.

"Honest Injun," Charlie said, putting his hand on his heart.

Josh was trying hard to look at the man's face and not his belly button.

"Hey, you wanna see something real cool?" Charlie walked across the dirt yard and banged on the metal side of the trailer. "Darleen, get out here."

A few seconds later, a woman younger than Charlie waddled out of the trailer and into the yard. Hooter and Cooter stood up straight and looked solemn and respectful. The woman was tall and skinny, but her belly was clearly swollen with child. Her large T-shirt formed a tent, and her legs looked like wooden baseball bats falling out below.

Standing next to Charlie, she reached over and tucked his hair behind his ear.

"Honey, my little buddy here is a fan of belly buttons. Would you mind showing him yours?"

Darleen looked at Charlie reluctantly, but he smiled, and she pulled her shirt up and revealed her stomach. Her belly button stood out as if at attention. Josh stared at the two of them, Darleen and Charlie, their twin bellies and buttons. Darleen's face gleamed, as did Charlie's.

"Almost nine months now," she said.

Josh tore his eyes away. "Wait, you're pregnant?"

They all three laughed, and she looked down at him sweetly. "Yeah, honey, I am."

Josh said, "Neat."

"You wanna touch it?" she asked.

His father took a step closer, now partially between Josh and Darleen. "You don't have to do that."

"I really don't mind."

"Please, Dad," Josh said. Darleen nodded, and his father stepped back.

Josh felt unchained, bonny and free, as he reached out his hand. Her belly was firmer than he had expected, like an over-filled waterbed. It sprang back to his touch.

"We're just waiting on the quickening now," she said.

"What's that?" His hand was tracing a small circle around her belly button.

"It's the moment when the baby decides she's ready to come out. My momma always said it was like a bunch of butterflies fluttering around and threatening to take off."

❧

As they were driving home, Josh's stomach began to ache. He bent over on the bench seat of the truck and groaned. He rolled down the window but immediately rolled it back up when he smelled the sweet sulfur coming from the paper mill.

"You all right?" his father asked.

"My stomach hurts bad."

"Okay. Just buck up."

"No. It really hurts."

"We'll be home soon."

Josh was rocking back and forth, gripping his stomach with both hands.

"You're fine. We'll be home in just a minute."

"No," Josh said. "There's something you need to know. I ate a roly-poly before we left the house. I swallowed it alive." Josh was groaning again, his stomach aflutter. He put his feet up on the dashboard, spreading them wide.

"Just hold on. Your mom'll know what to do."

"Dad," he said, "it's the quickening."

3

BAKE SALE EXPOSURE

Like most mothers of Pawleys Island in the mid 1990s, Josh's mom ate cottage cheese, drank Weight Watchers shakes, and, when she was feeling saucy, gave herself an extra toot of hair spray. Usually she loved to make dinner, but she hadn't cooked for the family in a week. Instead she was in the kitchen all day and night preparing for the bake sale, her face covered in flour and her apron streaked with dark chocolate.

Bake sales were constant during Josh's childhood. The moms, and occasionally the dads, would get together to hawk brownies and cookies outside local grocery stores to raise money for this or that school function. A proposed trip this fall to Washington, D.C. for the sixth-grade class had recently mobilized a bevy of concerned parents, baking into the wee hours.

Josh's dad ordered pizza every night that week.

On the Saturday morning of the bake sale, Josh's mother was all in a tizzy. There were pastries and cakes on every surface of the kitchen.

"What's for breakfast?" his dad asked, walking breezily into the kitchen.

"Fend for yourself for once," his mother said.

His father looked shocked and then deflated. "Sorry."

"No," she said, her voice softening. "I'm sorry. It's just that floosy Helen—you know, the one who runs the PTA—always sells more than anyone, and for once I'd like to beat her."

Josh was sitting at the kitchen table working on next week's homework. His mother looked over at him. "What does floosy mean?" he asked.

She rubbed her hands together, and flour blossomed in the air. "I didn't say that word, sweetie. You misheard."

Josh shrugged and returned to his long division.

"Go get in the car, Josh," she barked, as she began to stack boxes high in her arms.

When they arrived at the Piggly Wiggly, his mother realized that Helen was not even there, had signed up to work another fundraiser. "Well then," she said, straightening her sweaty hair and beginning to unpack her boxes.

Josh had a habit of balancing on one foot whenever he didn't know what to do with himself. He waved his arms around like a whirligig to keep balance. In front of the Piggly Wiggly, his mother saw him doing this, what she called his "little seagull routine," and said, "Joshua, I need you to act your age. I have work to do."

Other mothers were arriving, carting loads of baked goods. The women helped one another set up, their cakes, cookies, and pies mixing together as the plenty grew. The table was draped with a heavy maroon tablecloth, which fell to the ground on all four sides. The women surrounded the table, worrying over the display, and just before the sale started they pinned a sign to its front that read *Waccamaw Elementary School Bake Sale*.

Josh burrowed under the table, finding a comfortable dark cave there. Occasionally, he would catch a glimpse of a woman's shoe or ankle, but other than that he was alone in the darkness.

His mother was talking louder than all the rest above him. A man must have approached, because Josh heard her say, "Roger, I haven't seen you in ages. Now I know you're going to help our kids go to Washington, D.C. and learn about America's founding."

"I would, but I don't eat sweets."

"Why I've seen you helping yourself to a fair share at our Sunday suppers after church."

"Well, my wife says I need to stay away from sugar for a while. The old ticker, you know."

"In that case, how about a donation?" She laughed flirtatiously. "Surely these ladies are sweet enough."

Josh heard the women cackling above him, and he felt his

first erection coming on. His thoughts drifted to a conversation
he recently had with his mother. "A mind full of sex is like a
mind full of maggots," she'd said.

Under the table it was so dark that he couldn't see his hand
before his face. Desperate for something to divert his attention,
he started feeling the concrete and trying to count the number
of cracks in the sidewalk. He was almost to the end, when a
tunnel of light broke into the cave, and he saw Chloe mooning
in, her long dark hair framing her face.

"My mom says I'm supposed to hang out with you."

Josh and Chloe had always been in the same class. Back in
first grade they had been assigned to be on an "exploratory
team" together when they were studying dinosaurs. At that
time, Josh and Chloe had wondered how to tell a man dinosaur
from a woman dinosaur. They had plastic models of stegosauruses, and they searched them for any sign of genitalia.

"There's nothing to do in here," Josh said, as Chloe moved
into the cave and lowered the cloth behind her, enveloping the
space again in darkness.

"It's like night."

"I've been counting cracks."

He explained that if you went from one side of the cave to
the other, you could feel three deep straight cracks and another
six that zigzagged shallowly across the sidewalk.

"That's really boring," Chloe said.

For a moment, they were silent. Then Chloe leaned in and
whispered, "Let's play a game."

"What?" Josh was already nervous, fearful of anything he
had not planned himself.

"I'm a sick person, like a patient dying in a hospital, and you
have to save me."

"But how?"

"That's for you to figure out. That's the game."

Josh could not see Chloe, but he could sense that she was
now lying down on the sidewalk next to him. He heard a groan
that grew louder and louder, her sickness taking hold.

Josh felt both too old and too young for this game. But he steeled his nerves and forced himself into character. "Ma'am, what seems to be the problem?"

"My stomach hurts," she said, and again Josh heard the groan.

He reached out his hand to touch her stomach. He had expected to feel the material of her shirt, but his hand made contact with naked flesh. He drew back, the feel of it electric. His head was like the inside of a conch shell, and maggots crawled one by one into that empty, roaring space.

Chloe groaned. "My stomach!"

He reached out and again felt her hot flesh.

"Well," he began, "this stomach has a disease in it." Her belly button was a center around which he was making circles.

Chloe giggled. "Don't tickle."

Josh rubbed harder, and periodically he commanded the sickness to "Get out!" like the big tent preacher his granddaddy had once taken him to see. "Get out, thy demon!"

Chloe sat up and said, "All healed."

Josh exhaled. He was just beginning to breathe normally when Chloe asked, "You wanna see it?"

He went rigid, feeling the maggots beginning to twitch again. "The doctor's duty has been—"

"No, not that. Not the game. Do you wanna see *it*?"

He paused. "What?"

"My fanny."

Josh had only a vague notion of what the word meant. A vacation Bible school lesson bubbled up in his memory.

"Yes," he whispered. Chloe was already lowering the zipper of her shorts. He could vaguely discern the elastic pop of an underwear band.

"I can't see it," he said. He started to lift the tablecloth.

"No," Chloe said. "Our moms'll kill us."

"Later then."

"Okay."

❧

At recess on Monday, Josh caught glimpses of Chloe across the jungle gym. She was staring right at him.

When their bug-eyed teacher, Miss Marian, started organizing sides for a game of Red Rover, Chloe ran and grabbed Josh by the hand. It felt like a firecracker going off in his palm. "Come on," she said, leading him away from the group. "We're too old for Red Rover anyway." They walked to a corner of the playground. A puny boy named Spregg, who their parents said was "touched," watched from where he stood at the fenced edge of the yard. He picked a little crusty from his eye and slipped it into his mouth. Josh and Chloe grimaced, but Spregg said nothing. He then flipped his upper eyelids inside out, so that it looked like chicken cutlets bounced above each eyeball.

"Just ignore him. This way," Chloe said, tucking herself into a small structure they called The Igloo. "No one can see us in here."

"Neat," Josh said, following her inside.

Chloe shucked off her pants. They were a buttonless, elastic-banded number, and they came down quickly, undies and all. "See," she whispered.

"It's not what I expected," he said, thinking she looked a bit like the underside of a dolphin.

"Now let me see yours," she said.

Josh's mind was a-buzz, maggots dithering to and fro. "Mine is private."

Chloe glared back at him. "That's not fair."

"My butt then," he offered, lowering his shorts.

"Fine," Chloe said.

Josh quickly gained confidence. What they were doing didn't seem so wrong after all. He imagined an audience comprised not only of Chloe but also of stegosauruses looking on and seeing his bare ass. He shook it in the air, his gangly body doing a little skeleton jig. He wiggled his way into "The Charleston," the only dance he knew.

Josh was about to make each buttock go up and down, when Miss Marian poked her head into The Igloo, her eyes even buggier than usual. "Jesus, I call upon," she exclaimed.

Josh and Chloe were taken to the principal's office and forced to sit in silence while their parents were notified. As they waited, Josh reached out and grabbed Chloe's hand. He had meant to comfort her, to suggest that they were in this together. But she recoiled.

They were eventually separated. Chloe and her mother talked to Miss Marian, while Josh and his mother talked to the principal, Mr. Donaldson.

"I hope you understand the gravity of the situation," Mr. Donaldson said. He had a habit of tugging on his bushy eyebrows whenever he was giving a serious talk. "This is a public school, but we're all Christians here."

Josh's mother shot him an icy glance. "Our house is Christ-centered, I assure you."

She and Mr. Donaldson went on talking for a while, acting the whole time like Josh wasn't there. After they finally left, and he and his mother were in the car alone, she said, "Jesus is so upset with you right now."

He looked out the window, trying to hold the image of Chloe in his mind.

"Do you have nothing to say for yourself?" his mother asked. "Are you just going to sit there in silence?"

He thought for a second and then said, "Does Jesus not like fannies?"

Josh's mother drew in a sharp breath, her face reddening. "Did you say *fannies?*"

"Um."

"I don't want to ever hear you say that word again."

"I'm just wondering."

"Well, don't wonder things like that."

Josh looked out the window and watched the live oaks and

Spanish moss whizzing by. After a while, he asked, "So Jesus would say they're bad?"

His mother exhaled. "Jesus, Joshua. I mean, Jesus would say there's a time and a place."

He nodded, willing the time to be now, the place here.

4

MANEATER

Everyone arrived at First Baptist early on Sundays. While the parents crowded into the sanctuary to nab the best pews, the children of Pawleys Island hung out in the antebellum cemetery that stretched across the rear of the church's property. They frolicked obliviously amongst the graves of the enslaved and slaveholders, hiding behind moss-covered headstones and towering mausoleums.

Josh and his friends were obsessed with reciting ghost stories. Today they were fixated on the tragic tale of Alice Flagg. Josh began, "Alice was a young lady who fell in love with a poor lumberman, who her family said was beneath her." Josh and three others stared down at the grave in front of them, a long slab of marble that lay flat on the ground with just the word ALICE carved into its top.

"They were engaged," Chloe said, "in secret." Josh couldn't keep his eyes off her, so tall and dark against the backdrop of trees draped in Spanish moss.

Mary, a short blond girl who was friends with Chloe, took up the tale. "So she wore her engagement ring on a ribbon around her neck. It was covered by her clothes, and no one knew except for Alice and her one true love."

Josh chimed in. "Alice's family eventually found out, and they tore her away from the lumberman and sent her to Charleston where she slowly began to die of a broken heart."

Ryan, Josh's best friend, stepped forward. He was shorter than Josh and husky, but he was stronger than anyone their age and carried his weight in his shoulders and calves. Ryan's hair was as orange as a squash blossom and cut into the shape of a bowl. The freckles that covered his cheeks and the bridge of his nose were so light they were almost imperceptible. Ryan said, "She was sick and skinny and dying in Charleston."

"So they brought her back to Pawleys Island," Mary said.

"And she grew sicker and sicker," Chloe said.

"When she died, they buried her right here." Ryan's voice boomed, too loud for a graveyard.

"But," Josh said, leaning forward over the grave, "it wasn't a simple death."

"Her evil family," Mary added, "took the engagement ring from her neck."

"They buried her without it, and she rotted alone in her grave," Chloe said. Josh studied her face, her grin, the bunch of her heavy eyebrows. She had only recently started coming to church—forced there by her mother after the peekaboo incident with Josh on the playground. Now that she was joining in the game, Josh loved her dark turn of mind. She caught him staring, and his face flushed pink as a Christmas ham.

"But to this day," Ryan said, "Alice emerges from her grave each full moon, and by its light she floats along the saltmarsh, searching for the ring that was taken from her."

Josh raised his right arm high in the air and then drew a sharp line with the heel of his shoe in the sandy soil next to the grave. "And now," he trumpeted, sounding like some kind of diminutive carnival barker, "we begin the ritual." Josh loved the story, but hated the ritual and only performed it so Ryan wouldn't mock him in front of Chloe.

They all gathered closer around the grave and placed their arms on one another's shoulders. Once linked, they began walking backward, forming a conga line in reverse. Ryan was first in this procession, then Chloe, Mary, and Josh. They circled the grave, moving slowly backward. Josh was jealous that Ryan's hands were on Chloe's shoulders. He also hated that Mary was touching him; she'd made fun of him when she heard that he'd been too scared to show Chloe his penis on the playground.

"Okay," Chloe said. "Thirteen times around." They moved,

their feet working the bare dirt encircling the grave. "And then?" Chloe peered around and locked eyes with Josh. "And then?" she asked again, and they all erupted in a gale of giggles.

Ryan said, "And then Alice comes up from the grave, grabs hold of us, and drags us down to the pits of hell!" They tittered with laughter and continued their long gyre. They called out the number each time they passed the starting line. When they reached their tenth circle, the pace slowed, and they began to glance around at one another.

"Eleven," Ryan yelled. They continued around, even slower.

"Twelve," Chloe said. Their feet were dragging now in a sort of tentative moonwalk.

Just before Ryan reached the line marking their thirteenth turn, he stopped and said, "Now hell." He lifted up his left leg, angling it over the line. He taunted the rest, "Should I put it down?" Their eyes shifted uneasily. "Okay, I'm gonna do it," Ryan said. "It's going down." The procession held, but everyone was starting to twitch. Josh was silent, holding his breath. "I swear I'm gonna do it," Ryan said again. He kicked his leg back farther, waving it over the line. "On three I put it down! One, two—"

Before Ryan reached three, they all screamed and ran to far-flung corners of the graveyard.

Ryan and Josh trickled back to Alice's grave, surveying the area. "One day," Ryan said, "I really do want to cross the line."

"Yeah," Josh said. In his dreams, Alice loomed large, a witch out there haunting the marshland. She would beckon to him without words, and when he came to her, she would signal over the marsh. The water would recede, and he would see, amongst the pluff mud and oysters, human hands emerging, reaching up into the land of the living. Josh would start awake, still feeling fingers curling around his ankles, as he kicked off the bed sheets and rubbed sweat from his eyes.

"I don't complete the thirteenth circle," Ryan explained, "because I've heard that Alice doesn't always drag her prey to hell. Sometimes she'll come up out of the grave and bite your dick off."

"No way."

"My brother James told me. He saw it happen once." Ryan started dancing. He put his closed fist up to his mouth like he was holding a microphone and screamed, "She's a maneater!" He danced a little rock 'n' roll boogie, shuffling around the grave on one foot and then the other like a flamingo.

"That's not part of the story," Josh said.

"How do you know?" Ryan said. "You weren't there. This isn't even your story."

5

BIRTHDAYSUIT

Across the saltmarsh from Josh's neighborhood, Birthdaysuit and his wife Jaybird still lived out on Naked Island, though they hadn't had a guest in over a decade. The hotel lobby was dusty, and cobwebs clung to nude oil paintings of Marlon Brando, Cyndi Lauper, and Ronald Reagan holding a chimpanzee. Located in an undeveloped marsh north of Pawleys Island, Naked Island had once been South Carolina's premier nude vacation spot. People had flocked in droves, their suitcases nearly empty, to spend a skin-giggling week in the sun. Birthdaysuit would pick up groups from a shrimper's dock in Murrells Inlet and bring them back to Jaybird where she waited, naked as her name, in the side yard of the resort with lemonade, rackets for badminton, and acrylics for "Naughty Parts Painting." The sprinklers would be turned on for any soul brave enough for a game they called "Clean Insides."

Back then Birthdaysuit was an upside-down triangle, and Jaybird was a slender, slow-dwindling hourglass, and they couldn't keep their hot places off one another. Birthdaysuit loved to feel different textures and surfaces, and he was forever trying to convince Jaybird to make love in and on different things—rocks, grass, water, wood, air, upside, downside, blue, green, hot, cold. Birthdaysuit claimed his ass had experienced more textures than Sasquatch had hairs—Sasquatch being a hairy Italian from Long Island who used to come to Naked Island every sultry summer.

Now sixty-five, Birthdaysuit still loved surfaces, but he could rarely convince Jaybird to make regular bed sheet love with him much less sandy beach love or fiberglass boat bottom love or white oak bark love.

One morning Birthdaysuit was reading in bed and couldn't concentrate on the words of Henry Miller, his favorite, because he was thinking about Jaybird and the kitchen counter covered in sticky maple syrup.

So he went to her, moving through the house like so much water. His now pear-shaped figure did not sally forth quite as it once had, but for her he could still flow. He remembered the way Jaybird used to move, to float. Like Grace Kelly, he thought, as he ambled into the kitchen.

There was Jaybird before him at the sink. She was peeling eggs, and Birthdaysuit noted the shape of a shell as it came away in a long spiraling peel.

He pulled Jaybird close. He was wearing only a pair of leopard-printed underwear, and they tightened about the crotch, as he whispered, "I need you."

"Pshaw," she said. "You need to go check those traps is what you need to do."

Naked Island had never officially closed. But after the heyday of the '70s and '80s, Birthdaysuit and Jaybird made ends meet by catching blue crabs and selling them to shrimpers in Murrells Inlet, who then sold them to restaurants in Myrtle Beach and beyond.

"Later then," Birthdaysuit said, his voice strained. "I need to feel you and the hammock in all the right places."

"Go on," she said, shrugging his hand off of her arm. "We need money. After you sell the crabs, buy me some flour and sugar and coffee."

His shoulders slumped, and his underwear slackened as he walked toward the door.

"Hey," Jaybird called. Birthdaysuit turned quickly and reached out a hand to her. His inhalation of breath sounded like a sharp burst of wind moving through the grasses of the saltmarsh at low tide. She saw his excitement and knocked it from the air between them. "No, you old fool. I was just going to remind you to put some damn clothes on. Remember what happened last time you went into the inlet naked—all those poor children."

❧

Birthdaysuit left Naked Island in his flat-bottomed Boston Whaler, and once out in the marsh, he shucked off his jeans and shirt. He donned a heavy knee-length oilcloth apron to protect his downstairs from angry blue crabs. Underneath, he was nude, his ass exposed to the spray of the sea.

Birthdaysuit stalled the boat's motor by the first crab pot. He grabbed the floating buoy, an empty bottle of Aristocrat vodka, and dragged the pot up from the dark water. When he got it onboard, he dumped its contents into the bottom of the boat. Oyster shells, pluff mud, and small blue crabs spilled out in all directions. He leaned over to inspect his catch. Up close, the contents of the trap smelled fecund and raw, dried blood remixed with animal-rich salt water.

Birthdaysuit did this at three other traps, and each yielded a small menagerie of blue and stone crabs.

When he yanked his last trap from the salty depths, he at first thought it was empty. Just before throwing it back, Birthdaysuit noticed something large in a mud-covered corner. He put on a glove and reached in. The pluff mud was thick as cold grits. He fished around in it and pulled out the largest blue crab he had ever seen. He thought about rushing home to show it to Jaybird. She loved the big ones because the bigger they were the more brilliant the blue of their backs and claws.

When he looked up from the crab wriggling in his hand, Grace Kelly was sitting in the bow of the boat. The tulle of her Edith Head gown—black on the top and white on the bottom—blended with the shrimp nets she sat upon. There were fish scales, silver and iridescent, on the nets that complemented the pearls around her neck.

"Well, fuck a duck," Birthdaysuit said.

"I have a nose for trouble," Grace Kelly replied. She crossed and re-crossed her legs, tulle rustling with the nets. Birthdaysuit checked her ankles for tan lines.

"I should have my eyes poked out with a red-hot poker, Grace Kelly." He was still holding the crab.

"It's just a run-of-the-mill Wednesday," she said.

"You look the same as you did all those years ago."

"And yet you've gotten so old, Birthdaysuit."

Standing there before Grace Kelly, he held the crab up to the sunlight and ran his fingers over its cerulean shell. Imagining the widening of Jaybird's pupils as she saw this wonder of the deep, Birthdaysuit said, "I gotta skedaddle."

But Grace Kelly was already gone.

6

SWIMMERS

The overhead light flicked on, and Josh stared up groggily at the bright white ceiling. His mother climbed the ladder of his bunk bed and hovered in his field of vision. She was breathing heavily, her hair sticking out in the back like she had just gotten out of bed.

"Wake up, Josh."

"It's still dark outside," he muttered.

His mother put her hands on his shoulders and gave him a shake. "The turtles are here. They're hatching."

Josh threw back the covers and leaned forward in bed. He'd long anticipated the moment in early fall when the newborn loggerheads would emerge from the dunes of Pawleys Island and trudge to the sea.

He dressed quickly and made his way downstairs where his mother was waiting by the door, keys in hand.

"No one else is going?"

"Your sisters are at a sleepover, and your father—"

She paused, and Josh finished her sentence. "Doesn't care."

"No, that's not it," she said. She was drowsy and wasn't wearing any makeup, and as a result she looked kinder than usual. "Your father has to go to work early in the morning."

Once in the car, Josh sat next to his mother and picked little crusties from the corners of his eyes.

"Okay," she said. "The baby turtles will need us to help them find the ocean. You know what to do, right?"

"Direct them there."

"But don't interfere unless you have to. Nature knows what to do, but sometimes it just needs a little help."

The residents of Pawleys Island had recently started a campaign for the turtles, and Josh and his mother volunteered in the endeavor. Each Saturday in front of the Piggly Wiggly, they handed out bumper stickers that read, *Lights Out, Sea Turtles Dig the Dark*.

When they arrived at the beach, his mother swiveled toward him, seatbelt still on. "Your father wanted to come."

Josh shrugged, opened the door, and left her there. He made his way across the boardwalk, and the beach was surprisingly well lit. The moon burned so bright it cast a shadow as he strode through the floodcrest of washed-up sea oats and driftwood. In the distance, he could see people swinging the beams of flashlights over the expanse of sand.

He approached a gaggle of children. They were standing with a marine biologist named Hutch who often came to their school to talk about local ecologies.

"Slow down," Hutch yelled at Josh as he approached. The man was tall and had a quaff of white hair and a long beard that covered his chest.

Josh paused, one foot suspended in the air. He looked down and in the moonlight could see that the sand itself appeared to move. Silver-dollar-sized loggerheads were crawling this way and that. Hutch walked up gingerly and put his hand on Josh's shoulder. "Amazing, isn't it?" Josh nodded, canvassing the beach before him. "They're all making their way to the sea. But not many will survive."

"What will happen to them?"

"The world is a cruel place for a creature that size. Just about everything wants it for dinner."

Josh and Hutch stared out at the ocean. The moon above the horizon cast its light across the dark mirror of the water.

"There, son," Hutch said, turning and pointing back toward the dunes. He shone a light on the sandy hillside. At first Josh couldn't see anything. Then he spotted a small shape moving up the dune toward the row of houses behind it. "That one needs redirection. It believes the light from the houses is the moon."

Josh scurried up the dune and retrieved the turtle. He brought it back to where Hutch stood and placed it before him. Josh was careful to point the turtle toward the sea, and they watched it use its miniscule flippers to pull its way forward. Josh's mother was standing behind them now. "It's a miracle," she said. "Oh, your father should have come."

Josh's father had recently told him that he was an accident, that they hadn't been trying to have another child so soon after his older sister. His father, who had been a star swimmer in college, joked that out of all his little swimmers Josh had been the strongest. Josh had always had a large birthmark on his left shoulder covering his upper arm and spreading across his heart. The edges of the birthmark fizzled into small circles that resembled fish scales. This, his father said, was evidence that Josh was meant for the water.

Ahead of them, the turtle paused and, working just its left flipper, turned around. When it was facing them, it began pulling itself with both flippers through the loose sand.

"Some of them just don't get it," Hutch said, shaking his head. His silver beard lifted in the breeze and then settled back on the front of his shirt. Josh liked the look of his belly and wondered about the shape of his navel.

"You okay, buddy?"

"Oh yes, sir."

"Go ahead then."

Josh knelt down and turned the turtle again. It moved forward for a few seconds and then stopped, seemingly reluctant to continue to the sea. They all watched, transfixed, and Josh willed it forward.

Hutch said, "We don't like to meddle, but some of them need not only a push in the right direction but to be delivered headlong into their proper element." He looked down at Josh and nodded.

"You're part of a miracle, Joshy," his mother said.

Josh scooped the turtle up into the palms of his hands and walked it into the surf. He waded in, his shoes and blue jeans still on. The water was chilly, but Josh moved ahead until it was up to his waist. He lowered his hands, and the turtle hopped off and swam away. Josh watched until it seemed the dark water swallowed the turtle, and then he could see only the ripples as the moon spread glittering fireworks.

Josh imagined his mother as an ocean, he swimming desperately away from his father. He must have swum like hell to twinkle in her eye.

7

HOMEMADE THONG

During the Thanksgiving holiday, Josh and his family went to see his great-grandmother who had Alzheimer's and was in an assisted living facility. She no longer remembered to lock doors, and during the visit Josh walked in on her in the bathroom and saw her in the nip. The next day he began to sprout a thin nest of pubic hair, inspired, he was convinced, by the exposure. The sight had opened up some new part of his brain, and he felt he was now on a quest, for such flesh, once seen, demanded more.

So Josh began to draw. He knew vaguely the shape of the penis, based upon his own and his father's, which he had taken a gander at on occasion. And he knew of breasts, the parabola, the culmination of the nipple. But despite seeing his great-grandmother and despite the brief game of peekaboo with Chloe, a woman's genitalia was still beyond his imaginative grasp, and he wondered long at its orientation upon the human frame.

For days Josh drew men and women, their naked flesh dancing out of his pencil as he approximated where each bit would go. He drew men with breasts and women with penises in the attempt to capture the forms that meandered their way through the burlesque show of his imagination.

After a few weeks, the flesh materializing before him on the page grew stale, and Josh needed something to bring him out of the doldrums. Around this time, his older sister Jennifer started receiving catalogues full of all manner of underwear. Josh's mother disapproved, saying, "Why is this smut coming to our house?"

Jennifer rolled her eyes. "Mom, it's not smut. I need special bras for support." Jennifer was a star on the middle school cross-country team. She had large breasts that Josh deduced she was trying to wrangle.

He began volunteering to check the mail. He watched from his bedroom window and would run out to meet the mailman. When a choice catalogue arrived, he would stuff it down his pants and walk straight-backed into the house, throw the bills on the counter, and retire to his room, where, with the door locked, he could peruse the various unmentionables on offer.

Victoria's Secret came first and made of Josh a nipple detective, scanning the pictures for even a hint of brown, the faintest outward projection of flesh on lace. Later *Frederick's of Hollywood* arrived, and Josh discovered the thong. He had rifled through his older sister's and his mother's drawers but had never seen such a thing.

One day, when the family was away at one of Jennifer's track meets, he settled into the futon under his bunk bed and held a *Frederick's of Hollywood* close to his face, examining the brightly colored thongs. He considered once again drawing a series of people—men, women, boys, girls. He fancied already how the women would appear, but he had a difficult time imagining how he would draw thongs on men. Then an idea hit him: how could he draw it if he had never seen it?

Josh spread out a few pairs of his own underwear on the futon, next to the opened catalogue. He studied the thongs and then took scissors to his tighty-whities, carefully cutting out each buttock. When he was finished, Josh held up the bespoke thong and admired it front and back. He then took off all of his clothes and slipped it on. The underwear, well worn and long familiar, now seemed fresh and exotic. He tucked himself between his legs and pulled the slender back of the thong between his cheeks, enjoying the feel of it nestled there. Josh inched open his bedroom door, listened for a second, and then pranced down the hallway to his parents' room.

Standing before his mother's full-length mirror, Josh observed how the thong cupped him in the front. He then turned around and checked out the rear. He was pleased to see that his ass looked much like the models' in his stash of catalogues. For a moment, the image of his great grandmother flashed through his mind, but he quickly pushed it back down. He looked in the mirror again, and his skin turned to gooseflesh. He shuddered and skipped merrily in place.

"Oh yeah," he said to his reflection. "So sexy." Josh began to dance, gyrating his hips and watching this gorgeous, newly formed woman move in the mirror.

At precisely this moment Josh's mother walked in. She saw him spreading his cheeks before the mirror and humming a tune, the only one he could think of at the time, the hymn "A Mighty Fortress is Our God." He couldn't remember the words but manipulated the melody into something between a church standard and what he imagined the soundtrack at a strip club would sound like.

"Sweet Lord!" his mother cried, dropping a stack of folded laundry. They locked eyes, and she muttered, "But why, Joshua? Why?"

Josh grabbed each exposed buttock and fled the room, and as he did he felt a maggot mount in his brain. He legged it down the hallway and slammed his bedroom door. He grabbed the catalogue and threw it under his futon. He then shucked off the thong and put on a pair of sweat pants and a T-shirt. Breathing heavily, he sat down on the futon and listened to the sounds of the house, hearing the back door downstairs opening and closing.

Josh expected his mother or father to come in and have a talk with him, but they didn't. He sat there for a long time until finally he heard a knock at his door. Josh readied himself for a lecture. But when the door opened, it was only Jennifer.

"Come on, freakazoid. Dad got Domino's."

Josh followed her downstairs. Opened boxes of pizza lay on the dining room table. His father and younger sister Liz were already scarfing it down. Josh and Jennifer took a seat and pulled pieces of pizza from the boxes and placed them

on paper plates. They were taking their first bites when Josh's
mother walked in. She was flustered and looked at them with an
antic stare. "Why, I never," she said. Josh dropped his half-eaten
piece of pizza. "Have y'all even said grace?"

"Sorry, honey," Josh's father said.

The others, staring up at her, mumbled sorrys as well. They
all grabbed the hands of those closest to them and bowed their
heads.

"Thank you, Father, for all that you've blessed us with,"
Josh's dad began.

"No," his mother interrupted. "I'm saying the blessing tonight." She broke into the circle between Josh and his father,
roughly grabbing their hands. "Heavenly Jesus," she said, louder than anyone had ever heard her speak. "We come before you
today as sinners. The snares of the flesh beckon us, and we are
sorely ashamed that sometimes we are weak enough to answer.
Forgive us, Lord, for we are but vile earthly creatures not fit to
be in your presence." Josh's eyes were closed but he could tell
from her voice that she was facing him. "We humbly ask that
you lead us to the way of light."

She exhaled, and everyone opened their eyes, awkwardly
saying, "Amen" in muted unison. She looked around at their
stunned expressions. Josh felt his face go hot, and he hoped she
would not reveal anything in front of his sisters. "And thank
you, sweet Jesus, for the pizza," she added before walking briskly to the kitchen.

When they finished eating, Josh snuck back upstairs to his
room. He was hoping to go to sleep early, but soon there was a
bang on the door. His father came in and sat down on the futon
next to him. He put his head in his hands and sighed. "Josh," he
said and paused, kneading his forehead. "Your mother just told
me what happened."

Josh nodded and clammed up, not knowing how this was
going to shake out.

"What you were doing," his father said, "the thing with your
underwear…" Josh flashed red and felt the maggots of his

mind singing a little wild-haired, satanic ditty. "Whatever it was, you need to know that it's perverted. And Jesus frowns on that sort of thing."

"Dad," Josh said. "I didn't mean it to be bad. I just thought—"

"Nope," his father said. "I don't need any details." He looked at Josh. "You can't let sin creep in. If you do, it'll overtake you in the blink of an eye."

"I know," Josh said. "I'm sorry."

"Don't say sorry to me. You need to say you're sorry to Jesus."

"Yes, sir."

"All right. Good talk." He patted Josh's shoulder and left the room.

Before going to sleep, Josh prayed, pleading forgiveness for how much he had enjoyed the sight of his own flesh, how he had longed to be as beautiful as the women in the catalogues. Josh said he was sorry over and over, lying in his bunk bed and staring up at the ceiling.

But in the long night, Jesus never responded, which Josh took to be a sign. The next day he put the thong on under his clothes, and all throughout school, he felt it inching up and down. His asshole, he imagined, was exalted pink, and he was pleased as punch.

8

SKID MARKS

Word of Josh's skid marks spread through the school like wild fire. One of his younger sister's hollow-hearted friends had told everyone she'd searched Josh's chest of drawers during a sleepover and discovered that his undies, one and all, were be-nastied in the seat.

It could have been worse, of course. Josh felt lucky, because he had recently cleared his underwear drawer of a series of homemade thongs he'd created for himself. Josh buried the thongs in the woods. He covered their shallow grave in stones, a purple passage of his life laid to rest.

Today, in fourth period, home economics, the students were making brownies. Josh concentrated on the recipe and tried to ignore his classmates' leering, sidelong glances. He knew they were sharpening knives in anticipation of a slaughter.

"Hey, skid marks," one boy finally hissed at Josh. He had a face like an anvil, long and ending in a sharp chin. For years, he'd brought a Confederate flag for show and tell. It took the complaints of several prominent mothers on the PTA to put a stop to it.

Josh swiveled to him, looking away from his bowl of batter. The anvil-faced boy sneered and expelled a cheek-flapping fart sound. He then dipped into his bowl of batter with a wooden spoon and let it drip slowly down. "Skid marks," he repeated and again his slack-jawed face farted. "You some kind of fudge packer?" he asked.

The class erupted in peals of laughter. Josh knew what fudge packer meant, and he tried not to register that his mind was now aflush with maggots. The teacher, Miss Watson, at the front of the room, turned from an oven she had been tinkering with and faced the students. "Hush," she said. "That's about enough." Her eyes paused for a chilly moment on Josh. She hit the counter before her with a meaty paw, causing a cloud of flour to ascend in the bright florescent light.

Silence fell across the room. The anvil-faced boy went back to stirring his batter, and Miss Watson returned to checking on the oven.

Josh felt his eyes begin to burn wet, as the maggots stomped around in his mind. He stood and slunk from the room. The anvil-faced boy looked up briefly and seemed to consider mouth-farting again, but his eyes surveyed the teacher and he shrugged in resignation.

Down the hall in the bathroom, Josh dried his eyes and cursed the foppery of his bowels. He went into a stall, pulled down his pants, and sat down on the toilet. From the stall next to him, Josh heard the toilet seat creak. He bent over and tried to see below the divider. Whoever was there pulled up their feet. Josh heard a faint, high-pitched giggle.

"Who is that?" Josh asked.

"Babooshka."

"Seriously. Is that you, Spregg?" Josh sniffed the air. For some reason Spregg always smelled like cheese.

"Um. It's Big Boobs McGillicutty."

"Spregg, you chode."

"I'm feeling up my tig ole bitties right here in the stall."

"Screw you, Spregg."

"Wipey time."

Josh unrolled a lengthy piece of toilet paper, folded it neatly over and over in a thick square. He tucked the toilet paper into the hammock of his tighty-whities. He then pulled them and his pants back up, and the toilet paper cradled his pizzle in a manner he found unexpectedly pleasing.

He kicked the door of the other stall as he passed it. The boy inside said, "Not by the hair of my tainty taint taint."

As Josh walked back to class, the toilet paper began to move.

He sashayed a bit, to and fro in the hallway, a little cheeky two-step, working the toilet paper up into his crack. With each secret rub, the maggots leapt one by one out of his ears. He saw them there on the hallway floor, little Xs for eyes.

By the time he re-entered the home ec classroom, he was starting to feel a deep ache. He hopped into his seat, as he felt his pants getting tight.

"Nice of you to rejoin us, Josh," Miss Watson said.

The kids around him smirked but remained silent under the teacher's constant surveillance.

When the period ended, everyone filed out into the hall. They turned their heads like owls as Josh walked by, and several heaped insults upon him. The hallway seemed to go blue with their jeers.

But as he walked through the crowd, the taunts of "Skid Marks" filling the air barely registered. His body was not a font of shame, nor was it a frail mechanism made of meat. It was a sparkling funhouse. This toilet paper was ticklishly and devilishly fine, and Josh felt a-thrill with possibilities.

9

CODPIECE

Spregg's mom moved from room to room like a moth in search of light. Her hands shook, and she often had to walk discretely into the pantry to breathe into a brown paper bag. Tonight when she strode into the living room, she brought Spregg and the boys a plate of Bagel Bites. They were still frozen. She was drinking red wine and smoking inside.

Spregg gnawed on one of the frozen Bagel Bites. "Thanks, Mom," he said, as she walked back to the kitchen.

Josh and Ryan sat on the couch next to Spregg, staring at him as he ate. He smiled back. Spregg was the kind of kid who started running as soon as a pair of scissors was put into his hand. They were here to hang out with him because their parents made them. Spregg's mother had recently been in rehab, and Spregg had stayed with his grandparents for the last month in Sarasota Springs, Florida. Now Spregg was back, and Josh's and Ryan's parents said he needed their support. As far as they could tell, Spregg was fine, or as close to fine as he had ever been.

"Want some wine?" Spregg asked.

"Shhhh," Ryan said. "Your mom'll hear, dumbass."

"It's fine," he said, whispering now. "She buys enough to share."

Just then she walked back into the room. She'd lit a fresh cigarette, which she waved around in one hand like a sparkler. In the other, she carried a tray of shot glasses full of wine. She put this before them on a coffee table and said, "A bit of wine because you're such good boys."

Ryan and Josh grabbed their glasses and took them down

in a single gulp. Josh's eyes burned, and he began to blink un-controllably. With his head thrown back, Ryan burped loudly toward the ceiling.

"My, my," she said. "You boys sure are thirsty. I'll get one more wee dram for you. Just don't tell your mothers."

When she returned, she was carrying another tray of drinks, under which there was a large photo album. "I want to show you something." She flipped open the album to a picture of a tall man who was sitting on a motorcycle and holding a blond toddler. "It's the only picture I have of them together from the old days. Father and son. My little Gregg." Josh and Ryan both looked confused. Somehow it had never dawned on them that Spregg's actual name might be Gregg.

Spregg's mother mused at the picture for a moment and then turned the pages backward, with Spregg getting younger and younger until he was just a small baby. On the first page of the album, there was a piece of tape holding something in place that looked like the stem of a dried mushroom.

Ryan was no longer paying attention, as he was busy licking the rim of his second empty glass of wine.

Josh was still peering into the album. "What's that?" he asked, pointing to the dried thing.

"Why that," she said, "that's my baby's little umbilical cord." Spregg and his mother looked at one another and grinned. "His foreskin's not in here, because you know…" She pointed at him. "He's still wearing it."

Ryan looked over and said, "Jesus. Gross."

Josh was thinking about how he had until recently thought it was pronounced "biblical cord" and that it somehow had to do with one's religion at birth.

Spregg's mom shut the album and walked off without saying another word.

"That's so weird," Ryan said.

Josh shrugged and shook his head noncommittally. Lately he'd been saving his own belly button lint in the hopes of mak-ing a sweater from it for Chloe. Now, though, he wondered what Spregg's belly button looked like, what future he could divine from it.

"Wanna watch a movie?" Spregg asked.

"Thank God," Ryan said. "Anything to stop myself from thinking about your dried-up umbilical cord."

"I just got a copy of *Labyrinth* from my grandparents." Josh said, "Ryan and I used to watch that movie all the time. We haven't seen it in forever." Josh stood up and sang, "You remind me of the babe," and pointed at Ryan, who sang back, "What babe?" Ryan stood up now, and he and Josh launched into their best David Bowie impressions, singing, "Dance magic! Dance magic!"

When the song was finished, they collapsed together on the couch, and Ryan playfully slugged Josh on the shoulder.

"Maybe this night isn't going to suck as bad as I thought," Ryan said.

Spregg squealed, "Yeehaw!" and got up to put the VHS into the player.

"Any more wine?" Josh asked, feeling the alcohol and the Bowie spread through his veins. Spregg ran from the room and returned with a magnum.

"What's mine is yours, boys," he said in a high voice, pirouetting dramatically.

When the movie started, Josh and Ryan abandoned their glasses and drank straight from the bottle, passing it back and forth.

"I don't remember Jennifer Connelly being this hot," Ryan said, shortly into the film.

"She's gorgeous," Josh concurred. "Like an angel." His voice was beginning to slur.

"And that Bowie," Spregg said.

"Yeah," Josh replied, quickly and without thinking.

"Look at his junk," Spregg said.

"What's that thing he's wearing?" Ryan asked.

Josh said, "I think it's called a codpiece."

"I want one," Spregg said. He stood up and gyrated about,

moving his hips like Bowie. His T-shirt flapped up, and Josh caught a glimpse of his belly button. It looked pale and doughy like a tortellini, his all-time favorite pasta.

Josh poured more wine down his gullet, and Ryan did the same. They made eye contact and grinned at one another as Spregg pranced about.

The wine made Josh squint. For the remainder of the movie, he stared at the TV like he was looking down the barrel of a six-shooter. Through the sights, he eyed Bowie's codpiece and Connelly's young body by turns. When they appeared onscreen together, he wondered where to aim.

10

SMUT CABIN

Josh and Ryan spent most of the summer after sixth grade exploring the old logging roads that snaked their way through the woods behind their neighborhood. They could meander half a day without seeing any sign, other than the sandy roads, that humans had ever set foot here.

Today, while walking through a new part of the woods, Josh and Ryan came upon a small cabin. It had the look of a spook house about it. Ryan rubbed a hand through his red hair and said confidently, "Let's check it out."

Josh was hunkered down behind a fallen tree. He motioned for Ryan to join him. When Ryan was on his level, he whispered, "Wait a second. We need to scope out the situation."

"What situation? We're in the middle of nowhere."

"People could be here."

"Who?"

"I don't know," Josh said. "Let's just wait a second."

The two of them sat down on the pine needle floor of the forest. They listened for several minutes before Ryan had had enough and said, "All right, let's go. There could be some kind of treasure."

"Cut out the Tom Sawyer crap," Josh said, still whispering.

"Stop being a baby."

"I'm being cautious."

"Well, I'm gonna Indian rug burn the shit out of you if you don't come on."

Ryan reached toward him with both hands. Josh jerked back and then stood up. "Fine." He followed close behind as Ryan crept up to the cabin. There was a small clearing in front. Josh looked left and right and wondered if there may have been a road here at some point, many years back. The cabin was small, approximately eight feet by eight, and the entire structure sagged to one side like a wounded eye.

Josh and Ryan stood in the clearing. They listened and heard only the sound of squirrels barking in the trees overhead.

When Ryan looked over at Josh and nodded, they both forged ahead. The roof of the cabin's small front porch was rent down the center, and the porch's floorboards had rotted out so badly that they did not even try to cross it. Instead they went around to the back. The door there was missing, and they stepped in. The floorboards were dry and eaten through with termites. Their steps crunched more than creaked, and the floor yielded to their weight.

The cabin consisted of only a single room. Careful of their footing, Josh and Ryan moved into its center. In one corner, there was a dingy navy-blue blanket. Next to it stood a can of baked beans, a crumpled pack of cigarettes, and several empty Budweiser bottles.

Ryan walked over to the corner, bent down, and examined the trash. When he reached out to the blanket, Josh said, "No, wait."

"Why?"

"I'm not sure."

Ryan grabbed a corner of the blanket and then threw it back. There was a stack of magazines where the blanket had been. Ryan saw the woman on the cover of the top magazine and said, "Shit, dude, these are pornos." Forgetting his fear, Josh walked over and leaned down next to Ryan. On the cover of the top magazine, there was a petite blond woman dressed like a cheerleader. Josh pulled magazine after magazine off the stack. Each cover featured a nearly naked woman, all smiling suggestively. Josh and Ryan cut the stack in two, each taking four or five. They settled in opposite corners of the cabin and for a long time perused the magazines. Josh thought of maggots only when he looked up and Ryan caught his eye.

It was getting late and the sun was sinking low in the sky. They would be expected for dinner soon. Both boys' penises were beginning to ache.

"Should we bring some home?" Ryan asked.

"I can't," Josh said. "I think my mom searches my room. She'd find them and freak out."

"We can always come back, I guess."

Before leaving, the boys flipped through the pages one last time, finding their favorite images to store away in memory.

The next day when they returned to the cabin, the magazines were gone, as was the blanket. They found only a pile of trash on the floor.

The boys reconnoitered the woods, and soon they came upon another clearing, the saplings hacked down and a small area cleared of pinecones and sticks. The charred remains of a fire were still smoldering to one side, and on the other there were two spent cans of Campbell's and a gunnysack full of the empty rotgut whiskey bottles.

"Somebody lives here," Josh whispered.

"No shit."

"We got to go."

"Definitely."

The boys fled, running for all they were worth the whole way home.

"That was close," Josh said, when they were back in his own manicured yard.

"Yeah," Ryan said. "We'll return at dawn and see if we can get the magazines before this wanker leaves for good."

"What? No."

"You're right," Ryan said, thinking it over. "We'll give it a week and then return and claim what's ours."

❧

The boys never returned, because a few days later, Josh sold Spregg a Zippo, which he immediately used to burn down the cabin. Spregg claimed the Zippo was a gift for his father, and

Josh said nothing even though he didn't believe Spregg had a father.

Not much happened in Pawleys Island, so the burning of the cabin made the front page of the local newspaper.

A history professor at the College of Charleston named Isabella Davis found the article, came to study the structure's charred remains, and determined that it had been an immaculately well-preserved antebellum cabin. "This vandal has burned down a piece of our history. We could have learned so much about the life of enslaved individuals," she said on the evening news out of Charleston. She was a middle-aged African-American woman, whose short hair was beginning to turn silver at the temples.

Josh watched the program, sitting between his parents on the couch in their living room.

"We could have created a museum," his father said. He was a realtor and a member of the local architectural review board.

On TV the professor said, "The inner workings of the institution of slavery are still only dimly understood."

His mother let out a regretful sigh. "Can you imagine? And nearly in our backyard."

"The horrific exploitation of the enslaved cannot be overestimated."

"I'll talk to the other members of the board," his father said. "Perhaps we can erect a monument or a sign at the very least, one of those official-looking silver ones with the bold black type."

The professor nodded gravely on the TV. "Without understanding oppression in the past, it is impossible to combat it in the present."

Josh lowered his head so that his parents could not see him crying. But his mother heard him sniffle. "What's the matter, Joshy?"

"Nothing," he said. "Just my allergies."

"Come with me, sweetie. I'll get you fixed right up."

They walked upstairs and into his parents' bathroom where

his mother began rummaging through drawers. Josh could still hear the TV blaring downstairs. The news had switched to the weatherman, who said, "Today's clear skies will not last long, y'all. The region can expect severe storms ahead."

11

PANTIESLINE

The Fourth of July was tomorrow, and Josh's dad took the day off work to prepare for their annual party. His mother and sisters were out buying supplies, so Josh was left alone with him.

"Josh," his dad said, standing in the yard with a shovel in his hand, "we're grilling a whole hog tomorrow. What do you think about that?"

"Does hog mean pig?" Josh asked.

It was midday and hot, and his father's thinning hairline was beaded with sweat. He was breathing heavily. "Yes, Josh, hog means pig. Do you want to help or not?" He continued without even waiting for Josh to respond. "To cook a whole hog, we have to build a barbeque pit." His dad explained the design—a large hole in the ground that would be filled with hardwood coals, surrounded by four walls of cinder blocks, across which they would lay a metal grate. "You can start digging the pit." Josh nodded, and his father handed him the shovel. "Right here. Just follow the outline." He dug the heel of his boot into the grass and dirt, making a large rectangle.

Josh was good at digging; he'd been searching for arrowheads in the woods and riverbanks for years.

For the next hour, Josh dug alone, creating a deep moat around the perimeter that his dad had mapped out. When he came back, his father yelled, "What are you doing?"

"Digging," he said.

"You aren't digging the hole; you're digging around the hole."

"Right," Josh said proudly. "That's a safety moat. So a fire doesn't break out in the yard."

His father grabbed the shovel from Josh's hand. "We've got to have a pit, not a moat, to make barbeque. Use your head." Whenever he deployed this phrase, Josh knew his dad was angry. "I guess I wasn't," he said, grinding the toe of his shoe in the moat. "We learned about fire safety in Boy Scouts. I thought we'd do safety first and then dig the pit."

His dad muttered something Josh couldn't understand.

"Sorry."

"Fine," he said. "Tell you what. I have another job for you. You know our new neighbor?"

"Not really. I saw the moving truck last week."

"Well, go invite her to the party. I think her name is Mrs. Dallas."

Josh turned and trudged off in the direction of the house on the other side of the cul-de-sac. He knocked on the door and then stood back, as he had done last Halloween at the same house. After a few seconds the door opened and standing there in the doorway was a beautiful woman. She was fair and blond, and she wore what looked like a man's T-shirt and the shortest shorts Josh had ever seen.

"Hi there," she said. Josh was frozen, his thoughts scrambling this way and that. "Can I help you?"

"I'm next door," he managed. "We barbeque soon."

She giggled and pulled up her oversized shirt to wipe sweat from her brow. Josh saw a quick flash of her bare stomach. Her belly button was an inny, deep and dark like a crab's hole in the sand.

"Come on," she said, before stepping forward and putting a hand on his shoulder to usher him inside.

As he moved over the threshold, he heard her say, "So hot out there. Would you like a Coke?"

"I am in desire of one."

"My name's Janet," she said as she entered the kitchen, opened the fridge, and retrieved two Cokes.

Josh stood by the kitchen island. He noted that her hair was pulled up into a high bun on her head. Stray golden strands had escaped everywhere, surrounding her face like a wispy halo. She cracked open the cans and pushed one across the counter to Josh. He grasped the sweating Coke and took a swig. He fumbled for something to say and "I'm your neighbor" was all he could come up with.

"I figured. I'm just moving in."

"I figured, ma'am," he said. He made a grand motion with his hand, as if to survey her new kingdom. Josh imagined dialogue from movies. "What brings you to these parts?"

She smiled. "Well, I just went through a divorce back in Cincinnati, and I came to Pawleys looking for, as they say, a fresh start."

Josh looked out of the kitchen window over Janet's shoulder and noticed that there was a clothesline in the backyard adorned with colorful items. He had seen all manner of undergarments in his older sister's lingerie catalogues, and he could identify some on the line: baby doll, teddy, French knickers.

Janet was talking about the breakup of her marriage, something about her husband being a "lousy bastard." Josh heard little of it as he fixated on the clothesline.

Janet peered behind her and then back at Josh. "What did you say you needed?"

"Oh. We're having a Fourth of July party, and my parents wanted to know if you could come."

"That sounds nice. I'll see if I can get through some of this unpacking."

Josh stood on his tiptoes, straining to identify more items on the clothesline.

"Speaking of which," she said. "I should really get back to it."

The next day, the Fourth, Josh's parents were busy with preparations. Having proven himself a useless helper, Josh was left to his own devices. From his upstairs bedroom window, he could see the cul-de-sac. He was monitoring it in the hope that Janet would leave and he could hop her fence and get a better look at the clothesline.

When guests began to arrive at the barbeque, Josh was still looking out the window. His mother ran up the stairs and said, "Joshua, get outside. We have guests."

Josh went downstairs and out into the backyard. His father was standing over the hog, which had been cooking in the pit since dawn. His father's face was beaming, as he clapped his friends on their shoulders and peered down at the split, crucified-looking animal. "That's a hog," his father kept saying. "Have you ever seen a hog as pretty as that?" Josh was watching them all nod, when his father began recounting the story of Josh digging the moat around the pit. "Sometimes I don't know what to do with that kid. A real space cadet." His father's friends nodded at this, as if to indicate that they also had kids that didn't always act right.

When his father looked up, he saw Josh and hustled over to him. "Hey, bud," he said. "I got a job for you."

"I'll probably mess it up."

"No. This is a fun job." His father took Josh over to a fold-out table that he'd set up as a bar. "I can't make the cocktails, because I have to mind the hog. So I need you to make drinks for the adults whenever they need one."

"All right," Josh muttered.

"Great! We're making mojitos." His father showed Josh the cocktail shaker and the muddler, and how he could use them with just the right proportions of lime, mint, sugar, and rum. His father made one from start to finish, and then Josh replicated it. His father clapped him on the back. "Bravo. Smart boy."

For the next hour, Josh stood behind the bar and made one mojito after another for his parents' friends. It was the shank of evening, and the adults were standing over the barbeque pit, the fire still smoldering and billowing blue smoke up between them as they clinked their glasses and laughed. At one point, Josh heard his father again tell the story of his safety moat.

The guests howled when he recited the line, "I thought we'd do safety first."

Josh snuck away from the bar and kneeled down in the dirt at the foundation of the house. He removed a brick, and in the almost darkness he could tell there were several roly-polies writhing in the dirt. He grabbed four and went back to the bar. He threw the roly-polies into the cocktail shaker and muddled them with lime, mint, sugar, and a heavy glug of rum. He poured the cocktail into a glass, walked to the barbeque pit, and handed it to his father. "For you, Daddy-o," he said.

"Thanks, bud. I'm parched." Several of the women at the pit made an "aw" sound to indicate what a sweet boy he was.

A few minutes later Janet walked into the yard. The women at the party surrounded her, asking a barrage of questions and then saying things like, "Nuh-uh, girl," "Good riddance," and "Lower than a lowdown dog."

Night was coming on, and with it the liquid sounds of cicadas, frogs, and whippoorwills. Josh knew that this was his opportunity. He walked from the yard, making sure not to catch the attention of his parents or their friends.

Crossing the cul-de-sac, he could feel his heart beating like a timpani in his chest. The gate to Janet's backyard was unlocked, and he let himself in noiselessly. There was a single floodlight beaming from the back of the house, which enabled him to see that the clothesline was still full. But the items on it were different now. There were fewer pieces of lingerie and more T-shirts and jeans. At one end there were several pairs of panties. He counted them, five, and assessed their colors, mostly pinks and baby blues. Two were lace, one satin, and two cotton. Four had full-seated bottoms, and one cotton pair was a thong. Josh reached out and stroked them all in turn. He was not even thinking about the fact that a beautiful woman wore these. He was just fixated on the feel of the material and the impression the colors and shapes made in his brain.

The satin pair was light purple, and they were soft and

smooth. Josh touched his face to them, still hanging there on the line.

As he was doing this, he saw an arch of light move across the sky. It was the night's first Roman candle. The festivities were beginning, and he knew he would soon be missed.

Without thinking, Josh grabbed the satin panties, and knowing only that he had to have them, he pulled them from their clothes pin and stuffed them into his tighty-whities. As he ran across the cul-de-sac, Josh felt the panties doing delightful work.

Back in his own yard, Josh's little sister Liz and her friends had been given sparklers, and they were waving them about, writing curlicues in the night air and creating a strobe light effect in the yard. Josh's mother clinked her glass of chardonnay with a shrimp cocktail fork. "Gather round, everyone. Gather round."

The guests encircled the barbeque pit, some thirty members strong.

"Thank y'all for coming," she said. "I think we need some words to commemorate the occasion." She looked to her husband who was swaying a bit and had one eye clinched shut. She shook her head almost imperceptibly and searched elsewhere in the group. Everyone looked to the ground. Josh's mother waited several beats, and then her attention fixed on him.

"How about you, Joshy?" she said. "Give us a speech."

Josh looked around the crowd, their faces lit horrendously from the coals below. He watched his mother sip from her wine and saw his father take a long slug from his roly-poly mojito. Josh said the first thing that came to mind. "Thank Jesus."

Everyone clapped, but they continued looking at him.

"Thank Jesus for what?" his mother asked.

"Thank Jesus for..." Josh's mind went blank. He stuck his left hand in his pocket and felt Janet's panties rub up and down. "Thank Jesus," he said, "for all that America has to offer."

The crowd cheered wildly.

12

CAMELTOE

During the last few long-lingering days of the summer before seventh grade, Josh's friends were away on vacation; Spregg had gone to Florida to visit his grandparents, and Ryan was on a fishing trip with his family in the Caribbean. As a result, Josh was bored at home and spent his time exploring the large tract of woods that lay between his neighborhood and the Waccamaw River to the west.

Today he was searching for a Native American burial ground that he'd heard about from a kid at school. He was careful to avoid poison ivy as he made his way through a stand of loblolly pines. The understory was thick with bushes and choked with vines. He monitored these as he walked, dividing the five-leaf Virginia creeper in his mind from the three-leaf poison ivy.

When he had wandered farther than ever before, Josh came upon a neighborhood that he never knew existed. The houses were smaller and older than the ones in his neighborhood, and they had yards of dirt brushed into circular patterns. Josh meandered along the sandy road, which was washed out and bumpy as corduroy. Passing house after house, he noticed that most of them had African-American people in the yards and on the porches. Josh waved, and some of them waved back. At one house, there was a basketball court in the yard. It was unpaved but had two goals that appeared to be regulation height. Josh stopped and stared, wondering why no one was here playing. He was about to leave when he heard a voice calling from the house next to it.

Josh squinted in the direction of the voice and saw Carl, a short Black guy that he knew from school. They had worked together last year on a project in earth science. He was waving at Josh from an upstairs window and seemed to be indicating for him to hold on. Josh gave him an awkward thumbs-up, and moments later Carl ran out of the house and into the yard. As he neared Josh on the court, he said, "That really you, Josh?"

"Yeah, of course it's me."

"What are you doing here?"

"My house is close." Josh motioned vaguely in the direction of the woods.

"Cool," Carl said. "How was your summer?"

"Boring lately."

"Mine, too. Want to do something?"

Josh nodded. Carl was big-boned, as people said about kids before they knew whether it was just a phase. He was also one of the top students in school. Other kids made fun of him for how good his grades were and how much teachers lavished him with praise.

"What do you want to do?" Carl asked.

"We could go to the pool," Josh said. There was a pool in his neighborhood. Since his friends were out of town, he had found it depressing to go, bobbing there as he would alone all day on a flotation noodle.

"Sweet," Carl said. He then paused. "Is it—"

"What?"

"Is it okay for me to go?"

"Yeah, man," Josh said. "I got guest passes."

Carl eyed Josh for a second and then said, "All right then, let's go. I just got to grab my swim trunks."

Josh followed Carl into his house. After he entered, he realized that this was the first time he'd ever been inside the home of an African American. He had never even seen his parents with a Black person, although his mother was fond of saying things like, "All people are the same in the eyes of Jesus."

"Wait here." Carl ran upstairs to change, and Josh was left in the living room. He surveyed the pictures on the wall, the couches and chairs. It was pretty much like every other house he had ever seen. While he was leaning in to examine a picture of Carl and his brothers, both of whom were much older, Carl's mother walked into the room.

"Hey there?" she said like it was a question.

"I'm Carl's friend Josh. We're going to the pool."

"Well, it's good to know you, Josh. Have a seat." Carl's mother was tall and thin, the opposite of Carl. Her hair was short and slightly curly, and she had on a blue polka-dotted dress. Josh sat down across from her in the living room.

"So you're Carl's friend, eh?"

"Yes, ma'am."

"He needs a friend about now." Her eyes moved in the direction of the stairs.

Josh felt like he should say something nice about Carl. "He's really good at science. I've seen him in action."

She was about to respond, but at that moment Carl trotted down the stairs. He kissed her on the cheek and said, "We're going to the pool. Love you."

She smiled and blew kisses into the air. "Y'all be careful," she called. But they had already bolted out the door and were on their way.

Josh and Carl rode bikes to the pool. Carl got his from the yard, and they stopped by Josh's house to retrieve his. The day was bright and blue, and the few clouds in the sky were as round as the bellies of babies.

By the time they chained their bikes up at the entrance to the pool, Carl had fallen silent. He checked and re-checked his lock, as if stalling.

"Let's go," Josh said. "It's hotter than hell riding around in this weather."

"Okay," Carl muttered as he followed Josh to the pool house.

Once inside Josh signed into the membership ledger. No one was in the pool, and the lifeguard Amy was sitting behind the counter of the sign-in station. Amy grew up in the neighborhood, but she had just finished her freshman year at the University of South Carolina where she had a full scholarship for being on the swim team. She'd changed a lot since she left last summer. Josh noted that she was all lithe muscle like a tuna. Amy was smoking a Marlboro Red, which she started to hide when the door opened, before realizing that it was just Josh. The cigarette now hung from her mouth, and she squinted at Josh and Carl through the smoke.

"Hey," she said apathetically.

Josh nodded at her cigarette. "That good for the old swimming career?"

"Fuck off," she said. "I'm sick of people telling me what to do all the time."

"Okay, okay," Josh said. "Geez."

"College isn't as fun as you'd think, especially for athletes."

"That's a drag," Josh said.

Amy pulled hard on the cigarette and, canting forward, exhaled toward Josh. "Yeah, a drag," she said, mimicking his voice, which was softer and higher than her own.

"Anyway," Josh said. "This is my friend Carl." He indicated Carl with a wave that even in the moment felt overly dramatic.

Amy nodded to Carl and then stuck her thumb out toward Josh. "This guy's a pervert. I should know; I've been babysitting him for years. Watch out, Carl."

"Don't listen to her," Josh said. "Let's go take a little dip."

Amy put out her cigarette. "Fine, but I have to be on the pool deck while you swim. New regulation. They don't want any babies drowning, I guess."

Josh rolled his eyes and started out the door that led to the pool. "We're swimming," he called back to Amy. "You better make sure we don't drown."

Josh pulled off his shirt and threw it on the deck, and without even stopping, he kicked off his loose shoes. He then galloped headlong toward the pool. At the edge, he jumped high into the air, yelling at the top of his arch, "Cannonball!" before crashing down into the water. When he surfaced, his dark hair, which had been getting long and shaggy all summer, fell down into his eyes. He had to constantly fling his head sideways to see.

Carl walked across the pool deck, and he was careful in removing his shirt and shoes. He even folded his shirt before placing it on a lounge chair. Carl then walked to the stairs at the shallow end and lowered his body into the blue water, one slow step at a time.

Amy came out on the pool deck wearing a red one-piece. "Don't be a little shit, Josh," she said. "I swear to God I'll kick you out of here."

"Do you even have that power?" He was smiling and frog-legging himself around the deep end.

"I've done it before," she said, her arms crossed, standing on the deck and looking down at him.

Carl stood quietly in the shallow end. When Amy turned her back to Josh and took a seat on a high red chair, Josh swam over to Carl. "Can I ask you a question?"

"Sure."

"One about race?"

"I guess." Carl looked at him nervously, as he bobbed in the water.

"Is it true that Black people's hair can't get wet?"

Carl laughed. "Of course, it can. But probably not quite like yours."

"Can I see?"

Carl held his nose with his thumb and forefinger and lowered his head below the surface. When he emerged, beads of water stood out and rolled down his short-cropped hair.

"Wow. It really is like water off a duck's back."

Carl's mouth clinched.

"Is that okay to say?" Josh asked.

"I guess so. I've never really thought about it."

"Well, what I mean is just that your hair is really neat. Never wet, always dry—handy in all seasons."

As the day wore on, Carl and Josh discussed several possible games to play, but everything seemed lame with only two people. Even Marco Polo was best played with more than just a single Marco and a single Polo. While wallowing in the shallows by the stairs and wondering what to do, Josh sat up straight in the water. He was watching Amy as she stood from the lifeguard chair and walked toward the edge of the pool. "I'm going inside," she said. "It's hot as shit out here."

"Okay, boss." Josh looked up at her from the pool. Carl had his back to her and didn't turn around.

"Don't you fuckers drown while I'm gone."

She turned and Josh stared as she walked to the pool house. Once she was inside, he clapped his hands and looked at Carl. "Did you see that?"

"What?"

"She had a cameltoe, dude!"

Carl looked uncomfortable. He leaned in closer to Josh. "I didn't see it."

"That's a shame." Carl shook his head, and Josh continued, merry as a tree frog. "I know what we can do. I'll pretend to be drowning, and when Amy comes back out here, you'll be able to see."

Carl shook his head again, more vigorously now. "No, no, no."

Josh looked betrayed. "Why?"

Carl whispered, "My dad told me not to look at white women."

"White women are great."

"Shut up, man," Carl said. "Please stop talking about this."

"I'm just saying, a cameltoe is a beautiful thing. Once you start noticing them, it's hard to stop."

"Just because something's beautiful doesn't mean you have the right to look at it."

Josh thought about this and nodded. He and Carl went on swimming, but Josh said little and for the rest of the day found it difficult to look either Carl or Amy in the eye, seeing as he had the hideousness of his own heart.

SEVENTH GRADE

13

WHERE THE GOOD LORD SPLIT YOU

Shortly before starting seventh grade, Josh decided that it was time to grow up and fall in love. Not sure how one initiated this process, he consulted his friend Spregg. Everyone knew something was wrong with Spregg, but no one could pinpoint what exactly. Josh had once overheard his parents arguing about whether he should be able to hang out with Spregg, and his father had said, "That boy was born wrong." Josh's father said the same thing about him. Josh had been born breach, and his father liked to tell anyone who would listen at parties, "Josh was born wrong. Came out backward and has been that way ever since."

Josh was desperate, and he knew Spregg had made out several times with an older girl who sold popsicles out of a cart on the beach. So Josh was convinced there was some kind of wisdom he could glean from him.

On a clear, blue Saturday morning, Josh and Ryan rode their bikes over to Spregg's house. He let them in, and they walked into his room where he was blaring a Danzig album. "Have you heard this shit?" Spregg asked, air drumming away.

"Yeah." Ryan waited for the air drumming to stop but it didn't. "We have a favor to ask," he yelled over the music.

"Right on, man." Spregg's air drumming crescendoed, and he then walked over to the tape player and turned it down. "Lay it on me."

"Well, we were wondering." Ryan paused. "Shit, man, I don't know. You tell him, Josh."

"We're thinking about... Well, you've got a girlfriend, and

we were wondering how that happened. We need, like, some kind of catalyst."

Spregg laughed. "I have no idea what a catalyst is, but girls are kinda my thing. So you've come to the right place."

"Okay," Josh said. "So what do we do? We've been trying, but we can't even get girls to talk to us."

Spregg held out a hand to Josh and waved for him to be quiet. He turned the music back up and paced in front of them, air drumming again and periodically hitting himself on the head like it was some kind of accent cymbal.

After a full three minutes, he stopped and squealed, "Cha-ching! I've got it. We need to go see the witch out on Sandy Island."

Sandy Island was located on the Waccamaw River near Pawleys Island. It was mostly inhabited by African Americans, many of whom were Gullah. The kids of Sandy Island went to school with the boys, but they were ferried over the river in a boat, before being put on a bus. Josh had been told stories for as long as he could remember about the witches who lived there.

Josh was thinking about these stories when Spregg fled the room. Danzig was still playing as Josh and Ryan ran after him and out the door.

They all rode their bikes to the river, where, Spregg explained, someone's canoe was stowed near the landing. "These rich assholes never use it," he said. "It's ours for the taking."

To Josh's surprise, the canoe was exactly where Spregg said it would be. There were even life jackets tucked inside and two paddles. Josh took the front with a paddle, Ryan the rear, and Spregg the middle. "I can't paddle," Spregg informed them. "I'm about to take a little trip." He pulled a small Ziploc bag from his pocket. Three pills were in it, all different shapes and sizes. Spregg threw them into his mouth and swallowed. "Okay, men," he said. "Onward!"

Josh and Ryan paddled across the Waccamaw River, which was part of the Intracoastal Waterway. Large boats moved up and down the river constantly: fishing boats, yachts, sailboats.

As they rowed across the waterway, struggling through the wake as large vessels motored by, Josh looked across the water and saw a turtle surface. Someone had painted its shell, and each octagonal shape was a burst of different colors. "Shit," Josh said. "Look how amazing that turtle is." Ryan was paddling hard through the high wake. "Screw the turtles, Josh. We're gonna capsize here. You best be paddling at full titty."

Josh looked back, and the turtle was gone. He dug in with the paddle, and after a few minutes they made it across the waterway and into a smaller creek that wrapped around the back side of Sandy Island. They paddled on through calmer water and soon came to a flat wooden dock, where the children of Sandy Island got picked up each morning by the school boat. Ryan and Josh tied the canoe to the dock. Spregg's head was beginning to bob, as if without his consent. They helped him out of the canoe, careful not to tip it over.

When they got on terra firma, Josh turned to Spregg and asked where they were supposed to go. Spregg swayed a bit, but pointed a finger in the direction of a dirt road that led away from the dock. Josh placed an arm under Spregg's, and they stumbled down the washboard road. There were small houses on either side, squatting low under the live oaks draped with long strands of Spanish moss. Older African-American people eyed them from their porches. Some tipped their hats, and some looked at them suspiciously. Spregg was limping badly now. "Where do we go, Spregg?" Josh asked. "People are staring at us."

"This way," Spregg slurred. His head swayed like a balloon on a string. He pointed in the direction they were already heading.

They walked on, now both Ryan and Josh supporting Spregg. His arms were outstretched, one on each of them, like a drunken sailor, or perhaps Jesus. His feet were beginning to miss steps, drag, and make short straight lines in the dirt of the road. The houses grew fewer and fewer. When Josh was about to insist that they turn around and go home, Spregg looked up. Drool was falling from one corner of his mouth, but he mumbled, "Here." He pointed up ahead, and Josh could just make out a mailbox peeking through a row of azaleas.

By the time they got there, Spregg's eyes were dilated, large and dark as a shark's. Josh and Ryan lowered him to the ground by the mailbox. One side of his mouth had gone slack, and through his roping drool, Spregg hummed a Metallica song.

"Should we just leave?" Ryan asked.

Josh was thinking about Chloe, whom he'd been obsessed with since he'd seen her naked last year on the playground. "We gotta play this out."

Josh and Ryan walked off the road and past the row of azaleas. There was a clearing in the woods with a house. It was small but looked freshly painted a pale sky blue. Flanking it on either side were rows of well-pruned pink roses. This was not what Josh had imagined a witch's house would look like.

"Okay," Josh said, as they trudged through the yard, encouraging himself forward.

"Here goes nothing," Ryan said.

They walked to the door and knocked. A small Black woman wearing a peach-colored dress answered, "Can I help you?" She smiled but looked wary. She was old and for a moment she reminded Josh of his own grandmother.

"Yes, ma'am," Josh said. "We wanted to ask you about something."

She hesitated for a second and then said, "Well, come on in. Make yourselves at home."

Ryan and Josh sat down on a floral-printed couch, and she sat across from them in a high-backed rocking chair.

"We hate to bother you, ma'am," Josh began, "but we were hoping to get a love potion. There's this girl and I—" He stopped. The woman was rocking back and forth and looking up at the ceiling. She started to hum, and Josh recognized the song from church. When she looked down, she appeared angry.

"A love potion? Now why would I have a love potion?"

Josh looked to Ryan whose eyes were now glued to the floor.

"Let me guess," she said. "You think I'm some kind of a witch."

"Well. See our friend said—"

"That the drunk fool outside?"

"Yes, ma'am."

"And you trust a drunk fool?"

"I did."

"You know what that makes you?"

"I'm sorry," Josh said. "But it's just that there's this girl named Chloe."

"Lord Jesus. There's always a Chloe or a Katie somewhere. Boy, I'm as Christian as anybody."

"I didn't mean any disrespect," Josh stammered.

"Boy, you don't even know enough to know when you're disrespecting."

Josh stood, his shoulders slumped, and made his way to the door. Ryan followed. "I'm sorry," Josh said, turning back to her. "We won't come again."

She was humming and rocking. Josh knew the hymn now: "Abide with Me." As he was about to apologize again, the woman lifted one finger in the direction of the door and said, "Don't let the door hit you where the good lord split you."

14

BREAD

The weekend before he started middle school Josh got into a mess of poison ivy, and his body broke out in angry red blisters. On Monday morning he locked himself in the bathroom. His mother spoke to him through the door, assuring him that it wasn't that bad, that no one would even notice. But he refused to budge.

Josh heard her walk away from the bathroom door. When she returned a few minutes later, he could hear his father's heavy footsteps alongside her softer ones.

"Josh," his father said. "Open the door."

"I'm hideous," Josh replied.

His father banged twice and the doorknob jiggled. Josh was silent, sitting on the toilet, the lid down, in only his tighty-whities.

His father knocked again, harder this time. "You're going to be late for school, and I've got a house showing in less than an hour. Get out here this second." Josh stood up; he knew how his father could be when he got angry. He opened the door, and his father walked into the bathroom, surveying Josh's thin body, blotched everywhere with red. Even one half of his face was covered in bumps and blisters.

His father looked surprised and then laughed. "You really got it ass to elbow this time, son." He grabbed Josh by the chin and turned his head so that he could see the rash in the early morning light that came in through the bathroom window. He chuckled again. "Maybe this'll build character."

❧

In his first class, math, Josh made sure to sit in the back with the poison ivy side of his face turned to the wall. His next class was music, and Josh's heart sank when he walked into the room and noticed that the teacher, Mr. Morris, had arranged the chairs in a circle. Josh sat down, and all the other students streamed in and did the same. Some of the girls were snickering to one another, and Josh saw one of them point at him.

Chloe walked into the music room and sat down in the circle directly across from Josh. She looked different than he remembered, her dark hair streaked lighter and her skin sun-kissed. Penny-colored freckles formed a saddle across her nose and cheeks.

Josh was startled when a boy with a rat-tail and frayed cutoff jean shorts walked in front of him and said, "What kind of disease is that on your face?" He was the kind of guy that spit all the time—a sure sign, Josh's mother always said, of a lack of discipline as a child.

Mr. Morris was a new teacher, fresh out of graduate school, and he looked like a young, emaciated Kenny Rogers. He had black wispy hair and a short beard, and he wore a pink tie and a blue plaid shirt that was not tucked into his pants. When the bell rang, Mr. Morris picked up an acoustic guitar and sallied forth into the center of the circle. Without saying a word, he began strumming on the guitar and singing Bob Dylan's "Blowin' in the Wind." His voice was high and clear, and the class sat rapt, wide-eyed. When he finished, one girl started slowly clapping, and then several others joined in.

"Okay, okay," he said, waving for them to settle down. "My name is Mr. Morris, and this is music class. Do you know what we do in music class?"

Everyone was silent, some looking around nervously. "Come on. What do we do in music class?" Mr. Morris pointed at Josh. "Yes?"

"Um…make music," Josh said.

Everyone in the room laughed, and some began to whisper

about his rash. "Good job, hoss," the boy with the rat-tail said.

Mr. Morris clapped his hands. "Bravo, young man. That's the perfect answer. We make music in music class. Some of you will go on to pick your own instruments if you join band next year, but for now we'll all learn the basics." The tittering in the crowd diminished, as Mr. Morris turned back to Josh and asked for his name. "And, Josh, do you know who the song is by that I just played?"

Josh's mother would only let him listen to Christian music, but for as long as he could remember he'd been listening to his father's albums that were hidden in the garage. He also listened to a classic rock station out of Myrtle Beach whenever he was home alone.

"Of course," Josh said; this came out sounding more sarcastic than he intended.

"Well, come on then, who's it by?"

"Bob Dylan. 'Blowin' in the Wind' is one of his most important early protest songs."

Mr. Morris, grinning and impressed, looked around at the rest of the class. "Do you know anything else about Dylan that you'd like to share?"

Josh thought for a second. "Only that he's a folk-rock god."

The rat-tailed boy said, just loudly enough for everyone to hear, "Freak."

Mr. Morris turned a cold eye on him. "Why would you say that?"

"Look at his face," the boy said.

Mr. Morris walked closer to Josh. He bent down and examined the rash. He then took a step back and rubbed his beard. "Know what? That rash is perfectly in the shape of a guitar. Yep, a Fender Stratocaster."

The students all leaned in, eying the rash. Several of girls nodded and chirped. Chloe smiled at Josh from across the circle, and he smiled back.

"Stand up everyone," Mr. Morris said. They all did, and when Josh looked over Chloe was standing beside him. She braced a hand on his shoulder and whispered in his ear, "Every time you smile, that guitar on your cheek looks like it's breaking in two. Like somebody's smashing it at the end of a show."

"Like Pete Townshend."

"I was thinking Kurt Cobain. But yeah."

Mr. Morris moved around the room, handing out bongos and triangles, finger cymbals and spoons. Josh got a wood block and a small mallet. Chloe's hand on his shoulder had given him a jolt, and he felt it surging now through his body.

When Mr. Morris launched into "Like a Rolling Stone," Josh swayed to the rhythm of the verses, and when the chorus began he stomped around the room, beating the hell out of the wood block and singing in unison with Mr. Morris, "How does it feel?"

After class, Josh's steps were high, and he sailed through the hallway as if on air, for this, he felt, was his moment on the mountain. Students he had never even seen before came up to him and said, "I heard you have a Stratocaster on your face." He smiled and the guitar shattered in two.

At lunch Josh managed to secure a place behind Chloe in the cafeteria line. Feeling buoyed by the guitar on his face, he took a double helping of tater tots. One of the lunch ladies, a stout woman with a great quaff heaped up under her hair net, said, "Only one per person." She hadn't even looked up from the pan of spaghetti she was stirring.

Josh pretended not to hear and continued down the line. "Hey!" she yelled. Josh looked back, and she saw the rash on his face. "God, what happened to you?" Several students stopped to listen.

"Looks like a guitar, right?" Josh asked.

"Just looks like an ugly rash to me," the lunch lady said.

Josh put the tots back on the line and then walked to a table and sat down alone. He was thinking, *You better not cry, you pathetic baby*, when Chloe sat down next to him.

"Don't mind her," Chloe said. "I've heard that lunch lady's always mean."

"I guess." Chloe was sitting on his rash side, and he felt embarrassed.

She glanced around and then said, "My older brother says everyone calls her Bread."

"Why Bread?"

Chloe put her hands out in front of her torso, shaking them up and down. "'Cause her boobs are as big as bread loaves."

Forgetting the rash, Josh leaned in, and the two of them touched shoulders. He reached out under the table and took Chloe's hand. Her pinky wiggled around his and his around hers like two earthworms writhing on a summer sidewalk.

15

ALL MOUSES IN THEIR HOUSES

In late September, school was out for three weeks after a hurricane hit Pawleys Island and flooded the area. Josh and his older sister Jennifer could barely remember the last time they had been outside. Josh was crepitating, he wanted to see Chloe so badly.

To make matters worse, Spregg was staying with them for an unspecified amount of time, because his mom had recently gotten a DUI and was, according to Josh's mother, "taking some time to get right with the Lord." No one had seen Spregg's dad in years; some said that he was dead, and others that he was in prison.

For days they had had nothing to do but watch the few movies the family owned on VHS—*Grease*, *The Goonies*, and *Harry and the Hendersons*—and play UNO with a deck they suspected was incomplete. All the while the rivers rose, the saltmarshes filled, and the ponds overflowed around them.

One afternoon the rain paused. Josh, Jennifer, and Spregg were home alone. The sky was still gray and ominous, but they took the opportunity to go outside. Jennifer wore a pair of tall galoshes, and Spregg, who had always been pale and skinny as a plucked chicken, insisted on borrowing Josh's new L.L. Bean boots, claiming, "I catch a cold if my feet get the least bit wet."

Josh said, "It's like 80 degrees outside."

Spregg shot him the pathetic smile of an orphan in a TV movie. "Fine," Josh mumbled. He put on his regular tennis shoes, and they all three left the house. After walking through their cul-de-sac and then a dense forest of loblolly pines, they circled a pond, and the trees opened onto a wide field. Across

the green grass in the floodcrest lay waves of debris, pine nee-
dles and sticks networked with plastic bags and even a truck's
tire.

"Wow," Spregg said. "This place looks like shit."

"The flood waters came all the way up here," Jennifer said.
"It's amazing." They were a mile from the ocean, and about half
that to the nearest saltmarsh. With her toe, Jennifer nudged a
dead mullet that was covered in green oak leaves. "See. That's
a saltwater fish, which means the marsh backed all the way up
here." Spregg kneeled down in front of the mullet and poked
its bulbous eye with a stick.

"Get off it," Jennifer said, before swatting Spregg across the
back of his head.

"Ow," he yelled. "That hurt." Jennifer shrugged.

Spregg rubbed the back of his head as they continued
through the field, scanning the refuse for anything of interest.
At one point, Spregg dropped to the ground and rummaged
amongst a pile of soggy sea oats. When he stood up, he was
holding a condom, limp and fully unfurled. "Cool," Spregg said.

"God," Jennifer said. "Don't touch that filthy thing."

"Do you even know what it is?" Spregg twirled it through
the air in a figure eight.

"Yes, I know what it is. That's why I told you to drop it."

Spregg sniffed the air. "Smells like fart out here."

Jennifer rolled her eyes. "That's the paper mill in Georgetown. You can smell it sometimes when the wind blows north."

"Fart mill," Spregg muttered, before slipping the condom
into his pocket.

Josh walked a few feet ahead of them. He paused and said,
"Holy shit, guys." He pointed at something moving slowly
through a pile of palm fronds. Spregg and Jennifer ran over.
They stopped, and all three stood there trying to make out what
was stirring a few yards in front of them as it emerged into a
clear patch of grass.

"It's a giant turtle," Spregg said.

"No, it's a loggerhead," Jennifer said. "It clearly got caught up in the high water."

Josh cocked his head to one side, taking in the turtle's features: a long reptilian tail, broad head, and fierce beak-like mouth. "No," he whispered. "It's an alligator snapping turtle." They approached the turtle, which was more than three feet long including the tail. With just the balls of their feet touching the wet grass, they stepped lightly. Soon they could smell the turtle, like old, dried algae and fishy pluff mud. "That is stank," Spregg said.

For a long time, they just stood there before it, unable to move, overawed like dim beasts. The flood had coughed up this creature, a monster raised from a primordial bog. Its dark shell and clawed, gnarly feet appeared ancient against the spot of bright grass across which it moved.

The turtle paused and looked over at them. "Far out," Spregg said.

"I've heard of them," Jennifer said, "but I've never actually seen one."

"Me neither," Josh said.

"Get me a stick," Spregg commanded. "Get me a stick." Both Josh and Jennifer stared at him blankly, so Spregg turned and retrieved a stick for himself. "Watch this." He started toward the turtle, but Jennifer took two steps forward and caught him by the shoulder.

"No, Spregg," she said, curling her fingernails into the flesh of his shoulder. "Don't be cruel."

"I'm not. Swear to God."

Jennifer looked into his pleading eyes. "Okay. But hurt it and I hurt you." She released his shoulder, and Spregg made his way to within three feet of the turtle. Slowly he stretched out the long stick in its direction. It was bigger around than a grown man's thumb. When the stick was within two inches of the turtle's face, it threw its head sideways, much faster than they would have imagined possible, and snapped, cutting the stick clean through.

Spregg jumped back and caught one of his feet on a branch behind him. He stumbled, and a wave of terror passed over his face as he surveyed his proximity to the snapper's mouth. He scrambled to his feet and leapt farther away. "Fuck me sideways," he said as he fought for breath.

Josh and Jennifer both reached out, steadying him as he regained his balance.

"See? Cool, right?"

"I want to try," Josh said.

"No," Jennifer said. "Remember, Mom and Dad left me in charge. Once was fine, but we don't need to go on torturing this animal. It's already been traumatized by the storm."

"Just once more," Josh pleaded. He held clasped hands up before him, as if in prayer. Josh was imagining how he and Spregg would tell this story to their friends at school. "Pretty please." He thought of Chloe and bowed to Jennifer, shaking his hands up and down.

Her eyes softened. "Fine. But just once more, and that's it."

Josh clapped and then went in search of a stick. When he returned he had one even longer than Spregg's, but about the same diameter. Like Spregg, Josh approached the turtle slowly. After he had taken only a few steps toward it, he heard Spregg behind him say, "Make sure your mouse is in his house." Josh stopped and looked back at him, rolling his eyes.

Jennifer crossed her arms and frowned at them. "What is that supposed to mean?"

"Don't worry about it," Josh said. "It's something our gym teacher says to remind us to wear our jock straps."

Jennifer said, "He says that in class? Ew."

Spregg cut in. "Every day in gym he says, 'I don't want to see that mess. Make sure that all your mouses are in their houses.'"

"Gross," Jennifer said.

Josh was still paused, halfway between them and the turtle.

Spregg said, "My grandfather always told me that if a snapping turtle bites you, he won't let go until the next time it thunders."

"That sounds like an old wives' tale," Jennifer said. Spregg ignored her. "But in the case of your pants' pinkie, Josh, he might just bite it clean off." Spregg turned away from them. When he spun back, his hand was down his pants and his pinkie was sticking out of the zipper. "Oh no, a snapper's coming," he said. Spregg bent his finger at the second knuckle. "No!" He shook the nub to and fro in Josh's direction. "Shut up, Spregg." Josh returned his attention to the turtle. When he got close, he thrust the stick into its face. The turtle responded less swiftly this time. But within a few seconds, it snapped the stick in two.

As Josh sprang back, Spregg cheered, and even Jennifer let out a whoop.

All three of them followed the creature at a safe distance, until it got to the pond at the edge of the field. It flung itself off the bank and into the water with surprising grace. They continued to stare long after it disappeared into the muddy water.

Early the next morning Josh awoke drenched in sweat from a nightmare in which the turtle was in his bedroom, creeping around the walls, seeking out his flesh in the dark. He threw his head over the side of the bunk bed, scanning the floor in what little light filtered in through the window. His heart was pounding, and he was having trouble drawing enough air. He reached down past his belly button and plunged his hand into his underwear. He felt around and counted: bean, bean, frank. He breathed a sigh of relief, his mouse still securely sleeping the night away in its house.

16

HANGIN' BRAIN

Josh, his father, and two sisters sat around the table eating breakfast. His mother was pacing and looking out the front windows. "Wonder where she is," she kept saying.

On either side of their house lived two elderly widowers. Josh's father called one of them Mumbles and the other Shuffles. Mumbles wore a different colored bandana around his neck every day. People said that he had once tried to hang himself. They saw Shuffles more than Mumbles. He lingered by his mailbox hoping to see one of Josh's sisters in the yard. This occurred more frequently in the spring when the weather got warmer and their clothes scantier.

Both men were taken care of by the same nurse. She always parked her car in the cul-de-sac in front of Josh's house, rather than in either man's driveway, so that she was equidistant from each. Josh sometimes watched out the window as she went from one to the other. However, the nurse had not shown up for the past two days, and Mumble's daughter in Charlotte had called Josh's mother and asked her to check on the nurse's whereabouts.

"Wonder where she is," his mother said again. She turned from the window to the breakfast table. "Someone should go over and make sure they're all right. But I have to leave soon for Bible study. Can you do it?"

Everyone at the table was confused, not sure whom she was asking. Josh's father lowered his newspaper and looked at her. "Make Josh do it."

"Oh, Joshy, please."

"He'll do it. Right, Josh?" His father gave him a stern look, and Josh slowly nodded.

After breakfast, Josh put on his shoes and ventured out the front door toward the cul-de-sac. He decided that Mumbles was the scarier of the two, so he would visit him first to get it out of the way. Last summer Mumbles had tried to paint his house with olive oil, which had confirmed everyone's suspicion that he was insane.

Mumbles's house, like most in the neighborhood, was medium sized and well maintained. It was white with bright aqua trim and had architectural details common to the beach: Bermuda shutters on its windows, board and batten siding, and a tin roof. Overall, the house looked too cheery for a deranged widower.

Josh knocked on the door, and within seconds Mumbles opened it. He motioned Josh in as if he had something of great importance to show him. They walked through the house, first a foyer and then a living room that fed out into a sunroom. Each of these was immaculately clean. Unlike the exterior, the aesthetic inside was faux Italian, with a picture of Il Davide in the foyer and plastic grape vines sprawled out on the walls around the living room. The sunroom had a miniature version of the Trevi Fountain bubbling away in the corner.

Jabbering about something that Josh could not discern, Mumbles sat down at a table in the sunroom, and not knowing what else to do, Josh sat down across from him and tried not to stare at the bandana around Mumbles' neck. He wondered what noose marks might look like. A large puzzle was spread out between them. Pieces were separated into piles according to color, and Josh could make out the corner of a wine bottle emerging in one of the sections that Mumbles had completed.

"Mr.—" Josh stopped himself before saying Mumbles. He didn't know his actual name. "My parents wanted me to check on you, since apparently your nurse is missing." Mumbles looked at Josh and smiled. He then returned his attention to the puzzle.

"Does that mean you're doing okay?"

Mumbles snapped together two puzzle pieces and made the sign of the cross: head, chest, left, right. Catholics were foreign and ill-understood amongst the Baptists of Pawleys Island. Spregg's cousin had married a Catholic, and Spregg had attended the wedding in Myrtle Beach. He said the choir consisted of albinos and that everyone, even the kids, swilled as much wine at communion as they could stomach.

After several minutes, Josh got up and walked over closer to Mumbles. He stuck out his hand, thinking that he had never, to his knowledge, touched a Catholic. Without removing his eyes from the puzzle, Mumbles extended his right hand and shook. As Josh turned to leave, Mumbles again made the sign of the cross, this time as if aiming it at Josh.

Feeling lifted by his visit with Mumbles, Josh knocked confidently on Shuffles's door. For several moments, all was silent within the house. When he was about to head home, Josh heard a faint noise like a distant train. The noise grew steadily louder, and Josh realized that this was Shuffles moving toward the door. When it opened, Josh was shocked to see how tall Shuffles was. He had never seen him up close. Shuffles's height was augmented by the fact that he was rawboned and wore only a purple kimono. This hit him at the forearms just below the elbow, and it went down his thighs halfway to the knees.

"Do I know you?" He bent over and eyed Josh. Josh tried not to look at the abundance of white hair that grew out of his emaciated chest. Josh imagined counting his ribs, one by one.

"My name's Josh. I live next door."

"Of course." His face seemed to slacken. "Do come in."

Josh was momentarily blind as he entered the dark house, and all he could smell was mothballs and stale cigar smoke. The sitting room that he walked into seemed pitch black compared to the morning sun outside. As his eyes slowly began to adjust, he looked around the room. The walls were lined with built-in bookshelves. Josh had never seen so many outside of a library. Between the bookshelves the wallpaper was dark red, almost maroon, as were the heavy curtains that covered the windows. "Have a seat," Shuffles said. Josh sat in the first chair that he could make out, a large leather recliner. Across the small room from him, Shuffles sat down on a velvet love seat and crossed his legs. Josh surveyed the length of Shuffles's exposed thigh. His hair there was much darker than the hair on his chest. "What brings you here?" On the end table next to him, there was a taxidermic bird. Josh was trying to focus on this, rather than on the man's thighs. "You're admiring my bird, I see." Josh nodded. "A blue jay. Terrible, mean birds, but so beautiful. Don't you agree?"

Josh nodded and forced himself to explain that his mother wanted to check on him since the nurse was missing.

"What fine neighbors. How can I ever thank you?" This seemed like a question to which he was expecting an answer. Josh shrugged. "Well," he continued, "are you a reader?"

"Sometimes."

"I have precisely the book every young man should read. Just have to find it."

Shuffles jumped up from the love seat. He didn't dodder now as he made his way across the room. He leaned over a pile of books on the floor next to Josh. The purple kimono rode up, and Josh could see his testicles flopping against his thighs. Hangin' brain, they called it at school. Josh had never seen a brain hang so low.

Shuffles came up with a book and placed it in Josh's lap. He then moved across the room and sat down again. This time Shuffles did not bother to cross his legs. His penis poked out from under the kimono, and Josh saw where it ended but not where it began.

His mind was now well a-crawl with maggots. They began singing an evil, jaunty strain. He sat up dizzily from the chair, and the springs creaked. The sound seemed absurdly loud in the cramped space. Through the brain-fog and maggots, Josh trundled out the door and into the cul-de-sac. He looked down at the cover of the book, which he did not even realize he was still holding. He read the title: *Leaves of Grass.* Josh fled pell-mell into the woods, and after he had run so far and fast that his chest ached, he dropped to his knees. He quickly dug a hole and buried the book in the dark, dank dirt.

17

Hamsters

"Get a fucking bowl!" Amy screamed at Josh.

He stood, eyes wide, staring at the plump, blond hamster cupped in her hand. Blood was oozing out of the hamster's hind end. Josh's younger sister Liz nudged him. "Josh. Earth to Josh."

Their parents were out on a date and their older sister was at a friend's sleepover, so Amy was watching Josh and Liz. Josh felt he was far too old for a babysitter.

"What?" he asked. Amy had been testy with him all night, even since he told her that he collected his own belly button lint. One day, he had explained, he would fashion a sweater from the lint and give it to Chloe. "That's truly twisted," Amy had said, but Josh was confident Chloe would appreciate it.

"A fucking bowl," Amy repeated. "Or something, anything to put it in."

Josh felt like he was in a trance. He stared at Amy. She was leaning over the bleeding hamster, and he could see down her shirt. He thought often of the red one-piece she wore when working as a lifeguard at the neighborhood pool.

"Are you seriously looking at my tits right now?"

Josh gave his head a slight shake and turned away. He walked into the kitchen and came back with a small ice cream bowl. Amy looked at it and then at him. "What's wrong with you?"

"He's retarded," Liz said.

"What? You said get a bowl."

"Take this," Amy said. Josh put his hands together, and Amy gingerly placed the hamster into his palms. "Careful. Don't jostle it." She walked toward the kitchen.

"What happened to it?" Liz asked, leaning over Josh's cupped hands. "Why's it bleeding?" She'd gotten the hamster two weeks ago for her birthday.

Josh tried to see where the blood was coming from, but he got queasy and looked away. "Take it," he said to Liz.

She shook her head. "Heck no."

Josh looked in the direction of the kitchen, hoping Amy would come back. He heard her opening and closing cabinets. The hot wet made a puddle in his hands. Josh stifled a heaving sensation, and he began to shake. "Hold still," Liz said. "It's sick." Josh looked down again and something pink slipped from the back of the hamster. "What's that?" Liz put her face even closer to his hands. "A baby!"

All the air seemed to be sucked from the room. Josh tried to breathe. His face drained of color, and he slumped over, the hamster and baby tumbling softly to the carpet.

A few minutes later, Josh came to. On the coffee table next to him, the hamster was now in a large rectangular Tupperware container that his mother used to transport deviled eggs. Next to it were four bald babies.

"They look like teeny tiny pigs," Liz said.

"They kinda do," Amy agreed.

"You did so good, Amy. How'd you know she was having babies?"

"Just knew."

Josh stood beside her now, staring down at the babies. Amy had placed them on a clean white towel, and they looked smooth and naked and oddly lewd. The mother hamster seemed to be sleeping.

"I thought it was a boy," Josh said.

Amy rolled her eyes, and then Liz did too.

"You don't know anything about anything, Josh," Liz said. He shrugged and bent closer to see the baby hamsters.

"Especially not about girls," Amy said.

He teetered and for a moment thought he was going to faint again. He grabbed the edge of the coffee table to steady himself, feeling like Amy had ripped open his chest and seen the state of his tepid heart.

Before his parents arrived home that evening, the mother hamster killed all four of her young. Liz had already gone to bed, and Amy was reading a *Vogue* spread out on the kitchen counter. Josh found the dead babies in the living room, their bodies twisted and mangled in the Tupperware. The mother's once-blond face was now carmine. The sight made his knees go shaky, but he kneeled down, steadied himself, and picked up each of the dead. He put them into his pocket and then slipped out the back door and into the night, careful not to arouse Amy's attention. He buried the hamsters behind the garage, wishing them well with each shovelful of dirt.

In the morning, he would tell Liz that Amy had taken the babies with her, that they were sure to have long and happy lives.

18

SINLOCK

The week before fall break, Josh, Ryan, and Spregg skipped school and rode their bikes to the beach, ready for some bully adventure. Offshore there were a few container ships that they could barely make out on the horizon. They heard them, though, honking their horns like gigantic lowing cows. The boys bivouacked in the sand dunes, making a fire in a small valley sequestered from the wind. This formed an impromptu flophouse for the day.

Josh spread out a tattered blanket on the sand next to the fire, and they all threw down their backpacks and scattered their contents like soldiers revealing the spoils of war. Josh had a Boy Scout canteen full of Tang and a glug of his mom's chardonnay he had filched from the fridge that morning. Ryan had a few random pages from a *Playboy* he'd found under his brother James's bed.

They all gulped down the Tang and wine. "It just tastes like Tang," Ryan said.

"Well, I couldn't take too much wine or my mom would notice."

Ryan shrugged and passed around the pages from the *Playboy*. They moved from boy to boy quickly because they'd all seen them before. Ryan had been carrying them around for weeks.

Spregg waved his hands excitedly in the air and then pulled a crumpled pack of cigarettes from his backpack. "Check this out, boys."

"Menthols?" Ryan said.

"So?"

"So that shit is gross."

"Well," Spregg said, "I heard they're healthier than smoking regular cigs."

"Is that true?" Josh asked.

"Of course not," Ryan said.

"No, they are, dude. Like you clean your teeth with mint, these clean your insides. Like brushing your lung's teeth."

"That's insane," Ryan said, but he and Josh both reached out and grabbed a cigarette. Each took a turn leaning in to the small fire and lighting up.

By the time the boys were finished, they felt ill. "I need some air," Josh said, his face sweaty. He had been growing his hair long, and it stuck now to the sides of his face. Josh took off his shirt and swayed in just his cutoff jeans. Despite the smoke of the campfire, he could still smell the sweet sulfur blowing up the coast from the paper mill.

Ryan and Spregg shucked off their own shirts and followed him out of the dunes toward the beach, each walking as awkwardly as toddlers in the loose sand. When they emerged from the dunes, they felt a spanking breeze on their faces. It was early October, but due to the unseasonably warm weather a scattering of tourists remained on Pawleys Island. Josh walked through them as he made his way across the expanse of the low-tide beach. He entered the surf, splashing cool water on his face and feeling already less like death.

Josh sensed a presence, like some stranger's eyes were upon him. He looked to his left, and standing not far away was a man, over six feet tall, his form hulking. The man was wearing an eye patch and had the raffish cut of a pirate. He winked at Josh with his one eye. Josh waved and winked back but felt strange about it immediately.

"Hello," the man said.

"Hi."

"And hello to you two." Ryan and Spregg had waded into the surf and now stood behind Josh. They also looked refreshed by this new, briny world.

Spregg said, "What's under that eye patch?"

The man looked at Spregg for a second and laughed. "You're a direct little ragamuffin. I appreciate that."

"Sorry about him," Josh said. "He's just curious about what happened?"

"Lost it in Vietnam."

"Can we see it?" Spregg asked.

The man lifted the eye patch. Underneath, there was a fleshy pocket like a deep belly button in his face.

All three boys inhaled sharply.

"No glass eye?" Spregg asked.

"What?" the man said. He looked concerned and felt the fleshy pocket. "Had it there this morning. Must've fallen out somewhere." He looked around, as did the boys, but the water was not even transparent enough to see their own torsos much less the sandy bottom. The man shrugged and walked away, leaving the boys still peering down.

Spregg said, "I want to find that eyeball."

"He was just messing with us," Ryan said.

"You think so?"

"I know so."

Spregg looked unconvinced. He turned to Josh. "You think he's messing with us?"

"Probably," Josh said. But he too liked the idea of having the eyeball. For some reason, he wanted to hold it in his mouth before bed and then store it in a glass of water at night. "Let's look just in case."

The boys spent the next hour diving in the surf, which had turned rough since the morning. The sky was dark, the wind driving, and the temperature had dropped. The waves came on like relentless white-maned horses. The boys struggled to swim against them, and by the time they waded out of the water, their ears were a-fuzz and their eyes stung from the salt.

They looked for the one-eyed man on the beach, but he was gone, along with most of the tourists who had fled the gray sky and cooling winds. The boys hotfooted their way back to the dunes. The fire still smoldered there, and they each, as if entranced, lay down beside it, spreading their shirts out to form makeshift sleeping quarters on the sandy blanket.

Josh slept fitfully. Once, when he half-woke, he saw Spregg next to him by the fire, smoking another menthol. When he woke again, it was to the sound of beating wings. He opened his eyes, and the air was exploding with white. Seagulls were everywhere, diving at his body. Josh heard Spregg and Ryan laughing nearby. He looked over, and Spregg was holding an empty potato chip bag. He had spread the chips all over Josh's body while he was asleep.

Josh was about to scream at Spregg when a seagull dove and landed on his chest. The bird was heavy, and before Josh could swat it away, the seagull bent down and bit his nipple. Josh jumped up, clutching at his chest, which was beginning to bleed.

Josh had taken two long steps toward Spregg, when a pelican dropped from the sky and hit him squarely in the face. He fell to the ground, and all the world went dark.

When Josh came to in the hospital, his mother was sitting in a chair next to his bed. "Joshy," she said, seeing him stir.

"What happened?" he asked. His throat was dry, and his head throbbed.

"You were concussed by a pelican. Ryan rode his bike to our house and told me. Then we called the ambulance. You're in big trouble, young man, for skipping school. But for now—"

His father walked into the room. He stopped by Josh's bed, looked down, and said, "I'm going to beat the devil out of you, boy."

Josh blinked at the thought of violence, unable to fully process the threat.

"What he means," his mother said, "is you can't let the devil get a foothold in your heart."

Josh closed his eyes and pretended to sleep. He knew it was already too late.

19

THE LADY

Josh was all fidgety with excitement as he sat through his morning classes, because today was his day to play The Lady at recess. When the bell rang, he fled from the room and out into the fenced lot behind the middle school. The other students streamed out after him, laughing and yelling as they moved from shadow to sunshine. The girls organized a game of Four Square, and some of the boys were beginning to draw out bases in the sand for kickball. Josh and Ryan, though, were already hunting for the small color-changing anole lizards that sunned themselves around the schoolyard. Ryan ran up behind Josh as he scanned the brick wall of the school, hoping to spot one there.

"Find any?" Ryan asked.

"Not yet. You can search the fence. They like the wooden part over there in the sun." Josh motioned to where the fence tied into the brick school building.

Spregg approached Josh as well. Spregg was humming with excitement, lively as a flea.

"Be careful, Spregg," Josh said. "You know there's a real monster lurking around here." The boys had seen, in recesses past, flashes of a large lizard.

Josh swore to their teacher, Miss Palmer, that it was over two feet long, but she always said, "Oh, you're just joshing me." This was her favorite pun.

"I'll keep an eye out," Spregg said. "And if I do see that monster…" He turned his back to Miss Palmer who was leaning against the brick wall of the school. Spregg flashed an eight-inch Bowie knife he had hidden in his pants. He slipped it back in, saluted Josh, and ran away.

The boys searched for a few minutes in different corners of the schoolyard, before Spregg called out, "Heyo!" The others ran over and saw that there were two small lizards clinging to the trunk of a pine tree. They were brown and blended in almost perfectly with the bark.

"Payday," Ryan said, grabbing one of the lizards, which moved slowly in the mild early fall temperature. He held it just behind the head, its neck swelling into a red semicircle as it continued its silent mating ritual. Spregg reached down and grabbed the other lizard, turning it from side to side in the sun.

"Two of them," Josh said. "My lucky day!"

Ryan reached up and tucked Josh's long brown hair behind his ear. He then held the lizard up to it. The lizard's mouth gaped, and he placed either side of its opened jaw to Josh's lobe. The lizard clamped down, and Josh involuntarily let out a squeal. When Ryan released the lizard and pulled his hand away, it remained attached to Josh's earlobe. It would stay, gripped there, until someone pried it off.

Spregg had just attached the second lizard to Josh's other ear when a kickball came whizzing by. The ball bounced off the fence and rolled back nearly to their feet. A tall, athletic boy named Jordan ran up. Jordan was the kind of kid that tore the tails off lizards and put *Kick Me* signs on people's backs in the lunch line. Josh stooped to pick up the ball, but Jordan charged at him.

"Get away from that," he said.

"I was going to give it to you," Josh said.

Jordan grabbed the ball. "I don't need your help. Go back to whatever gay-ass shit you're doing here."

Ryan was the first to shrug as Jordan walked away. "Let them play kickball. Our game is better."

Josh had turned red and was trying hard not to flinch at the pain the lizards were inflicting now on his ears. He cleared his throat, and he, Ryan, and Spregg formed a huddle. "The lizards are in place," he began as if addressing a ballroom full of resplendently dressed guests. "The Lady has her earrings." The boys clapped, and Josh gave a careful, shallow bow. He then paraded around, lifting his arms into long slow arcs the way he had seen his sisters do in ballet recitals.

"What an elegant lady!" Ryan said, his voice high and feminine and cracking just a bit. Josh smiled at him and feigned shyness. He waved his hand at Ryan as if to say, *Go on, you.*

The boys then took turns with The Lady. Spregg copped a feel of Josh's breasts, squeezing each of them in turn, pretending they had some heft. He looked back to Ryan and said, "These melons. Oh, these melons." He pretended to faint. Josh gave a delirious little scream.

Ryan bowed low and, as he came up, said, "A kiss for The Lady." He put his full open palm over Josh's mouth and then kissed the back of his own hand. Josh looked around nervously. No one had ever done this to The Lady before.

A cry rose up from the other end of the schoolyard, and the ball whizzed by again. It stopped before a dead, hollowed-out tree along the fence line.

Feeling confident from his kiss with The Lady, Ryan ran over to grab the ball next to the old tree. Bent over the ball, he peered into the hollow space in the tree's trunk and saw an enormous green iguana. Ryan screamed bloody murder, and Spregg ran over. Josh pranced with his head held high, careful not to shake loose the lizards. The girls playing Four Square nearby heard the commotion and ran over as well. As soon as they witnessed the massive iguana, they started screaming, and their screaming spread, until all the girls, along with Josh, Ryan, and Spregg were yelling and hopping around and pointing at the iguana.

The only person not screaming was Chloe who had walked up behind the group. While everyone was taking turns peering into the tree at the iguana, Chloe was staring at Josh with his lizard earrings.

Miss Palmer walked briskly over, got one look at the iguana, and shouted, "Oh, my sweet baby Jesus! You children stay away from that thing. I'm going for help."

Within a few minutes, Miss Palmer was back with Mr. Samuel, the school's janitor. Mr. Samuel had long greasy hair and a face like a possum. Nonplussed, he reached into the tree trunk with his bare hands and came out holding the back of the iguana. Its feet stuck out away from Mr. Samuel, kicking as if trying to run off into the air.

"What is that?" Miss Palmer asked, barely able to catch her breath.

"It's fine," Mr. Samuel said, as if annoyed more by the question than the iguana. "Probably somebody's escaped pet."

With that Mr. Samuel began walking back across the schoolyard, the iguana held out before him, its legs still kicking. The students followed behind him at a close but comfortable distance.

Josh had walked ahead and was now standing by the schoolyard gate. He still had the lizards clamped on each ear. Mr. Samuel stopped and stared at him. "You better quit that perverted stuff before it's too late. And cut your hair. You look like a dang hippie." He continued out of the schoolyard, and Miss Palmer and his classmates followed, even Josh's friends. They had forgotten all about The Lady.

But Josh lagged behind the group, touching his lizard earrings lightly to make sure that they were still there. He straightened his back and sashayed across the lawn, making ballerina arcs with both arms like flowers blooming in time lapse.

"Don't listen to Mr. Samuel," Chloe said from just behind him. Josh was startled and turned around. His face softened when he saw that it was Chloe.

"I wanted to be The Lady for a moment longer. While I could."

She stood on her tiptoes, leaned in, and kissed him high on the left cheek, nearly where the lizard, now green as grass, clung to his ear.

20

A BULGARIAN FURRY

On an overcast spring day, Ryan's father George motored his boat up to the dock in Murrells Inlet, and Georgi jumped out, his long legs arching over the water before he landed gracefully. George crawled down from the flybridge and threw the bowline to Georgi, who tied the vessel to a large cleat on the dock. Georgi then walked along the dock to the stern, and George threw him another heavy rope. Georgi pulled and the boat snuggled up to the dock. Georgi put out his hand, which George grabbed and hopped down next to him.

"Quite a day, boss," Georgi said.

"Epic," George said. They were beaming. The two men were roughly the same age, both in their early forties. George was of average height and, though once statuesque, had developed a belly the size of a well-inflated basketball. He still possessed all the strength, brawny arms and muscular legs, but he had gone "round at the middle," as his wife enjoyed saying. Georgi was thin and wiry. His arms and legs appeared almost too long, like he had been born with limbs that wouldn't stop growing.

Their names were part of the allure of their business. Tourists, usually men from the Midwest, got a kick out of George and Georgi's Deep Sea Charters; the novelty of their names coupled with the unexpected exoticism of fishing alongside Georgi, a Bulgarian.

George had lived in the area his entire life. Georgi grew up working with his father who was a professional fisherman on the Black Sea. Georgi had fled Bulgaria as a teenager; no one knew why exactly, and his story often changed. But he had traveled throughout the United States and eventually landed here and married a local woman named Anna.

On days like today, when they had no fishing tours booked, George and Georgi went out to the Gulf Stream, just the two of them, and brought their haul back to sell to restaurants in Murrells Inlet.

"Should we get the fish out now?" Georgi asked.

"No, Georgi. I think we deserve a drink." Sitting on ice in the hull of the boat was a tuna that easily weighed 200 pounds and a swordfish that was pushing 400.

"Sounds good, boss. Let me just go get my wallet from my car."

Georgi walked to his car in the marina's parking lot. He opened the trunk and was rummaging around in his backpack when George walked up behind him. As George reached out to pat Georgi on the shoulder, he saw the contents of the trunk and jumped back like he had stumbled upon a copperhead. Inside there were two costumes laid out in dry cleaner's plastic; each looked like a taxidermized cartoon character, one rabbit and one elephant.

Georgi slammed the trunk. "Let's get that drink, boss."

George was silent as they walked down the boardwalk that snaked its way around the saltmarsh. The air was burdened with the rank perfume of pluff mud and rotting sea creatures exposed by the tide. They entered a bar that was dark despite the fact that the sun had not yet set. The bar was called Hot Tony's, still a locals' hangout, even when it was overrun with tourists in the summer months.

As George and Georgi bellied up to the bar, the place was nearly empty. At the other end of the bar's long mahogany curve, an old man in a red sailor's beanie sat playing video poker.

"What'll it be, guys?" a young woman said from behind the bar. She was wearing a tank top, and a Confederate flag tattoo billowed across her heart.

"A beer," George said.

"A whiskey," Georgi said.

"A beer and a whiskey for each of us." George's face was twisted into a tight smile.

"Coming right up," the bartender said, her eyes lingering for a second on George.

The man playing video poker gave a whoop and clutched his gnarled fist into the air. "Sailors have gone the way of cowboys, or perhaps cowboys the way of sailors," he mused to no one in particular.

Their drinks arrived, and George took his whiskey in a single gulp and then stared down into his bottle of beer.

"Epic day," Georgi said. He had only a faint accent.

George remained silent.

"That tuna will bring in a lot of money. And the swordfish too."

"Yeah," George muttered.

"Remember that guy last summer who caught a marlin? He couldn't fit it in the boat, so he lashed it to the side and drug it into the bay."

George said nothing.

"And the sharks ate it up before he even got to the dock."

The old man in the beanie stood up from his barstool. He pumped his fists in the air, as the poker machine made a sound like cathedral bells going off.

Staring ahead at the dark row of liquor bottles behind the bar, George took a long drink of beer. "What the hell was that in your trunk?"

Georgi hesitated. "It's complicated."

George held up a hand. "Let me stop you right there." Georgi nodded. "Is that a sex thing?"

"It's complicated. I wish my English was better."

"You're English is just fine, Georgi. Don't fuck around. What was that?"

"Okay. They're costumes. They're—"

"I know, man. For what?"

"Sometimes I'm involved in a community that dresses up."

"A sex thing?"

"No, it's not a sex thing. I drive to Charleston and sometimes Columbia and even Asheville. It's a community. A pretty big one."

"I hate this *community* bullshit. People always call groups of weirdos communities. It's a sex thing, right?"

"No," Georgi said. "We just get together."

"And you wear animal outfits?"

"And we wear costumes, yes. It's not a sex thing, though. We just meet."

"You meet *and?*"

"We commune."

George was gripping his beer and twisting the label off. Damp pieces of red and white paper littered the bar in front of him. "Come on. You get together and do what exactly?"

Georgi tried to touch George on his shoulder, but he pulled away. "We dress up and we...we just cuddle. That's all."

"You cuddle with other adults. Male or female?"

"One never knows."

"That's fucking perverted, Georgi."

"Listen, it's not like it sounds. It's—"

"Wait a second. You used to come over to my house dressed like the Easter bunny for my kids."

"Yes."

"They called you 'the clothes bunny,' Georgi. My kids. My goddamn kids!" George waved his hand in the air. The bartender walked over. "Another whiskey and beer," George said. She nodded toward Georgi, but he shook his head.

George looked directly at Georgi for the first time since they had arrived. "You go to my church."

"This is not a violation."

George's drinks arrived. He downed the whiskey and looked across the bar. A few tourists had come in and sat down between them and the old sailor. They had ordered piña coladas, and the bartender was noisily buzzing at the blender. George looked away from them in disgust and squared down on Georgi. "What about Anna, man? She married you. She and I have been friends since we were kids. She got you a green card, for God's sake. Does she know about this?"

Georgi nodded. "She does."

"What? How does she stand for it?"

Georgi drained his beer and stood up. He was so tall he had to stoop to George's level. "Anna always says, 'I don't care what gets it up as long you bring it home.'"

George slammed his fist down on the bar. The mahogany shook. The tourists turned to them and went silent, as did the old man at the poker machine. The bartender walked their way, her Confederate flag bouncing.

"Keep your shit together, guys," she said, "or you're out of here."

Georgi nodded.

"I knew it," George said. The bartender looked at him again. "I knew it was a sex thing."

Georgi sat back down again at his stool. "It's not not a sex thing, okay?"

George pounded the bar again. The tourists looked over, and he shot them a withering glance. "We're dealing with some local shit here," he said to the room. "Direct your attention back to your fucking girly drinks."

The tourists huddled together, and one of them said, "Let's get out of this shithole."

Georgi stood up again, towering over the bar. "I'll be going too."

George, now almost serene, said, "You know you'll never see my kids again."

Georgi nodded. "Okay, boss."

"And, Georgi…"

Georgi was walking away but he turned back to the bar. "Yeah?"

"I'll be at the docks in the morning."

"Okay, boss."

"You better not be."

21

WAKEY, WAKEY, HANDS OFF SNAKEY

"Can you please go with us, Dad?" Josh whined. They were sitting at breakfast, Josh leaning over a bowl of Frosted Flakes. His dad had a cup of coffee in one hand and a folded newspaper in the other.

"Camping's not my thing, Josh." He hadn't looked up. Josh had asked several times by this point.

"But we need chaperones. Dad, please. Plus, you love history. You should see the area one last time."

Since he was old enough to take his bike wherever he wanted, Josh loved riding to the Waccamaw River and scouring its bluffs for arrowheads and shards of pottery. One of the largest undeveloped tracts along the river was now on the cusp of becoming a gated community. It was going to be called Legacy Plantation, although it had never been a plantation.

To mark the occasion before the loggers and backhoes arrived, the local Boy Scouts troop arranged a campout during spring break, a last huzzah before the forests were decimated to make way for retirees, second homers, and the burgeoning families of young professionals.

Josh's mother walked over to the breakfast table. She put one finger on the edge of her husband's paper and lowered it. "We talked about this. You said yes last night. Remember?"

His father smiled. "Can you remind me?"

"Just before bed. Remember now?"

"Will it be possible to have that conversation again tonight?"

His mother smiled at him and then turned to Josh. "He's going, Josh. Tell your scout leader to sign him up."

Josh gave a little wolf's howl. "This shit will be the kicks," he said, not knowing why. The phrase had spread through school lately.

"Joshua!" both his parents said in unison.

"Sorry," he said, shoulders slumped for a second. He then whispered, "But it will be."

The entire Boy Scout troop caravanned from First Baptist, where they regularly held their meetings, to the property. There were seven cars, all crammed full of boys. Josh's dad had a new convertible, and several boys had fought, almost coming to blows in the parking lot of the church, over who would get to ride with them.

At the entrance to the property, the caravan stopped. The troop leader Mr. Cooper was at the front with his son Marcus; Josh's dad's convertible was next and then the rest of the fathers. Stretched across the road was a cow fence with a sign on it that read *TRESPASSERS WILL BE PROSECUTED*. Mr. Cooper got out of his Bronco and gave the caravan a thumbs up. He was dressed like Crocodile Dundee, with a dirty tan vest and a cowboy hat with sharks' teeth running around the band.

"What's going on?" Josh's dad said, leaning out of the convertible as Mr. Cooper approached.

"We're all good," Mr. Cooper said. He waved to the other cars. Smiling back at Josh's dad, he said, "I'm dating a woman who works for the development company. They won't be around this weekend."

"So we don't have permission to be here?" he whispered, hoping Josh and the other boys in the convertible wouldn't hear.

Mr. Cooper leaned in. "Fuck the rich, right?" He turned before he could see Josh's father's incredulous expression.

Mr. Cooper opened the gate, which was unlocked, and led the caravan onto the property. They drove for at least a mile down a winding sandy road lined with live oaks.

The troop made camp in a tall-grassed field that ran for some two hundred yards along the Waccamaw River. Josh's dad produced a two-person tent from the trunk of the convertible. It still had the price tag on it. "All right, Josh," he said. "You read the instructions, and I'll put her together." His father was already sweating in the spring heat.

Josh read aloud, "Choose a flat open space." His father looked at him impatiently. He wiped his brow with the tail of his shirt and gestured around to the enormous wide-open field.

"Right," Josh said, returning to the instructions. "Roll out the main body of the tent. Position the door in the direction of your choice." Josh's father faced the door toward the broad slow-moving river. "Done," he said.

Josh continued, "Snap together the connected sections of the main support rods." Josh's father opened a canvass bag and dumped its contents onto the grass; a dozen rods of all lengths and thicknesses lay before him. He looked at Josh, and again wiped his brow. "It's hot out here," he said. "Your grandmother used to say that it was so hot the hens were laying soft-boiled eggs. That's what kind of day it is. Anyway," he said, returning his attention to the rods in the grass. "How in the hell do you tell which ones are the support rods?"

Josh and his father were still pondering this when Mr. Cooper sauntered up. His tent had already been erected, and there was a fire blazing chest high before it. He had even somehow found large stones and had formed a safety circle around it.

"Need help?" Mr. Cooper asked.

"I need a drink," Josh's dad said. Like magic, Mr. Cooper produced a flask from his back pocket. Emblazoned on its front was the Boy Scout motto: "Always be prepared." He handed it to Josh's dad who took a long slow draw.

"You finish that," Mr. Cooper said. "Josh and I will have this tent up in a jiffy. He needs to learn anyway. It's part of the curriculum."

Josh's father sat down in a folding beach chair and poured the contents of the flask down his eager gullet. Normally on weekend days this hot, he would be hiding in the garage, secretly drinking beers and listening to records.

As promised, Mr. Cooper had the tent done in a matter of minutes. After that, Josh's dad and the rest of the chaperones went to drink with Mr. Cooper at his tent, leaving Josh and the boys with free reign of the woods. As the sun set and the darkness began to settle, they arranged a massive game of Capture the Flag. The campsite was no man's land, and each team's flag was hidden in the woods on either side of it. Periodically the boys ran into no man's land, and their fathers would shout, a bit drunkenly now, little nuggets of wisdom.

"Watch out for poison ivy," one father said. "Never trust a three-leaved plant."

Another said, "Copperheads are the ones that look like they have rusty leaves glued to their backs, and water moccasins are those dark fat fuckers."

Yet another said, "Lyme disease is no picnic, y'all. Best check one another for ticks."

After Capture the Flag, the boys ate ham sandwiches on white bread that one of their mother's had made.

When it was fully dark, Mr. Cooper produced a box of Roman candles and gave each scout three of them. Eyes aglitter, they lit the Roman candles and ran around the clearing shooting them at one other, purposefully aiming for faces despite the drunken bellows from their fathers. "Cut it out, goddammit. Aim lower. Not at the eyes, you little fools."

One boy ended up with a long red and black slash across his neck, and another briefly caught on fire. By the time the Roman candles had all been discharged, the boys were exhausted, and the dads drunk and ready for bed.

Josh's father, like most, slept alone in his tent, while the boys all crammed into the larger tents the troop owned.

In the tent where Josh ended up, they were packed in like cordwood, feet to face, six deep in two rows, twelve boys in a tent designed to sleep eight. For a long time before the last ones struggled off to sleep in the sultry spring heat, the boys made a game of sneaking a hand out of their sleeping bag and slapping their neighbor. The slaps were, without exception, aimed at the neighbor's balls.

Wack! Josh heard throughout the evening, and then someone would inevitably say, "That's gotta smart."

Josh lay in his sleeping bag, hot and twitching with anticipation. There was a boy to either side of him, Ryan to his right and a boy he barely knew named Sam to his left. Sleep came for Josh once or twice, but each time he started awake with the sound of a slap, and someone saying, "Oh, boy, I think a heard a nut bust."

Josh listened to the river babbling and the crickets in the woods surrounding the tent. He wondered why no one had tried to slap him, and as he did, he felt a tingle spread through his midsection. He stared up at the top of the tent and could just make out a fly buzzing up against the netting. Josh looked left and right to be sure Ryan and Sam were asleep. He then eased his hand down into his pants. His tighty-whities were standing out and away from his body, forming their own little tent.

He gave himself two tugs and one hard flick, and even that, the sharp pain of it, felt marvelous. But Josh drew his hand away, not wanting to get caught. Although all seemed quiet, he was not convinced that the slapping had ceased.

In the morning, Mr. Cooper snuck up to their tent, unzipped the main flap, and peered in. The boys were all asleep, still crammed in together, some limbs draped over their neighbors. Mr. Cooper put a bullhorn to his mouth and shouted, "Wakey, wakey, eggs and bakey. Wakey, wakey, hands off snakey."

The boys began to stir, some of them pleading for Mr. Cooper to go away. Josh emerged from sleep the second time Mr. Cooper shouted the phrase into his bullhorn. At "hands off snakey," his hand made the same path it had the night before.

His penis had gone slack, once again a useless fleshy tube. Josh feared that he would never regain the feeling.

But the next night the slapping would begin again, and lying there in the hot dark, he would think to himself, "This shit is the kicks."

22

FEATHERS

Pawleys Island was already lousy with golf courses. Now the forest behind Ryan's house was being ravaged in order to put in another one, and the boys decided to investigate. When Josh rode up on his bike, Ryan and his older brother James were already outside waiting. They were sitting in the driveway, their bikes in the gravel next to them. They were in the shadow of their father George's charter fishing boat, perched there on its massive metal trailer.

"What took you so long? Come the fuck on," Ryan said. The seventh graders had taken up "fuck" with confidence and abandon, peppering their every conversation with the epithet.

James was silent. Josh and Ryan worshipped him. He had long blond hair and wore flannel shirts, even now in late April. James claimed to work as an oyster pirate, and while Josh and Ryan weren't entirely sure what that meant, they knew it was a vocation to admire. He had also just gotten both of them copies of Guns N' Roses' *Appetite for Destruction*, which Josh's mother had expressly forbidden. Josh kept the cassette in a box hidden under his bed and only brought it out, to strut and sing along with, when no one was home.

"Chores," Josh said. "Mom made me vacuum the fucking house."

"Well, come on," Ryan said, mounting his bike. James did the same and rode off ahead of them through the backyard. Josh followed close, and after they cleared a small strip of trees, he witnessed the devastation. The forest, which had been their playground for as long as any of them could remember, was gone, and in its stead only a scarred landscape, dark red earth pushed this way and that into small artificial hills.

They rode through the thick mud, moving the gears of their bikes lower and lower. Josh got bogged down, but the other two kept upright, pumping as hard as they could. Josh ended up walking alongside his bike, his shoes caked heavily.

James made it up the highest hill in the blighted landscape and stopped. Ryan followed close behind, but Josh was another two minutes before summiting. They looked down the opposite side of the hill, their faces reverential, as they examined the slope that plunged down to a newly dug pond.

"Shit," Ryan said. "That's steep as hell."

Josh said nothing, scared of what was to follow.

James eyed the slope like some sort of junior cartographer, noting the subtleties of the downward face, sizing up every bump and crevice left by the dozer's tracks. "All right, boys," James said, still looking down the hill.

Then he was gone, he and his bike careening downward. At the bottom, he hit a small lip and went flying. The bike went out from under him, and for a second he was alone in the air. His body extended like a flannelled bird in flight. The bike hit the water first with a mighty splash, and then James dove in just beyond it.

Ryan and Josh watched him resurface. His arms outstretched, James flapped the water to keep himself afloat. Flinging the wet hair from his eyes, he looked back up the hill. Ryan and Josh stared down with glassy eyes. "Fuck," Ryan whispered. "We gotta do it."

Josh was already shaking. He gripped the handlebars of his bike, his knuckles white. "Fuck that," Josh said. "This is mental."

"My brother will never let me live it down if I don't."

"Go then."

"You go with me," Ryan said.

"That's nuts. We'll collide in the air. Probably die."

James whooped from below. He went under like a hungry duck. The pond bubbled and boiled. His feet emerged, the water so murky they appeared detached from a body. Seconds later James turned and surfaced, struggling to gain breath. He was dragging his bike up from the deep, holding it with one arm, while flailing with the other to keep his face above the water. When he reached the shallows, he stood up. The T-shirt under his flannel, previously white, was now the same brown color as the water.

"Come on, you goddamn scaredy-cats," he yelled.

"All right," Ryan said. "That's it."

He took off down the hill. His bike made incredible speed, even as he maneuvered to avoid exposed rocks. Ryan hit the lip at the bottom and like James before him, launched through the air. But he and his bike crashed into the water at the same time in a graceless cannonball of man and machine. When he emerged from the water, he was laughing and coughing at once. James swam out to him and gave Ryan a dramatic high five, the two of them bobbing like seagulls. They almost hugged.

Josh knew it was his turn. He looked at Ryan and James, smiling up at him expectantly.

"You can fucking do this," Josh whispered to himself. But he remained still. He thought about all the things that could go wrong, and he saw his mother crying at his funeral, his sisters clutching one another, his father sitting stoically. They would coat his bike in gold, enshrine it, keep it in the living room in memoriam.

"What are you doing?" Ryan yelled.

Josh didn't look at him, but instead locked eyes with James. He was in high school, where Josh would be year after next. Josh needed James: protection from wedgies, a hookup for cigarettes and pornos and albums labeled Parental Advisory.

Josh put a foot on one pedal and then the other, and with that he was coasting down. He gripped the brake with all his might, but he was still going down faster than he could control.

A double whoop barely broke through into his mind. He looked up and smiled at James, and at that moment, he hit the lip. Rather than flying out over the water, man and bike, as he had hoped, the bike stalled, and he alone sailed over the handlebars. The bike clung to the lip, and he rolled in the air and came down not in the water but in the mud at the edge of the pond. He landed with a hollow thud.

Josh sat up, wheezing and struggling for breath. He imagined the shape of his ribs; he had felt them rattle as he connected with the ground.

James and Ryan, just a few feet from him now in the shallows, were doubled over, spanking one another, moving in and out of high-pitched giggles and low, barely audible man-guffaws. They were wet, but Josh, writhing in the mud and struggling to gain control, looked like some half-formed creature emerging from reptilian slime to test itself on terra firma.

He stood and raked the mud from his eyes. His long hair was so dirty and matted that he parted it in front of his face like a curtain.

Josh drug his bike off the lip of the hill; its chain had come loose, and the gears were clogged with mud.

Ryan stopped laughing long enough to say, "Again. Again, dudes." Ryan and James were already making their way back up the hill.

"My bike," Josh managed, holding his ribs. They looked back. "It's fucked."

James stopped. He stared at Josh the way a disappointed dad looks at a kid who can't even manage to get a hit in tee-ball. "Okay," James said. "Pack it in, boys. Let's shove off home and get Josh fixed up."

Ryan huffed. "Fine."

When they got back to the house, they all entered the garage. Ryan and James's mom Marie came out of the door that led into the kitchen. She shook her head at them. She took a particularly long look at Josh, noting his mud-covered clothes. "Take those off, all of you, and put them straight into the washing machine." Her eyes moved to the washer and dryer that hunkered in the corner of the garage. "Don't step foot in this house until you do."

She went back inside, leaving the door open.

Ryan shucked off his clothes. He and James were the kind of guys who were completely comfortable being naked in front of God and everybody. Josh looked at Ryan's privates, his penis and balls swinging hairless between his legs as he struggled with his wet T-shirt. Josh's gaze followed Ryan's naked ass as it bobbed up the stairs and into the house.

Even more than the hill and the fall and the pond, this was what Josh had been dreading. He had made careful study of all scenarios of late, eliminating the need to get naked with his male friends and classmates.

James disrobed now, and again Josh glanced between his legs, while trying not to be noticed. James's penis emerged from a whisper of blond peach fuzz.

Josh felt a maggot drop down into the yawning space of his brain. He shook in his wet, muddy clothes, despite the dense heat collecting in the garage. James smiled at him, and Josh started to disrobe as well, his shirt first and then his pants. Finally, he stood in just his tighty-whities. James said, "You got to take those off too. Or Mom won't let you come inside."

Josh inched down his undies, and James watched, standing next to the open door of the washing machine.

Naked, Josh's thin pizzle lay nestled in a thick mess of hair, a black bear's quaff.

"Holy fuck," James muttered.

"I know, I'm sorry."

"Sorry for what, dude?"

"My pubes. These awful pubes."

James looked admiringly. "Don't be sorry. You've gotten your feathers."

"My feathers?"

"Yeah," James said. "That's what Native Americans used to say—getting your feathers."

"Oh." Josh was still shaking, one hand now cupping his penis and balls.

"Like a bird. Like an adult bird, dude."

James turned and ran up the stairs and into the house.

Josh's mind was all fireworks now. The maggots screeched and fled as if from fire. He followed James up the stairs and entered the kitchen. James and Ryan's mother was there, stirring a pot on the stovetop.

His body was singing electric, aquiver with some new energy, as he walked through. He was naked and for once not ashamed. There was a large fan blowing from the ceiling of the kitchen. Josh felt the breeze stir his feathers; they lifted and resettled and lifted again.

"Don't mind me, Mrs. Marie," he said, pivoting slightly to her before swaggering on toward Ryan's room. "I'm just flying through."

23

TAINT

On the wall, there was a picture of Jesus's face made out of dried beans. The picture was behind Pastor Ben's head, and Josh focused on it as Ben finished the opening prayer of the special Bible study that his mother had forced him to attend. Several other guys were there that Josh knew from school. They were all sitting in small desks in a room of First Baptist ordinarily used for children's Sunday School.

Ben looked just like Sonny Bono in the 1970s, except tall. He had a thick brown mustache and thinning hair. He never wore a blazer, even on Sundays, but he had a different colored vest for every day of the week. Today it was paisley and baby blue.

"The point of this meeting," Ben said, after he finished his prayer, "is for you to have a Christ-centered space in which to discuss sex." The boys knew why they were there, but they blushed nonetheless. "Sex is a wonderful thing, but it is only to be shared between a man and woman, and only within the confines of marriage. I can't tell you how happy my wife and I were that we waited for one another." Ben looked around the room. He licked his moustache in concentration. "You're undoubtedly hearing a lot about sex from school and TV. We're meeting so that you can learn how Jesus fits into your desires."

Josh instantly imagined Jesus, sweaty and wearing only a loincloth, between himself and a naked woman. Jesus was ghost-like, nearly transparent, as he hovered there. Josh had to reach through His chest to fondle the woman's nipple.

"Earth to Josh," Ben was saying. "Earth to Josh."

Josh's attention snapped back to the room. He first saw bean-faced Jesus on the wall and then Ben.

"I was asking if you had a question. You looked rather quiz-zical."

Josh drained of color as he realized he now had a full-on erection, and that Jesus had played some role in his achieving it. Ben and the others were staring at him, and he was thankful that the desk hid his arousal. Desperate for them to look away, Josh asked the first question that came to mind. "Why do men have taints?"

Ben was taken aback for a second, and in the pause, several of the boys began to giggle. Ben waved at them to cease and said, "No question is off limits here, as long as we approach it maturely. So, please, no laughing. We need openness, honesty, and, above all, maturity."

The boys nodded and quieted down. Like Josh, they too were curious about taints.

"Good," Ben said. "The taint exists because in the womb, there is a moment when all babies could become men or women. They have, in other words, both sets of parts."

Josh thought briefly of his tendency to tuck his penis between his legs and ogle himself in his mother's full-length mirror. He felt his mind begin to squirm with maggots, and his pants tightened again.

"During gestation, God decides, in His infinite wisdom, whether you are to be a boy or a girl. If you are to be a boy, God magically sews up your vagina while you are still inside your mother. The taint is a sort of reminder of what could have been."

At that point, Josh stopped paying attention. For the rest of the meeting, he locked eyes with bean-faced Jesus and considered this miraculous new discovery.

When he got home that evening, his family was downstairs preparing for dinner. Josh made a beeline to the upstairs bathroom that he shared with his sisters. There he found a small hand mirror, a pair of scissors, and a pink razor in his older sister's drawer. He locked the door and shucked off all of his clothes. He tucked himself between his legs and did the "Dance of the Seven Veils" before the mirror. Satisfied with the jig, he proceeded to trim his pubes as short as possible. He moved carefully when he got to his testicles and even more carefully when he got to his taint. Within moments, he was almost clear of feathers.

Josh swept up his pubes from the floor with his hands and placed them into a plastic bag he found under the sink. He would scatter them outside tomorrow. He was thrilled by the thought that one day birds of passage might make nests from such leavings.

He got into the shower and felt the hot water careen down his body like so many hands. He backed away and lathered from his ass around to the happy trail that led up to his belly button. He shaved himself until he was as bald as newborn hamster. In the hand mirror, he observed his taint. The seam was there, evidence perhaps of God's own hand.

Needing to pee, Josh imagined Jesus cutting the sutures, and the vagina that could have been opened up.

24

WHALE TAIL

At the arcade in Garden City, Josh bowled his final ski ball and hit the 500-point hole dead on. "Fuck yeah," he said, reaching down and retrieving the tickets that belched out of the machine. "Wanna play again?" he asked Ryan.

"No. I'm bored." He drew the words out in an exaggerated manner.

"All right, all right. Where's Spregg?"

"He's out on the pier. Should we go?"

"Yeah. Just let me redeem my tickets."

Josh and Ryan walked up to the counter at the back of the arcade. A teenager wearing a Marilyn Manson T-shirt looked at them apathetically. She had on eye makeup dark as ash. Her black hair was shaved on both sides, and her top bun had a bone holding it in place. When she crossed her arms over Manson's face, Josh noticed a name tag that read Shanelle. "What do you want, fuckhead?"

"All I want is what I have coming to me. All I want is my fair share," Josh said. It was his favorite line from *A Charlie Brown Christmas*. He slapped his tickets down on the glass case full of brightly colored candies and plastic toys.

"I bet your mom is real proud," Shanelle said.

"One Chinese finger trap, please," Josh said. Shanelle gave him a pink one. Josh knew she did this to annoy him, but he just smiled, and he and Ryan left the arcade. They walked past a row of beachwear shops and a diner called Sam's Corner. They then crossed the street and went up a flight of wooden stairs to the pier. It was nearing sunset, but the pier was still full of old men fishing, their lines descending a hundred feet to the sea. Down the center of the pier teenage couples promenaded, holding hands and pointing out the softening colors of the sky.

"See," Ryan said. "That's what we should be doing. We're too old for the arcade, too old for candy and fucking Chinese finger traps. And don't you dare say you're saving yourself for Chloe." Josh put the finger trap to his lips like he was preventing himself from answering. Ryan rolled his eyes. "Why'd you get that thing anyway?"

"They're hilarious," Josh said. "Wanna do it with me?" He held the finger trap out to Ryan.

"No. This is exactly what I'm trying to say. You're too old for that shit. You never act your age."

"Fine." Josh slipped the finger trap back into his pocket.

They continued along the pier, farther out into the briny world. At one point, Ryan nodded his head to the left. An older guy they vaguely knew was leaning against the railing of the pier with a beautiful blond woman they had never seen. She had her T-shirt knotted high on her stomach, and Josh could see the top of her thong sticking out of her cutoffs like the tail of a humpback in the ocean of her lower back.

"A whale tail," Josh said in amazement. He and Ryan slowed their pace and continued to leer. The couple was looking away from them and out over the water. As Josh and Ryan passed, the guy put his hand into the girl's back pocket. The whale tail flicked ever so slightly.

"Something to celebrate."

"Something for poets to warble about."

They moseyed on in contemplation. When they reached the end of the pier, Spregg was standing there with a group of old fishermen. They were drinking beers and had apparently shared some with Spregg, even though he was only thirteen. He swayed and slurred, "Check it out!" He pointed to a man at the center of the group. His rod was bent, and he was struggling to reel in something. Josh and Ryan peered over the railing. The light was beginning to fail, but they could just make out a three-foot long eel writhing at the end of the line.

"That guy caught a fucking snake out of the ocean," Spregg said, slapping Ryan on the upper arm.

"Cut it out," Ryan said.

"That's not a snake," Josh said. "That's an eel." Spregg stared at him as if trying to decide if he was joking. Josh shrugged. "What?"

"What do you mean, 'What?' Eels don't exist."

"Of course, they do."

"Only in fairy tales."

"Are you serious?"

"Do you honestly believe eels exist?" He laughed and looked around, hoping one of the old men would back him up. "My dad's a snake expert."

"Of course, eels exist," Josh said. "Something's really wrong with you."

"Something's wrong with both of you," Ryan said, before stomping back down the pier.

Josh watched him for a moment and then turned to Spregg. "You coming?"

"Fuck no," Spregg replied. "Not when they're catching ocean snakes."

Josh walked back down the pier alone. He checked but the girl with the whale tail was no longer there. He could see Ryan up ahead and followed him down the steep steps, across the road, and into Sam's Corner.

Josh sat down next to Ryan at the counter. The diner was 1950s themed with black and white tile and red, sparkly booths. There were pictures of young shiny-haired Elvis everywhere. Josh and Ryan looked ahead into the kitchen. The man working the flat-top grill had no ears, just holes on either side of his bald head.

All of a sudden a spitball whizzed between Josh and Ryan. They turned around and as they did, another spitball smacked Josh in the forehead. Two girls in a booth behind them giggled and tried to look nonchalant. Then one held a straw up and shrugged flirtatiously. Josh and Ryan scrambled from their barstools and sat down in the booth, Ryan next to a blond girl and Josh a brunette. The blond said, "I'm Meg."

The brunette, barely stifling a giggle, said, "I'm Megan."

Ryan said, "I'm Ryan."

And Josh said, "I'm Ry."

Both girls laughed. "Great to meet you, Ry and Ryan," Meg said. "Glad our spitballs didn't turn you off."

"Nope, not us," Ryan said.

They sat in silence for a moment until Megan piped up, "Before you got here we were discussing that guy." She pointed to the cook with no ears. "What do you think happened to him?"

A waiter came over, and they all stopped staring. "What'll it be?" He looked like fat old shaggy-haired Elvis and was wearing a glittery red jacket and pants that matched the booths.

They ordered vanilla milkshakes, and when the waiter walked away, Ryan said, "I know. He used to run bets for a gangster in New York City. One day, when the gangster lost a boatload of money on a horse recommended to him by that guy, he burned off his ears and told him he better never see him around New York again."

"Good," Megan said. She looked over at Josh beside her. "Now your turn." Josh's thoughts ran crabwise. He started to sweat, and he searched the diner for some inspiration.

The waiter arrived and placed four milkshakes on their table. They all slurped for a moment.

"Refreshing," Josh said.

"You can't get off that easy," Megan said. "Let's have it." She nudged him with her elbow.

He could think of only one word. "Leprosy," he blurted out.

"Gross," Meg said.

Josh continued, "When I was young, I used to think that Jesus was always going around healing leopards. Then later my mom told me it was lepers and described to me what leprosy meant. Lepers' bodies basically begin to rot, and over time their parts fall off—noses, fingers, toes. They stink to high heaven, I bet, with all that rotten flesh." Ryan sliced his index finger across his own throat. "So the point is that the cook could have leprosy, and his ears were just the first to go."

Meg was making a horrendous face at Josh from across the table. He turned to Megan, and she looked flabbergasted.

Not knowing what to say, Josh took the cherry from his milkshake and tossed it in his mouth. He then forced a laugh, but when he did a chunk of cherry launched onto Megan's chest. Time slowed to a creep as Josh watched the cherry slide down her cleavage and into her bra. Then time began to move at a frenzied rate.

Megan said, "Ew, ew, ew." She pushed Josh from the booth, and Meg did the same to Ryan. They both fled from the diner. Josh and Ryan watched them through the window as they ran around the corner in the direction of the beach.

"That girl in the arcade was right. You are a fuckhead," Ryan said. "Actually, I take that back. I can't tell if you're truly a fuck-head, or if you're just so obsessed with Chloe that you sabotage your chances with any other girl you meet."

That night Josh lay sleeplessly on the futon under his bunk bed. He held the Chinese finger trap before him in the dark bedroom. He thought of the whale tail and the chunk of cherry, and he slipped his penis into the finger trap.

He gave it a tug and the trap tightened. Josh smiled, and his penis began to swell. Within a few seconds, though, the trap was too tight. He tried to pull it off, but it dug in. "Shit." He pulled harder, and the trap cut into the base of his penis. "No, no, no," he said.

Moments later his mother burst into the bedroom. She saw the Chinese finger trap cutting into her son's half-erect penis. Eyelids fluttering, she braced herself against the frame of the bunk bed. "Heavenly Jesus."

"Get out," Josh cried.

She dashed out the door but came back a minute later. Josh had covered himself with a blanket. His mother handed him a pair of scissors. "Cut yourself free."

"Thanks," he whispered. He couldn't make eye contact with her.

"You know I love you," she said. "But I just don't understand why everything has to be so perverted with you."

"I can't seem to help it."

"Remember the maggots, Joshua. No woman's going to want to be with a man who has a mind full of maggots."

25

BUZZARD PARTY

Even late in the afternoon, it was still hot, as Okefenokee Job drove the back roads of the Georgetown County. Out past the Black River, the road turned into little more than a levee that rose out of the swamp. His blond hair was long, stringy, and sun-bleached, and his face dark and swarthy, like a lightweight prizefighter gone to seed. Job opened a beer and drained half of it. "Hot as fresh milk out here," he murmured to himself. His truck had neither air conditioning nor a radio. The mute antenna on the side of the hood was decorated with a number of squirrels' tails he'd picked up along the road. They fluttered in the breeze like a furry flag. Inside it smelled like damp earth and mushrooms, nearly rancid. He rolled down the window. With the wind in his face, Job drank and focused on the road, scanning for snakes.

He laughed at a sign that read *Speed Monitored by Aircraft*. This coastal land was flat as a bed sheet. Only an idiot would fail to consider the fact that you could see a plane coming from a mile away.

A snake, long and dark, lay up ahead on the road. He stopped the truck and killed the engine. He hadn't seen another person on this road all day, so he left the truck there in the middle of the lane. Job reached into a cooler in the bed and pulled out another beer. He popped the tab, and the vibration made a rattle go off in a wooden crate next to the cooler. "Whoa there, big boy," he said.

Job walked out to the front of the truck. The snake was still there, but even from twenty yards away, he could tell that it was a water moccasin, not the rattlesnake he had hoped it would be. "Well, damn," he said. He took a long swig of beer, making bubbles fast in the can, and then he walked forward and goosed the snake with the toe of his boot. It reared back, coiling itself like a spring. The snake seemed to consider striking, but then went limp and slithered off the blacktop. Job watched it drop into the water. It made a small wake as it moved along the surface, disappearing amongst the cypress knees.

He'd never been known as Okefenokee Job when he lived in Florida, just plain Job. It was when he moved away and began roaming the country that the name gained traction, used by a number of comrades in different states. It really stuck when he started doing snake demonstrations for Boy Scout troops throughout the South, telling youngsters which snakes to avoid should they run up on them during camping trips. Word spread, and within a few years he had bookings with schools throughout the region. "Okefenokee Job" was precisely the kind of name principals could showcase to get kids excited about educational assemblies.

Back in the truck Job drove on. He thought about his wife. She lived in Pawleys Island, not thirty miles from here as the crow flies. And yet he hadn't seen her in the two weeks he'd been back in South Carolina. He'd run into a little trouble in Florida, arrested for illegally trapping snakes and alligators in the Everglades. The police and game wardens couldn't pin the charges on him, though, after they searched the fish camp where he was squatting and failed to find any hard evidence. But the ordeal was enough to make him get out of Florida. He had a good gig going with the school demonstrations, and he knew that might be over if he was convicted of a felony.

Drinking and dreaming of his wife eventually made him think of his son. The boy needed him, he knew that, and yet he couldn't bear to be around him for more than a day or two. It was the boy, more than his wife, that made him take to the road. And he always had snakes, his livelihood, as an excuse for leaving. He had never known his own father, although his mother often told him what a piece of shit he was. His mother was no picnic either, and sometimes Job was happy he'd only had her to contend with.

As he drove, Job opened another beer and thought about the many burdens he could place on the shoulders of his own son. "He's better off," he said.

Job slammed on the breaks and swerved to the left. He'd come upon some kind of carcass on the blacktop. The truck skidded to a stop. "Fuck," he said, noting how close to the edge of the road he had come.

The still swamp was a black mirror, reflecting the blue sky and the clouds, small and plump like floating popcorn. In the reflection he could see a buzzard hanging in the air. Another joined it, and then another. Job turned from the swamp and looked up at this buzzard-haunted sky.

He grabbed a bottle of bourbon out of the glove box and took a deep slug to calm his nerves. He got out of the truck and walked up to a twelve-point buck. It had been hit in the flank, and through a tear white maggots oozed beneath shiny black flies. Job put his hand over his face. He felt his spit go hot in his mouth, and he regretted the bourbon. In all his years riding around backcountry roads, he'd never seen a roadkill deer this large. Job considered removing its antlers. But he was queasy now and thought he might vomit. "Maybe in the morning."

Job neither wanted to touch, nor leave the deer. What he wanted to do was drink and think about his son. So he backed the truck up about thirty yards. His vision was a bit blurry, he noticed, as he looked out the back window in reverse. He was happy to not be driving anymore and believed the buck was a sign that he should no longer be behind the wheel.

Job set up a pup tent on the small shoulder between the road and the swamp. He unfolded a camping chair and sat down with the bourbon in one hand and a beer in the other. He went back and forth between the two, chasing the bourbon down his willing gullet. The tree frogs sang out as the light began to dwindle.

The sky was swarming now with buzzards. Ultimately, a funnel of them formed, and like water going down a drain, they gyred to the earth. At about the time the buzzards lighted on the buck, Job's vision began to fail, both due to the drinking and the end of twilight's gloaming. He stumbled into the pup tent, and as he faded into sleep, he heard the buzzards out there rending flesh from bone.

When Job decamped in the morning, the buzzards were still there. He saluted them as he walked back to his truck. He called them by the names he had assigned them last night as they descended from the heavens. One of the names had been his father's.

26

THE ASSES OF THEIR YOUTH

During the summer after Josh's seventh-grade year, the youth of Pawleys Island took to mooning one another. If one walked the length of the island, you could see groups of boys or girls standing on the roofs of beach houses. They waited for passersby, and then pants came down and asses out.

Since the mooning epidemic began, Ryan and Josh were hanging out more than ever with Spregg, as his house was the closest to the beach and thus the action. Today the three of them roamed the sand. Around noon they found a house with four girls on the roof, and when they walked by, the girls gave them an eyeful. Josh grinned madly, recognizing Chloe among them. He, Spregg, and Ryan cheered from the beach, dropped their own pants, and returned the favor.

"Walk on," Ryan said. "We gotta leave them wanting more."

The boys continued down the beach. The girls' whoops followed as they sauntered along. When they were out of earshot, Ryan asked, "Have you heard of sunning?"

"What's that?" Josh said.

"It's mooning your front."

"Nice," Spregg said.

"I'd like to see that," Josh said, thinking of Chloe.

"Yeah. But we need to figure out how to make it catch on."

They pondered this for a moment, and then Josh said, "I have an idea. Follow me."

He led Spregg and Ryan up the South Causeway to a wooded area along the saltmarsh. They dogtrotted amongst the trees until they came to a stand of live oaks dripping with Spanish moss. "Grab as much of it as you can," Josh said, already reaching into the lower branches to retrieve the long gray strands.

૭

When they arrived back at the girls' beach house, they had festooned their heads and faces with Spanish moss, and they now looked like prophets from another age.

Our Father, who art in the flesh, the boys all thought, as if in prayer. Chloe was still on the roof, serving as lookout. She had binoculars trained upon the beach. When she saw the boys, she called into an open window and the other girls came out.

The boys launched into a rudimentary dance they had choreographed back in the woods, doing a sort of pig ankle waltz.

"Ho, ho, ho," Josh said. "We're Father Christmas."

"Show us those butts," Chloe called.

"Strip, boys," another girl said.

"Wanna see the sun?" Ryan asked. With that, all three boys pulled down the fronts of their pants. Spanish moss flowed out over their zippers.

The girls on the roof laughed and catcalled. "Love those old man pubes," one screamed. Another yelled, "Santa's carpet matches the drapes." Chloe walked to the edge of the roof and, looking directly at Josh, said, "Meet us on the dock in exactly one hour."

Their beach house was on the south end of Pawleys, which was so narrow that there was only a single row of houses. On one side of them, there was the beach, and on the other the road and then the saltmarsh that split the island and the mainland. Each house on the south end had its own dock that stretched west into the marsh.

The boys waited at the dock for two hours, but the girls didn't show up. Josh was despondent. He'd imagined walking off with Chloe, hand in hand, to some secluded spot in the dunes. Plus, chiggers had gotten into his underwear from the Spanish moss. They'd found the forest of his pubes and were worrying him to distraction.

"Why do you keep scratching your balls?" Spregg asked.

"I got fucking chiggers, man."

"I feel fine."

"I've got 'em too," Ryan said. "Let's get out of here. I need a shower."

They got up and had just begun walking toward the road when they heard a boat coming fast across the saltmarsh. They ran back, and the boat slowed near the end of the dock. On it there were six people, all facing away from the boys. Chloe whooped, and in unison everyone on the boat dropped their pants and bent over. Josh couldn't tell which ass belonged to whom, or even whether they were all girls.

Later Spregg would swear he saw at least one of them "hangin' brain." And later still they would recall these halcyon days and how beautiful they all had been, the boys equal to the girls. But in the moment, they thought only of the myriad moons, orbiting so close they could have seen an asshole winking in fart.

27

JAYBIRD

Through the large bay window in the kitchen, Jaybird spotted the boys in the yard. It was late afternoon, and the three of them were darting from tree to tree on the lawn of the Naked Island Resort. Jaybird was cutting up bag after bag of ripe tomatoes. "Birthdaysuit," she called to the adjoining room. "Put on some clothes. We've got visitors."

Birthdaysuit threw down the biography of Marquis de Sade he was reading and shot up. He peered out the window and was about to run outside. "Clothes," Jaybird reminded him.

"Right." He skittered off to get a bathrobe and then headed out to the porch. Birthdaysuit had been knocking back cocktails since noon, and he swayed a bit as he shaded his eyes and surveyed the lawn. "Hey there, boys," he said. There were whispers issuing from behind a row of wax myrtles. "Don't worry. All are welcome here."

Spregg stepped out from behind the shrubs and into the clearing of the lawn. He walked toward Birthdaysuit, passing a small sign pointing to nowhere that read *Esteban's Island*. Spregg's pupils were large and black as onyx despite the sun. He had been popping his mother's pills all day. He claimed he was so scared of drowning that he couldn't cross a body of water unless stoned. "This Naked Island?"

"Sure is," Birthdaysuit said.

"Where's the sex party?"

"What sex party?"

"The lace and leather? Whips and chains? Where are the dancing gypsies?"

"Hasn't been anything like that out here for a long time."

"Fuck," Ryan said, stepping out into the clearing. Josh

skulked for a moment longer and then followed. "Spregg, you said this place was going to blow our minds."

Josh said, "We paddled all the way out here, Spregg. For nothing?"

Birthdaysuit motioned to them enthusiastically, and the boys joined him on the porch. "The swingin' party is pretty much dead these days. Just me and Jaybird left." He saw the disappointment on their faces. "Tell ya what, though. I can give you a tour, show you what used to be."

Ryan murmured, "I don't know."

"We should probably go," Josh said. "It's getting late, and we've gotta paddle back."

Birthdaysuit stepped forward. "Ever seen a Masturbatorium? How about a Dildo Dungeon?"

"You, sir," Spregg said, curtsying and feigning a British accent, "had me at Masturbatorium."

"Come on then."

The boys followed Birthdaysuit inside the resort, and they went straight to the kitchen. Jaybird was still there, wearing a floral dress that she had put on while they were outside. "Here's Jaybird," Birthdaysuit said. "Prettiest lady this side of the Mississippi."

Jaybird smiled. Her dark hair was long for her age and without a hint of gray, and as a result it looked like a wig. "My name's Maude, but this one still insists on calling me Jaybird."

The boys all mumbled that it was nice to meet her. Spregg was swaying back and forth, and Ryan slugged him in the arm.

"Fuck you, fucktard," Spregg said.

"You're the fucktard, fucktard," Ryan replied.

Birthdaysuit stepped between them. "We're all pacifists here at Naked Island," he said and turned back to Jaybird. "I'm going to give these young'uns a tour. Tell them about the good old days."

Jaybird said, "Oh, pshaw. I don't remember them being quite as good as you do."

"Come on, Jaybird." Birthdaysuit tottered over to her and put his arms around her waist. She batted him away with a wooden spoon, but she grinned while doing it. "You remember the good old days," he said. "Parties every night, the never-ending flesh parade." Birthdaysuit began to dance in front of Jaybird, moving his grotesque midsection first as if he were hullahooping before then moving into a series of thrusts, punctuating the beat of a country reel only he could hear. Josh watched as if mesmerized until Jaybird cracked Birthdaysuit on the forehead with the spoon. She smiled and winked at Josh.

"Get out of here, you ole horndog." Birthdaysuit balked and doddered from the room. Ryan and Spregg followed closely behind him.

"You hang back," she said, pointing a large knife at Josh. He was keen to see the Dildo Dungeon, but something about Maude made him want to stay.

"He's a fool," she said. "But God knows I love him. Amazing that love could be erected on this foundation of dung." She motioned around at the resort with the knife. "Anyway," she said, returning her attention to the giant pots on the stove. "Help me out." This was a command, and Josh nodded. "These ones are full of tomatoes cooking down, and this one is full of boiling water." Josh had never seen pots so large. "I'm going to fill each of these Mason jars with the stewed tomatoes. What I want you to do is take the jars and put a lid and ring on each one. You got to do it fast now. Don't let the heat out." Eying the dozens of jars on the counter, Josh nodded again.

Jaybird sang a pleasant shape-note ditty at the tomatoes, wishing them all the best as they stewed away. When she and Josh started the operation, they worked in silence for a while. Josh was enjoying himself despite the fact that this was not how he had imagined his first day at Naked Island.

"Can't even grow a decent tomato," Jaybird murmured.

"What was that, ma'am?"

"I was just saying that I can't grow a decent tomato. I had to buy these from a farmer on the other side of Georgetown. My daddy would be ashamed if he could see me now. The sandy soil here doesn't wanna grow anything. Wasn't much better where I grew up. Mountains of North Carolina. Hard to grow them there too. Always too cold or too damp. But Daddy managed to do it, even up in musty old Appalachia."

Josh watched her fill the jars, and going behind her, he carefully fastened each lid. The sun hit the jars as he placed them back on the countertop, and the tomatoes shone out like liquefied rubies.

"Growing up there was hard. Not because of the place, mind you. Appalachia is like everywhere else, man stinking the same stink. It was hard because I was a girl—a girl raised by people who knew nothing about girls, and that includes the women. My mother told me that petting leads boys to be over-excited and that toxins back up in their bodies. Well, for sure, the petting was never going to cease, so the girls that I hung out with, even my sisters, were forever relieving boys of those toxins. They relieved them all over the yard. My momma used to have to turn a hose on boys to get them to simmer down and go home. But that didn't do any good. Not really; not in the long run. One after another, my friends and sisters fell pregnant. But not me, boy. I was smarter than the rest."

Josh focused on the jars, on the lids, hoping she would continue. He'd never heard anyone utter words such as this.

"I was smart—until he came along, that is. Birthdaysuit. In my little holler, where I'd never seen anybody except those that were from there. Birthdaysuit rode up one day on a motorcycle. He had a spider monkey that went around with him in a sidecar. But it wasn't anything he said or did. It was just him. I fell hard, and so did he. *Wham.*" She clapped her hands. "Like two trains on the same track coming together head-on. Wham." She paused for a second and wiped sweat from her brow with the back of her tomato-covered hand. "Anyway, he had just inherited this land from an uncle, and we took off on his motorcycle. We got hitched right over there." She pointed out the kitchen window. "There was nothing here yet. We camped for a few years before we started building the resort. The wedding was quite the party. The spider monkey—his name was Zucchini—was part of the ceremony. That's the sort thing we did back in those days. There was a man in a purple unitard too; he did an interpretive dance during the ceremony. My fourteen-year-old niece got so hot and bothered she had to excuse herself halfway through and run off to the bathroom." She paused. "You still listening?"

"Oh yes, ma'am," he said.

"I do go on sometimes."

Jaybird had finished distributing the tomatoes, and Josh had screwed on all the lids. They washed their hands, first Jaybird and then him.

"I can tell what kind of boy you are," she said. "Not like those anyway; not as forceful and petulant as the one, and not as glassy eyed and stupid as the other."

"Thanks." He didn't know what else to say.

"You got good parents?"

"They're okay, I guess."

"You guess, huh? Doesn't sound like they're too great."

"They're really strict," Josh said.

"That's why I never had kids. I'd hate to control someone else's life."

"My parents don't seem to mind."

"They probably wouldn't be too wild about you being here, eh?"

"Oh god," Josh guffawed. "They'd kill me."

"Sounds like it."

"They never talk to me about anything, especially things like girls and…" He paused and blushed.

"Like sex, you mean."

"Yeah," he said. "My mom always says, 'A mind full of sex is like a mind full of maggots.'"

"Hot damn, parents can be cruel." Jaybird shook her head and seemed to be considering something. "Hey, you ever seen a curio cabinet?"

"No."

"Follow me."

They went down a hall, at the end of which was a large wardrobe. Jaybird opened it and flipped a switch inside. Light filtered down through a Chinese lantern and illuminated its contents: a long blond wig, a glass eyeball, the skull of a bonobo, an antique wooden dildo, a turtle shell painted like a barn quilt, pornographic playing cards, a stuffed piranha, a kidney stone the size of a quarter, a statue of Durga with penises for arms, a bird's nest made of human hair.

Jaybird said, "You can take one thing and one thing only."

Josh surveyed the cabinet. He reached out and ran his fingers through the hair of the wig, wishing his own was this long and this blond. He clasped his hands together to steady them.

"Mind if I choose for you?" Jaybird stepped forward and retrieved from the top self of the wardrobe a tattered, well-thumbed paperback that said *Leaves of Grass* across the cover. Josh shuddered faintly, recognizing it. A single maggot scudded quickly through his mind.

"Closest thing to a bible I've ever found for myself," Jaybird said. "I swear old Walt had it all figured out. The world would be a better place if more folks read this."

Josh took the book in his quivering hands, turning it over like it was magic. Jaybird rapped the cover with her knuckles. "Read his work, but never his biography. Got that?" Josh nodded. "Come on then. Let's have a drink."

She grabbed a bottle of wine and two glasses from the kitchen, and they walked out to the porch. She poured the glasses so full he had to approach his like a hummingbird, bending his head down to it and slurping.

"Cheers," she said. "Good to know you."

"Good to know you, Maude."

They looked out over the lawn. Birthdaysuit and the other two boys were making their way over to the porch. Birthdaysuit whistled Donna Summer's "Love to Love You Baby" while smiling up at Jaybird. The sun was beginning to set, and the clouds were as fine as gossamer. The light reflected off them in pinks and purples, and for a moment the resort glowed, looking pastel and sanctified. Josh thought that the ruins of Naked Island might one day be viewed by antiquaries searching for some sign of progress in a region restrained as this.

28

HYDROTHERAPY

Josh had taken to baths each night, a form of hydrotherapy of his own design. Walt Whitman was his only companion. He held the worn volume before him, reading the words that gave tongue to his wildest fears and desires. The maggots in his brain disappeared one by one as he read.

This night Josh's rude flesh came to life, a muscle beckoned by the old graybeard and now with warf and woof all its own. He read, "...while they discuss I am silent, and go bathe / and admire myself. / Welcome is every organ and attribute of me, and of any man hearty and clean / Not an inch nor a particle of an inch is vile, and none shall be less familiar than the rest."

Josh was a pent-up, aching river. He stood in the tub and soused forward. Tiny pearls were broadcast before him and dissolved in the water. He felt slain in some spirit made of God but not in His service, doing in His stead an anointing new to the boy and old to the devil.

He looked to the door to see that it was locked. He then settled back into unalloyed satisfaction.

He always knew his first time would be in the bath.

29

Wet Business

Just after dark on a summer evening, Josh and Ryan rode their bikes to the south end of Pawleys Island. Ryan had recently started putting worthless baseball cards in his spokes, and they made a sound like a dozen miniature machine guns that slowed to nothing as the boys reached the boardwalk. They stashed their bikes in the dunes before running out onto the beach. It was low tide, and the expanse of sand stretched a long way out to the sea.

Their pockets were bulging with heavy flashlights, and they lumbered awkwardly. When they reached the middle of the beach, Ryan pulled out his light. He flicked it on and made the sound of a light saber. Josh did the same.

They circled one another holding their lights up, two-handed and high on their chests. The lights shone upward and danced off the low-hanging clouds. A few small bats made random, spastic arches across the sky.

Ryan cocked a hip and leaned in to Josh. Poking out his bottom lip, Ryan blew upward to get the quaff of hair out of his eyes. It was dark enough that his red hair looked brown. Josh squared off, too, bouncing on the balls of his feet and trying to look mean.

"On guard," Ryan said.

"On guard."

"Luke, you're a disappointment, my son. Now you must die!" Ryan was always Darth Vader, devoid, as he was, of fidelity to good guys in films. Josh favored Luke because he, too, despised his father.

The boys stepped toward one another. "You're going to die, Vader," Josh said, low and stern.

Josh and Ryan bellowed, and their lights came together. They slung their sabers back and forth, and each time they met, both boys made clashing electric sounds. After a few minutes of this, they moved in closer, holding their lights firmly against their chests, pretending that their sabers were locked. Gritting their teeth, they stared menacingly at one another.

"Okay," Josh whispered, as if in aside. "Vader has to go down now."

"Why? You go down."

"That's not the story."

"Is now," Ryan said, as he took a step back and kicked Josh in the stomach. Josh dropped his flashlight in the sand and fell, struggling for breath. Ryan stood over him and looked to the sky where his light shot up to the heavens. "Now I will be my own son's undoing." Ryan brought his light down and cut it across Josh's midsection. "Son, how does it feel to lose your very bowels?"

Josh held his stomach, pretending that his innards were bubbling out. Ryan turned off his light and bowed his head reverently.

Still struggling for breath, Josh hobbled to his feet and brushed the sand from his shirt. He was about to make Ryan promise that Luke could win the next round when he saw a figure walking along the beach. As it drew closer, Josh could see by the hazy light of the moon that it was a man. Ryan turned, and they both stared. The man was dressed in a gray three-piece gabardine suit, shabby and worn at the pockets.

"Holy fuck, dude," Ryan said. "That's the Gray Man. He's come to warn us that there's a storm on the way."

"Shut up, Ryan," Josh said. "It's not a ghost; it's just some old man." Josh eyed him, willing that he himself cut a less pathetic figure in the night.

"If that's not the Gray Man, then I'm a fucking trombone."

The man was walking slowly, but he had changed his course ever so slightly and was now coming straight toward the boys. Josh could see that his eyes were dark and that he had a wispy gray moustache the same color as his suit. His trilby hat had a hole in the front just above the brim through which thin white hair blossomed. He coughed and it rattled dryly.

Josh's heart began to palpitate, and he sidled up to Ryan. "Howdy, boys," the man said, stopping just before them. They said nothing. "Appears you were having quite a fierce battle there." The boys continued to stare. "You look like smart boys? What are your names?"

"Smith," Josh said. "And this is Murphy." Ryan looked at Josh incredulously and then shrugged.

"Well, Smith," the man said, addressing Josh. "You from around here?"

"Yes, sir."

"Good," he said. "You should think about heading home soon. The rain's coming. The old wet business. Promises to be a doozy."

Josh looked off toward the horizon where indeed a storm was beginning to gather. The moon was rising higher over the ocean, but the dark clouds obscured it. When Josh looked back, Ryan was gone. He rollicked down the beach casting his light this way and that for ghost crabs.

"A lively fella," the man said. "He seems the sort to go in for games. You, though—" He looked Josh up and down, his fingers worrying his moustache. "You seem clever. You like to read?"

"Sure. I like books."

"Like what?"

"C.S. Lewis mostly. And Tolkien."

The man's eyebrows rose sharply. "You can't go wrong with them. Who else?"

Josh wanted to sound sophisticated. He thought of the book stashed under the covers of his top bunk and said, "Whitman."

The man laughed. "Whitman seems a bit racy for a boy your age."

Ryan capered around the beach, following the small white crabs as they scurried in search of their holes. Josh wished that

Ryan would come back. He shot him a pleading look, but Ryan was now trying to bury a crab alive in its hole.

"Yes," the man said. "Best not to accelerate the loss of boyhood. There are some books that boys must be careful to avoid."

"I'm grown enough," Josh said.

"Oh, I bet you are. I was just thinking about myself at your age." The man looked out over the horizon, the lightning beginning to flash in the clouds. Josh took the moment to wave an imploring hand in Ryan's direction. He either didn't see or didn't care.

The man said, "I bet you have lots of girlfriends. Or perhaps just one main squeeze. Smart boy like you. Serious boy like you. And so good looking. Must have the pick of litter."

Josh shook his head and began to walk in the direction of Ryan, who was so far down the beach now that Josh could just make out his light dancing along the edge of the dunes. The beach was too breezy for fireflies, but Josh could see them winking their lights in the dunes beyond Ryan. He had taken a few steps in that direction before he felt a heavy hand on his shoulder. He turned, and the man was stooped down, his face level with Josh's. He could see the man's gray teeth, barely discernable in the dark below his moustache. Josh's arm whipsawed, knocking the man's hand from his shoulder.

"Come, now, my boy," the man said. "I want to hear all about your sweethearts. How many have you?"

"I've already told you."

"You mustn't be coy. How many?" Josh was silent. The man sucked in his breath and waved a hand dismissively. "No bother. They'll come soon enough. You'll give and take the old wet business soon enough."

Josh thought of the storm, of the rain. He remembered the book in his bed.

Ryan was coming back to them now, walking slowly, still scanning for ghost crabs. Josh had never felt happier to see him. The man stood silent and still.

"Come on," Ryan said. "I'm starving." Without saying a word to the man, the two boys walked away. As they reached the boardwalk, Ryan noted how strange it was to be wearing a suit on the beach on a warm summer night. Josh nodded and looked back. The man was gone, but the storm was moving closer, and the rain had nearly made it to the edge of the water.

"Want to stay at my house tonight?" Ryan asked as he bent over to pick up his bike.

"No," Josh said quickly. "I need to go home."

As they rode back to their neighborhood, the rain caught up with them, drenching first their clothes. Then the baseball cards in Ryan's spokes softened. The sound of tiny machine guns dwindled until the cards fell away leaving behind a trail of tattered paper. Small, dismembered faces stared up from the pavement into the underbelly of the storm. They followed the boys all the way home.

30

Bobby Brown, Corndoggin' It

Bobby Brown's mother sent him to the neighborhood pool each day of the summer with a backpack full of freshly microwaved corndogs. Once a week, Mrs. Brown went to Sam's Club in Myrtle Beach to replenish the supply, and she encouraged him to share. "You'll make friends, Bobby." She called him Bobby, but the students in his seventh-grade class last year all called him Bobby Brown and liked to sing "My Prerogative" to him in the hallways.

In truth, Mrs. Brown was less concerned about him making friends than she was about getting him out of the house. Since he'd sprouted his feathers last winter, she was forever after him to put on deodorant and powder his balls. "You smell pube-y," she told him almost every morning, particularly since the weather turned hot. "And God doesn't like it."

Her husband, Bobby Brown's father, also named Bobby Brown, had left her, which is why she and her son had moved to Pawleys Island a few months back. Mr. Brown worked as a high school gym teacher in San Francisco, and Mrs. Brown used to make him shower each day when he arrived home and again each night before getting into bed. But Mr. Brown fell in love with a waiter named Federico at the family's favorite restaurant. Federico never made him shower.

Today, when Bobby Brown pulled up to the bike rack outside the pool's chain-link fence, his back was already drenched in sweat both from the humid day and from the heat of the corndogs radiating out of his backpack. This made him worry about the state of his balls.

Bobby Brown walked through the pool house and was

stopped by Amy, the lifeguard, who was standing behind the counter reading a magazine about college swimmers of the SEC. Like most days, Amy was wearing a red one-piece that drove the local boys to distraction. "Hold up," she said to Bobby Brown. "You've got to sign in." Bobby Brown wrote down his name and address in the ledger. "All right, go on," Amy said from behind the counter. Bobby Brown started walking through the vestibule to the pool. "Wait," she yelled. He turned back. "You got any glass in that backpack?"

"No, ma'am."

"No, *ma'am?* I'm nineteen goddamned years old." Bobby Brown looked up at her like she was a math equation he couldn't crack. "Any booze?"

"No, ma'—"

"Fucking don't."

"No."

"Any cigarettes?"

"No."

"Good." Amy lit a cigarette herself and waved him through the pool house, her eyes blinking against the smoke.

As Bobby Brown walked out onto the pool deck, he surveyed the teenagers scattered around. He first waved to a group of girls who pretended not to see him. He then waved to some older boys who saw him and collectively shot him the bird. Next he saw Josh and Ryan sitting on lounge chairs and sipping beer they had funneled into Sprite cans. Bobby Brown waved at them; Josh waved back, and Ryan made a friendly farting noise with his mouth. When Bobby Brown walked over, Ryan said, "You're the one with the corndogs, right?"

Bobby Brown opened his backpack and corndogs spilled out onto Ryan's chair, their plastic wrappers beaded with condensation from the inside.

"I'm starving," Ryan said. "Join us, Bobby Brown."

Bobby Brown doled out corndogs. He had enough for each of them to have three. Ryan broke into one first and took down half of it in a single bite. Josh tucked into one as well, but Bobby Brown didn't touch his.

"Wish we had mustard," Ryan said.

"Wish we had ketchup," Josh said.

Bobby Brown seemed to make a mental note. "I'll bring those tomorrow."

"You're in our grade, right?" Josh asked.

"Yeah." Bobby Brown had a wispy Dutch boy haircut that made him look significantly younger than others their age.

"Where'd you come from?" Ryan said.

"San Francisco."

"What brought you to these waters?" Josh said. He'd heard this on TV.

Bobby Brown nibbled the end of his corndog, but only down to the pink. "My dad, he… I mean, my mom…"

"Real good storyteller we got here," Ryan said. Josh tried not to laugh.

"My mom wanted to move here," Bobby Brown continued, "because she said there aren't enough Christians in California."

Josh shrugged. "What's the deal with the hotdogs?"

"My mom, she…" He hesitated again.

"What?" Josh asked. Bobby Brown's discomfort was making him nervous. "Spit it out."

"Well, she won't let me stay in the house now that it's summer. She wants me out, and she says the corndogs will improve my chances of making friends."

"Well, that's a—" Josh began.

Ryan cut him off. "Why does she want you out of the house?"

"She says I smell funny?"

"What does that mean?"

"Like pube-y. And ungodly, I guess."

Josh chimed in. "Is pube-y a word?"

"I think so."

Ryan snorted. "Your mom sounds insane, dude."

Josh said, "You smell fine from here."

"It's since I, you know, became a man. She says she can smell my stink all over the house."

Ryan said, "You shouldn't stand for that shit."

Bobby Brown looked around shiftily like he was scared someone would overhear.

"He's right, Bobby Brown," Josh said. "You're fine."

"How do you know?"

"We're standing right here."

"Yeah," Ryan said. "You're fine."

Bobby Brown looked unsure. He nibbled his corndog, revealing more of its pink.

"I can prove it," Ryan said.

Josh and Bobby Brown looked at him in confusion. "To the pool house, boys." Josh and Bobby Brown followed Ryan inside. They all waved at Amy, as they passed the sign-in desk, each discreetly sneaking a peak.

"Don't do anything weird in there," she said as they entered the Men's room. "Yes, ma'am," Bobby Brown replied.

Once they were in the bathroom, Ryan took control. "Okay, Josh. You're going to have to take off your bathing suit."

"What?"

"So Bobby Brown here can smell your balls." He said this like it was the most obvious statement ever uttered.

"No, not me. What about you?"

"He can't smell me," Ryan said. "I was in the pool already. I just smell like chlorine."

"Definitely not."

"Come on, Josh. You like helping people, don't you? Bobby Brown needs to know what a healthy young specimen he is."

"Are you on board with this, Bobby Brown?" Josh asked.

Bobby Brown nodded. "I'm not sure how God would feel about it. But I'd like to know if Ryan's right."

"All right, fine. But quick."

Josh turned away from them and pulled down his bathing suit, but only in the back, careful to keep his penis hidden.

"You gotta spread it, Josh," Ryan said. "Waft it out."

Josh leaned forward, bracing himself on a wall of lockers. Just as Bobby Brown was enjoying his first whiff, Amy walked in without knocking. She did this all the time to try to catch them smoking. Although smoking wasn't allowed in the pool house, she smoked there all the time.

She took in the whole tableau—Bobby Brown mere centimeters away from Josh's balls, as Ryan looked on. "What are you doing in here, you little faggots?" They all went still and mute. Water dripped slowly in one of the showers. Josh's breathing halted, as he turned to her, his eyes saucers. The water drip, drip, dripped, and when Josh emerged from what felt like a coma, he leapt upright, hustling up his bathing suit.

"What the fuck?" Amy said, still standing just inside the doorway. The boys were all in love with her even though she called them terrible names all the time.

"It's not—" Josh began, fidgeting with his bathing suit.

"You. Fucking. Kids," Amy said, drawing out each word.

"We're not kids," Ryan said.

"No. You shut the fuck up. You're done. Your time at the pool is over. All of you."

Josh and Bobby Brown were looking at their feet. But Ryan stepped toward her and said, "You can't kick us out. This is none of your business."

The two squared off. Amy said, "I certainly could kick you out if I wanted to. But I honestly can't stomach relaying this story to anyone, especially not your parents. So you can get the fuck out right now and don't come back for a long time. Got it?"

"Yes, ma'am," Bobby Brown said.

"Yes," Josh whispered.

"Fine," Ryan said; his voice, too loud for the space, seemed to echo off the bathroom's wet tiles. "But for the record you don't even know what's going on here. We're helping him."

"Helping him along the road to becoming a pervert," Amy said.

"Don't listen to her, Bobby Brown. You don't smell nasty, and even if you did, who cares? It's your prerogative." Josh screwed up his courage and added, "Your scent is aroma finer than prayer."

Bobby Brown looked confused for a second, but their words had given him new pluck. He led the way out the door, his head held high.

The boys would be back at the pool tomorrow. Amy would forgive them, and they would hate and love her by turns—these being two sides of a coin they would finger smooth the rest of their days.

31

Two-Pump Chump

On a Sunday morning just before sunrise, Josh woke to the sound of pebbles pinging off his bedroom window. He descended groggily from his bunk bed and looked out. Ryan and Spregg were sitting on their bikes below, each with a leg akimbo to keep balance. Josh threw up the window and said, "What the hell?"

Spregg cawed like a bird, and Ryan said, "Come on," waving at him.

Josh checked the clock and saw that it was 5:30. He dressed quickly, descended the stairs, and walked out the back door, careful to close it softly so that he wouldn't wake up his parents or sisters.

Once outside Josh approached Ryan and Spregg in the cul-de-sac. "What are you guys doing here so early?"

"Get your bike," Ryan said, "and come with us."

"My parents'll kill me. I've got to go to church with them today."

"You'll be back before they even wake up."

Spregg stepped forward and said, "Trust me. You don't wanna miss this." He opened his backpack and flashed the cover of a *Penthouse*. Josh reached out to grab the magazine.

"Not here," Ryan said. "Not now."

"Fine. But we better be back before church."

"Done deal," Spregg said. "Shoulder your duds, and let's get the fuck on with it."

Josh retrieved his bike from the backyard, and the three of them rode first to Ryan's house and then cut through his yard, through a stand of pines, and into a clear-cut area along the edge of a new golf course. Ryan led the way, slicing through the loose red mud, where ancient live oaks had until recently stood. The boys rode single-file down a logging road and at the end of it came to a new housing development. The roads and cul-de-sacs were already paved, and the lots were demarcated with a series of numbered wooden signs. At the end of one cul-de-sac, there stood two houses that were already under construction. Ryan steered toward the one on the left, which had completed walls and a roof but no siding.

"Hide your bikes around back," Ryan said, as he hopped off his and walked it through the construction site. Piles of plywood and loose bricks were everywhere. Josh stepped lightly, thinking of rusty nails penetrating his tennis shoes. When they got around to the back of the house, Ryan motioned toward the door, which was propped open with a cinderblock. They stashed their bikes behind a pallet of shingle siding and entered the house. The door led directly into a large room that Josh assumed was the kitchen. There remained large holes in the cabinetry where the stove and dishwasher would go.

"Behold," Ryan said, making a grand Vanna White gesture with his arm. Vanna was the closest thing to a celebrity to ever come out of Myrtle Beach, and even the people of Pawleys Island begrudgingly claimed her as local.

Mounted on the wall next to Ryan was a phone with a long cord that looped down to the floor. Spregg gazed at the phone like it was a god and he some hotheaded acolyte.

Josh looked from Spregg to Ryan quizzically. "So what?"

"Dude," Spregg said, pointing wildly at the phone.

"A phone. I see it. Why would you get me out of bed for this?"

"It's already installed," Spregg said.

"I'm still not getting it. We could get in trouble for even being in here."

"It's Sunday, Josh. No one works on Sunday." Ryan looked to Spregg. "Show him."

Spregg pulled the *Penthouse* out of his bag and flipped to

the back. The pages there were carved up into smaller squares. Each one featured a naked woman alongside an 800 number.

Josh's eyes grew large. "Oh," he said.

"Exactamundo," Spregg said.

"No one will ever know it was us," Ryan added. "And the schmuck who's building this house will get the bill."

"Serves him right for ruining our woods," Josh said.

"Let's do it," Spregg said. He slapped the *Penthouse* down on the countertop next to them. The boys perused the ads. Josh picked an ad for Italian Beauties, and Ryan chose one for Catholic Girls Gone Wild. They were about to play Rock, Paper, Scissors, when Spregg snatched the *Penthouse* off the counter and said, "My mag, my choice."

Josh and Ryan nodded. "Fair enough."

Spregg flipped to the very last page of the magazine and pointed to an ad that featured a large woman eating a banana. Next to her was a pile of peels, and above that the words, *Big Girl Fun.*

Ryan began to protest, but Spregg raised a hand between them. "Y'all agreed it was my turn."

"Fine," Ryan said. He grabbed the phone from the wall and dialed the number. Ryan held it between him and Spregg. Their foreheads were touching, and they braced the phone between their cheeks. Josh leaned in; he could hear a faint voice, but he couldn't make out her words. Ryan and Spregg began laughing hysterically, and within a few seconds, Spregg bent over and the phone clattered to the floor.

"What'd she say? What'd she say?" Josh asked.

Spregg was sprawled on the floor now, laughing and pounding the tile with abandon. Ryan struggled to catch his breath. He stood up straight and inhaled deeply. "She said, 'Pick a fold and fuck it.'" Ryan dropped to his knees. He smacked Spregg on the ass as he lost himself again in laughter.

"Pick a fold and fuck it," Spregg repeated.

Josh grabbed the phone and put it to his ear. "Who is this?" the woman asked angrily.

"I'm…"

"Is this a bunch of fucking kids? God, I hate when this happens. This line is not for kids."

"We're not kids, ma'am," Josh said.

"Did you say 'ma'am'?"

From the floor, Ryan asked, "What's she saying?"

"She sounds mad."

"Damn right, I'm mad," she said in Josh's ear.

"Ask her about the folds," Ryan said. Spregg was moaning, and Ryan was spanking him again.

Josh returned his attention to the phone. "…curse you, you little bastard," she was saying. "When you're older and in love, you'll forever be a two-pump chump."

"What's that mean?"

"You'll find out soon enough," she said. The line went dead. Josh held the phone for several seconds, listening to the dial tone.

"Who's next?" Spregg asked. Ryan was already flipping through the *Penthouse*.

Just then a car door closed outside the house. "Holy fuck," Ryan said.

"We're outa here," Spregg said. He grabbed the *Penthouse* and ran out the back door. Ryan followed. Josh, still stunned from the phone call, was slow to stir. But when he heard the front door of the house open, he too fled.

All three boys grabbed their bikes and slipped around the side of the house, careful to stoop under each window. When they reached the cul-de-sac, they mounted and rode like hell back to Josh's house, their clip tremendous.

32

Marco Polo

When Josh walked out onto the deck, the girls were already in the pool doing the Mary Washington. They bent over and dipped their hair into the water and then in a single motion flipped their heads backwards, creating a folded wave of hair in the front. Josh looked around for Ryan and then turned his attention back to the girls. He saw Chloe, her long hair nearly black with wet. She spotted him on the pool deck and motioned for him to join them. Josh held up a finger and removed his shirt and threw it on a nearby lounge chair. He quickly moved toward the water and descended the stairs, submerging himself up to the neck. The birthmark on his left shoulder had darkened of late like it had been painted with iodine, and he tried to hide it as much as possible. He had to bend his knees dramatically so that only his head remained above water. He monkey-walked in this way toward Chloe and two other girls in the shallow end of the pool.

"Hey, Josh," Chloe said.

"Hey, Chloe." He waved to the other two, but they had turned to one another and were discussing their Mary Washington hairdos.

"You can do it," Chloe said, nodding toward Josh's hair. He'd been growing it out for over a year, and it was now nearly shoulder-length. Josh leaned forward, soaked his hair, and then flicked it back.

"Check him out," Chloe said. The other two girls giggled.

Josh looked eagerly at Chloe, and she too began to laugh. "My name's Mary," he said in his best womanly voice. "Pleased to meet you." He took Chloe's hand and gave it a shake. Josh felt his penis begin to harden, and a single maggot gained purchase in his mind. He looked down to see if his erection could be detected through the water. His Mary Washington flopped forward, and he had to hold it back with one arm. Josh's bright blue bathing suit stood out like a subaqueous tent. Hoping not to draw attention, he dropped Chloe's hand and took a step back.

"Aren't you forgetting something?" one of the girls asked, eyeing Josh now and grinning.

"What?" He was pleading with his penis to go down, to leave him and these girls alone. Josh thought of road kill, a pus-filled wound, a baby basting on a spit.

"Kiss her hand," the girl said.

Chloe held out her hand demurely, and Josh leaned in and gave it a smooch.

"Nice," Josh heard Ryan say. He had arrived at the pool and was watching the scenario play out from the deck. Ryan shuffled several steps back and then ran forward and cannonballed into the water, splashing Josh and the girls.

Josh rubbed the Mary Washington wave from his hair.

"Let's play Marco Polo," Chloe said, as Ryan surfaced and they moved into a circle. Josh's penis had gone slack, for which he thanked Ryan and his cannonball.

"Cool," Ryan said. Josh nodded, trying not to look at Chloe, trying to keep limp.

"No running," Amy, the lifeguard, yelled from the pool deck. She made eye contact with Ryan and then Josh. "No running, you little fuckheads." Amy sat down on a lounge chair and started thumbing through a *Vogue* that was open across her lap.

"Boys are Marco first," Chloe said. Josh and Ryan played Rock, Paper, Scissors, and Josh lost.

"Blindman's buff rules," Chloe asserted.

Ryan and Josh shrugged in confusion. Chloe swam to the edge of the pool and heaved her long, thin body out of the water and onto the pool deck. Her bikini bottom was caught between her cheeks, and she pulled it out nonchalantly as she ran across the deck. Josh struggled not to stare.

"No running," Amy screamed again.

Chloe shot her the bird as soon as Amy looked back down at her magazine. She grabbed a pink tank top from her bag on a chair, ran back to the pool, and jack-knifed in.

"No fucking running, or y'all're outa here," Amy said.

Chloe gave Amy a thumbs up, without even turning back to look at her. Chloe approached Josh in the water. She pushed the hair from his forehead and tied the tank top around his eyes. Josh could smell Chloe on it and saw only pink now. He tried not to think of his bathing suit tightening and the maggots, which had turned from one into two and then four, all now roiling in glee.

"Okay, go," Chloe said, and Josh heard several bodies swift-swimming away.

He counted aloud to ten and began wading through the shallow end, his hands outstretched before him. Someone giggled from behind. He turned and everything went still and silent. He moved ahead and bumped into the concrete side of the pool. He shifted directions and ventured forward, an explorer now, searching out new terrain, his destiny becoming manifest. He took a few more steps, and his right hand stopped on something unyielding, yet fleshy. Josh tore the tank top from his eyes with his left hand. His right was resting squarely on Chloe's breast, which was so small that he had assumed he was touching Ryan. Josh pulled back his hand, and as he did, he grazed her nipple, as hard as a Tennessee pearl.

"I'm so sorry," he blurted out. The tide was advancing in his mind and on it sailed myriad maggots.

Chloe smiled and did a backflip in the water. He watched her breach and subside as seamlessly as a sea creature. His pulse racing, Josh moved across the shallow end toward where Ryan was standing. He knew now that he'd been simmering, simmering, simmering, and Chloe had brought him to a boil. "By my life-lumps!" he said.

The other girls were standing next to Ryan, and they were all laughing and pointing at Josh. Chloe swam in the other direction. She reached the edge of the shallow end and braced her arms on the concrete ledge.

Amy walked over to her on the pool deck, bent down, and whispered, "You shouldn't associate with Josh. That guy's perverted."

"What makes you think I'm not?"

"Look, you're cute, and cute girls have it the worst. It's time you learn to juggle wolves."

"The thing is," Chloe said, "I'm the wolf, and these boys need to learn to juggle me."

EIGHTH GRADE

33

Sex Ed

When Mrs. Jenkins walked into the small classroom off of the gymnasium, cleared her throat, and said, "Okay, let's get started," Josh thought someone was staging an elaborate prank. A petite, middle-aged African-American woman with her hair in long braids, Mrs. Jenkins was not who he and the other boys had expected to teach their eighth-grade sex ed class. They had anticipated a man, first and foremost, and they had hoped that he would be young and could teach them about women, maybe even show them a blue film or two.

Mrs. Jenkins clapped her hands loudly, and the hubbub of chatter mellowed. A few boys still giggled, but when she cut them a side-eyed glance, they too went silent. "Thank you," she said, before turning to write her name on the board.

"My name is Mrs. Jenkins," she said. "Welcome to sex education." Giggles and guffaws bubbled up again here and there amongst the group of about twenty boys, some in desks and some in rusty folding chairs.

"Why's that funny?" she asked. When no one answered, Mrs. Jenkins pointed at Ryan. "Why?" she said, making direct eye contact with him.

His face went beet red. "I'm not sure," he said. "Just is."

Mrs. Jenkins swept her eyes across the class. "What about you?" she said, pointing to Spregg who was sitting in the back of the class. "What's funny?"

Spregg's body contracted into a ball, and he hugged his knees to his chest.

"Okay," Mrs. Jenkins continued. "Anybody else?" All the boys looked down and were silent. She walked gracefully as a jaguar back and forth in front of the class, finally stopping before Josh. He had gotten much taller over the past summer, and he was skinnier than ever. He had also grown his hair out, hoping to look like the professional surfers in the posters that hung on his bedroom walls. He looked more like a dirty mop sitting upright in a desk. Mrs. Jenkins leaned down and rapped her knuckles on his desktop. "What about you? Do you find the idea of sex education funny?"

Josh looked up at her reluctantly and shrugged. "I don't know, ma'am," his voice quivered.

Mrs. Jenkins smiled and stood up straight. "So no one seems to find it funny anymore. Great. This is a serious class. I would wager that it's the most important class you'll ever take. Do you know why?"

A few boys had raised their heads, but no one answered.

"Because if you get some girl pregnant, your life is over. All right?" They nodded. "And if you get an incurable STD, your life is over." They nodded again. "Any other dangers of sex you can think of?"

A shy blond boy in the middle of the group raised his hand. "The Bible says it's wrong."

Mrs. Jenkins asked, "What's your name?"

"Bobby Brown, ma'am."

She stifled a laugh. "Well, Bobby Brown's point here is one that I guess we should address early on. This is not Bible school. This is not a religious institution. This is public school, and you're beginning eighth grade. There is no room for God or Jesus or any of that in this class. We're going to be talking about real world stuff here. I can't say how Jesus feels about what you do with your penis, nor do I give a damn." The boys nodded enthusiastically. No one had ever heard a teacher curse in the classroom. "But I can tell you about what syphilis looks like and herpes, and how having a baby at fourteen will ruin whatever life plans you think you have."

Josh already loved Mrs. Jenkins. On a couple of occasions lately, he had asked his parents questions about sex. Both times his mother had left the room, muttering about the "maggots of his mind," and his father had told him to ask a friend.

"So this is an academic class," she said, "and I trust that you will treat it accordingly. Now my guess is that none of you have talked to a woman about sex. And I would wager that with the exception of the two Black men in the class—" She paused and waved to their only two Black classmates, Carl and Fred, sitting to one side of the classroom. "With those possible two exceptions, I doubt y'all have ever talked to a *Black* woman about sex."

The white boys nodded and looked surprised, as if Mrs. Jenkins had read their minds.

"Now that we've named the elephant in the room," she said, "do you have any questions?"

Ryan raised his hand and, without being called on, asked, "Can you go blind from jacking off?"

"Wow," Mrs. Jenkins exclaimed. "I meant more like do you have any questions about the course. About grades and assignments and such."

There was a pause, and then Fred asked, "But can you?"

"No, man," she said. "Do people still believe that? There would be a lot of blind boys running around this school if that was true."

The class erupted in laughter. Several hands went up around the room.

"Good lord," she said. "Y'all really have no one to talk to, do you?" She looked around at the hands and pointed to Josh.

He sat up straight as an arrow and asked, "If a man ejaculates in the ocean, can it get women swimming around him pregnant?"

Mrs. Jenkins paused, wiping away a few beads of sweat that were starting to form on her brow. "Okay," she said more to herself than to Josh. "The answer is probably no. But my question is: why are you ejaculating in the ocean?"

Josh blushed. "No! Not me. It's from a poem I read."

Mrs. Jenkins said, "Sounds like quite a poem."

Carl asked, "After semen has dried, if it then gets into a lady, could she get pregnant?"

"No."

"How many little people," Spregg asked, "are in each ejaculation?"

"You mean sperm? I don't know exactly. A lot. Millions."

Jordan, the star of the soccer team, followed up. "And all those little people swim into a lady's body and fight to become a baby?"

"Sort of."

"Like a game of King of the Hill."

"Maybe. I guess."

Another boy asked, "Can a penis ever get stuck in a woman's thing?"

"Vagina?"

"Yeah. And need to be, like, surgically removed?"

"No."

Bobby Brown asked, "What is onanism? And can you go to hell for it?"

"What did I tell you about religion, Bobby Brown?"

"Is that a no?"

"Religion has no place in this classroom."

Ryan asked, "Can a man impregnate an animal if they have sex?"

"No."

"Can a woman be impregnated by an animal?"

"Still no."

"Can a woman's vulva wink like a horse's?"

"No."

Josh asked, "Is it possible for a woman to be impregnated if she's facing into a full moon while she has sex?"

"Yes."

"What about away from a full moon?"

"Yes."

"What about at dead low tide?"

"What? Yes. Of course"

"King tide?"

"A woman can get pregnant in any weather event."

Carl asked, "Can a man pee and have sex at the same time?"

"No."

"Can a woman pee and have sex at the same time?"

"Maybe."

Ryan asked, "Can a man and woman have sex more than once a day? With each other?"

"Yes."

Carl asked, "Have you heard of those little fish that swim up men's penis holes in the Amazon?"

"Yeah, so?"

"Do we have them in Pawleys Island?"

"No."

Josh asked, "Do circumcised men live longer?"

"I don't think it's relevant to how long you live."

Bobby Brown asked, "How do priests who are celibate—" Mrs. Jenkins cleared her throat, cutting him off. "No, this is a real question," he said. "Do celibate men ultimately fill up with semen and explode? Or die at least?"

"No."

An anvil-faced boy who already had a full beard asked, "Can girls get pregnant if you have sex in the butt?"

"No, but you can still get and spread STDs."

The boy replied, "Is it dirty, though?"

"Are you talking about morality? As in, is it morally objectionable somehow? Because, again, that's not the point of this class."

"No, I mean, like does it get all over the place?"

Mrs. Jenkins paused for a second. "That kind of question is probably not the point of this course either."

Just then the bell rang. "Thank god," Mrs. Jenkins said. The boys all gave her a round of applause before they packed up and filed out of the room.

❧

At the end of the semester, the boys unanimously nominated Mrs. Jenkins for an award for Teacher of the Year. When she won, her picture was placed in the main entrance hall of the school.

One morning Josh and Carl walked into the building together and saw an older boy drawing a mustache on the picture. "What are you doing?" Josh yelled. Carl slapped the marker from the boy's hand. He was much bigger than Carl and Josh, but it was two on one, and he didn't seem eager to test his luck.

"Get out of here," Carl said. The guy gave both of them a confused look and scampered off.

Josh put his face close to the picture of Mrs. Jenkins and breathed out heavily, covering it momentarily with fog. He then rubbed his sleeve across it until the mustache was completely gone. He stood back from the picture, and Carl nodded approvingly.

"She's the best teacher we've ever had," Josh said.

"Chicken shit stuff like that," Carl said, pointing toward the picture, "is exactly what you would've done before Mrs. Jenkins got ahold of you."

34

Snake Charmer

"That's my dad," Spregg said, pointing down out of the bleachers toward the center of the gym. A tall, gaunt, long-haired man in buckskins was holding a rattlesnake behind the head with one hand and by the tail with the other.

"What?" Josh asked.

"Bullshit," Ryan said.

Josh leaned forward in his seat and looked at Spregg who was on the other side of Ryan in the bleachers. Spregg shrugged. They were surrounded by the entire eighth-grade class.

"Snakes around here are easy to identify," Okefenokee Job was saying into a headset microphone. His voiced boomed, echoing throughout the gym. "Not many poisonous ones to remember. Rattlesnake, coral snake, copperhead, and water moccasin." Josh sat transfixed and had already forgotten what Spregg said. "You'll probably never see the first two. Around here what you need to look out for are copperheads and water moccasins." Job dropped the rattlesnake into an enclosure on the gym floor, which looked like the playpen Josh remembered his sister having when she was little. "The other thing about rattlers is that they usually let you know they're there. Ever heard one rattle?" Job asked the assembly.

"No," several of the students answered.

"Want to?"

"Yes!" they all yelled.

In the enclosure, the snake was still and silent. Job hung his headset microphone on a long metal pole and extended it over the enclosure. Within seconds, the snake's rattle exploded, first so rapidly that it sounded like a buzz and then it slowed to a discernible rattle, dry and raspy.

The students clapped and cheered. When the applause subsided, Spregg again said, "That's my dad."

"I called bullshit," Ryan shouted. Their teacher, a woman named Mrs. Jones, was two rows down in the bleachers. She turned around and looked at Ryan, her glasses clinging to the tip of her nose. She put her index finger to her lips, and Ryan mouthed, *I'm sorry.*

Okefenokee Job was now beginning to talk about how to identify a water moccasin. Josh looked over at Spregg. He was watching the man pull a fat black snake from a crate. Its tail was in his left hand and he held its head away from him in the hook at the end of a metal pole. Spregg's eyes were glassy, and he'd gone grim about the mouth. He soon left his seat, and Josh stared as he walked down the bleachers and slumped out of the gym's side door. No one saw him again that day.

When Spregg didn't show up to school the next day, Josh decided to go over to his house. He rode his bike that evening just before the sun began to descend behind the trees.

Josh knocked on the door, and when it opened, he was shocked to see Okefenokee Job standing there in Spregg's foyer. He was wearing the same buckskin pants and shirt he had worn at the assembly. Job eyed Josh suspiciously from the doorway.

"I'm Spregg's friend," Josh said.

Job's face relaxed and he opened the door wider. "Any friend of Gregg's is a friend of mine."

Josh followed him into the living room. On the floor stood a pyramid of glass tanks. Each contained a snake, camouflaged amongst sand and leaves. "Sit a spell. Gregg and his mother'll be home soon." Job nodded toward a chair on the other side of the snake tanks, and Josh sat down. The movement of him lowering into the chair seemed to agitate the snakes. Multiple rattles went off; the sound was muted by the glass, but sustained and constant because of their number.

"I wasn't even sure Spregg had a father."

"Well, he does," Job said. He pulled a flask from his pocket and took a pull.

"He never said who you were until the assembly yesterday."

"He a good kid?"

"Sure, he's the best," Josh said, perhaps too enthusiastically. Then to underscore that he was genuine about this, he added, "You'll see."

"I'll be on my way tomorrow morning. I've got gigs from here to Texas."

"Are you taking Spregg?"

Job shook his head. "He's better off without me."

"What? Why?"

"Trust me."

"But he needs you. Spregg struggles…has issues. And it's getting worse."

"You look after him for me. Will you do that?"

"I'm not his father," Josh said. "Besides you can't just take off. You don't have that kind of freedom if you've got a kid."

"I'm the freest man on earth. You know why? 'Cause I understand what a piece of shit I am. I'm a shit dad, a shit husband. That doesn't make it right, doesn't make me happy, but it does make me free. What separates me from the herd is, I know I got dick coming to me in this world." He paused for a second and pulled his long hair back into a ponytail. "Men have gotten too much for too long. I'm of the mind that we deserve the very worst fates this world can muster. Remember that. Treat women well or go ahead and kill yourself."

"But you're not treating Spregg's mother well by leaving her."

"You're wrong about that. Her life'll be happier without me in it."

"That sounds like an excuse."

"Could be, kid. Could be. You religious? Believe in God and punishments for the wicked, all that?"

"I don't know."

"You gotta have the right kind of eyes to see through things."

"I need to go," Josh stated.

"Do what I said, okay?"

"We'll keep an eye on Spregg."

He nodded. "And one more thing."

"Yeah?"

"His name is Gregg. That was my father's name."

Josh stood up from the chair, trying not to make a sound. He walked gingerly toward the door, passing the tanks, where the snakes all lay, their rattles for the moment still.

35

STREAMS

Hutch's beard was long and white, and his worn felt hat was always perched atop his head at a rakish angle. Stout and nearly ursine, Hutch struck a powerful profile. He hadn't had a proper job in years, except that he taught local kids about ecology at school functions, usually around Earth Day, and he played Santa Claus at Christmas. He had hit his left thumb so many times with a hammer that the nail refused to grow back. As a result, it resembled a bald mouse, and he hid this from children at Christmas, out of fear they would find it upsetting.

Hutch's wife was nearing retirement, but she still worked long hours as a nurse at the county hospital in Georgetown. So Hutch's days were his own, and he spent them outside. Each morning he paddled across the Waccamaw River in his canoe to a swampy uninhabited island. He liked to feel himself dwarfed by the wide river and was refreshed each time he reached the far shore. Scattered about in the forest of the island were jugs of homemade wine, stashed there so he could imbibe when the spirit struck. At the center of the island was a broad deep pond with turtles milling constantly around its surface. He had studied cetology in his youth but now found himself content with nature's smaller offerings.

Hutch and his wife had long given up on sex, and his one remaining bodily pleasure was urinating in running water. He refused to pee in the pond, but rather saved his morning water for a stream that fed away from it, clear and quick. Today, slightly stooped with age, Hutch straddled the stream, his berry-brown face beaming. He held himself in his hand, as he did each morning, the sun hitting in dappled beams through the cypress trees overhead. After following the sunspots there for a time, he released, allowing his flow to become one with the stream.

The vast sky was a clock face, and Hutch could tell the time by watching the sun and the clouds. 9:30 a.m.

He stripped naked and slipped into the pond. He moved slow and soft so as not to disturb the turtles. He dove deep, all the way down to the bottom. The water was brown and silty, but from beneath Hutch could look up and eye the turtles that floated on the surface. Spotting a choice one, he pushed off the bottom and went up and up until he emerged from the water with the turtle grasped firmly in both hands.

Hutch brought the turtle to the shore and placed it in a small pen he had made out of smooth driftwood. He then opened a tattered Sierra Club backpack and laid out an array of brushes and small cans of paint.

As the turtle dried in its pen, Hutch imagined his design, following and yet augmenting the colors and patterns of its plated shell. He wanted the shell to resemble a barn quilt that he had seen as a child growing up in Appalachia.

After he finished and the paint had dried, Hutch released the turtle into the pond. It swam away quickly. He leaned back on a log and began to drink from a jug of wine. He kept his eyes ever on the surface. He waited and napped and looked again. Finally, he saw the morning's turtle break the surface, joining with myriad others, bobbing, their backs all shining barn quilts.

These painted turtles were spotted from time to time, and rivergoers believed this to be a good omen. Twice Hutch's turtles appeared in the local paper; the second time an intrepid reporter revealed this to be Hutch's handiwork.

Years later Hutch would die in this very spot, slightly drunk on his homemade wine and staring up at the sun, after a morning of painting barn quilts on the backs of turtles. His wife and two daughters would not be present, but his turtles were, swimming around out there in the pond, their colorful backs festooned before all of creation.

Hutch's canoe would be found, as would his body, by hunters seeking wild boar on the river's islands.

And Pawleys Island would mourn, though few of its inhabitants had ever shared more than a passing nod with Hutch. Many refused to believe that he had been interred in the graveyard behind First Baptist. Instead they imagined him always out there waiting for them, a box turtle in one hand and a paintbrush in the other.

36

DIANA OF THE CHASE

Although it was nearly the end of September, it was hot as Hades when the students filed off the bus and into the parking lot of Brookgreen Gardens. "Gather round," Miss Garner said, motioning with her hands. "Gather round. Form a circle." The students clustered into an amoeba-like shape with her at its center. "Good enough," she said, then under her breath, "for South Carolina."

Josh and Ryan had drunk two Mountain Dews each on the bus. Nearly vibrating, they stood next to Miss Garner. Ryan rolled his eyes, before leaning in to Josh and whispering, "It's hot as balls out here."

Josh nodded, wiping sweat from his brow. He retrieved a Boy Scout canteen from his backpack and chugged down its contents in two long gulps. He stood up on his tippy toes and craned to find Chloe in the crowd.

Miss Garner had recently moved to Pawleys Island, hot off a master's degree in English from UNC–Chapel Hill. Convinced North Carolina was the superior Carolina, she and her boyfriend were always saying, "That's some South Carolina shit," whenever they saw the worst of this place on display. This had begun one day while they were at the Piggly Wiggly, and she started counting Confederate flag T-shirts on the shoppers around her. The seventh one she spotted featured a Confederate flag draped around a Christian cross. In shock, she whispered, "That's some South Carolina shit."

Miss Garner had taken it upon herself to educate the young citizens of the lesser Carolina, including this trip to Brookgreen Gardens, a former rice plantation that had been converted into a sculpture garden in the 1930s by the son of a northern railroad magnate. Miss Garner believed that since many of the sculptures depicted figures from Greek and Roman mythology, it would be an ideal way to illuminate their current language arts unit.

"Now, class," Miss Garner said, "when we enter the sculpture garden, we'll see Diana, Dionysus, Pegasus, the Muses, Pan, Mercury, Neptune, Icarus, Bacchus, and many more. You'll recognize these names, I presume, from the Edith Hamilton book we've been reading."

Ryan rolled his eyes again, and Josh said, "I've gotta pee like crazy." He looked around for a bathroom, and when he did he saw Chloe in the crowd. She flashed him a smile.

The amoeba began to move, following Miss Garner through the main entrance into the gardens. Josh and Ryan slowed their pace to fall back in the crowd, where Spregg was bouncing along on the balls of his feet.

"Y'all think Miss Garner is pretty?" he asked. He'd been suspended earlier in the semester for giving her the leg of a frog, wrapped carefully in lined notebook paper, that he'd severed during a science class. The dissection had occurred the previous year, and he'd saved the leg for some reason.

Josh and Ryan both shrugged, and Spregg then ran ahead of them to be closer to her.

Throughout the gardens, the live oaks stood enormous. Draped as they were with gray Spanish moss, Josh thought they must resemble the hanging pubes of some ancient, gargantuan race of men.

Up ahead, Miss Garner stopped in front of a statue. Josh and Ryan pulled up the end of the amoeba. In the sweltering heat, Josh held his long damp hair in a ponytail and was feeling rather indifferent until he saw what Miss Garner was pointing out: a topless bronze woman stood in a pool of water holding a bow to the heavens. With the sun nearly at its meridian, her nipples cast distinct shadows down her ribcage.

"Diana of the Chase," Miss Garner said proudly.

"What is this?" Josh uttered.

"Shit, man," Ryan said. "Get a load of that." He elbowed Josh and snickered.

Josh's pants went tight, and he felt a maggot crawl up his spine like a ladder.

Up ahead, Spregg said, "Ooh la la. Miss Garner, these na-ked-ass statues are cheeky."

Miss Garner started to reprimand him, then mumbled, "South Carolina," and moved on.

Josh and Ryan walked to the front of the amoeba, as did several other boys. The next statue featured two nude women in white marble, both gazing suggestively into one another's eyes. Josh tried not to stand still. He pivoted left and right, believing that somehow a moving erection would be more difficult for people to notice.

From statue to statue, Miss Garner was lecturing, but Josh absorbed nothing about mythology. His aching erection hurt so much that he could barely concentrate enough to see a large nude man, gold and blazing radiant in the sun, followed by an-other nude man, this one a stone figure sitting atop an alligator, his penis and balls flopped out onto the back of the giant rep-tile. Josh needed to urinate, which made the ache of his erection all the more intense.

When the amoeba approached another statue of Diana, which portrayed her running alongside a wolf and shooting a bow and arrow, Josh went red, thinking it was the spitting image of Chloe. The marble statue had long flowing hair and small breasts, and its face had a faraway look that he had seen in Chloe. He sat two rows behind her in Miss Garner's class and watched her each day as she stared out the window.

His erection was standing out now like an unholy dowsing that divined stone rather than water. *Jesus*, Josh thought, *this fucking urge, always this fucking urge.*

He shook his head, turned to Ryan, and said, "Cover for me. I gotta pee."

Josh waited until Miss Garner began moving to the next statue and then slipped away from the crowd. At the edge of the gardens, he found a break in the brick wall and exited through an unlocked gate.

Outside the wall he found himself at the edge of a swamp. The live oaks gave way to cypress and still black water. The grass was knee high, and Josh tried not to think of snakes and alligators.

He was back to being limp as a boiled noodle as he unzipped his pants. He had just begun to urinate when Chloe walked through the same break in the wall.

"Fuck," Josh muttered, as he saw her. She stared at him and doubled over in laughter. "Oh, Christ," Josh said, struggling to zip his pants back up. She laughed so hysterically that she couldn't catch her breath and began to wheeze.

"Don't laugh at it," Josh said.

Chloe's laughter slowed enough for her to say, "I'm not laughing at *it*."

"You clearly are."

"I'm not. I swear." Chloe smiled and took a step closer, her eyes a-sparkle. "Remember that time in The Igloo?" Josh nodded. "Our little peekaboo?" He nodded again. "Well, this is just like that. I want to see."

Josh giggled awkwardly. "What? Are you—"

"I'm serious. You know I am."

"Come on."

"No, you come on."

Chloe leaned in and kissed him on the neck. She then shucked her own shorts and panties down to her knees. Josh followed the smooth flesh of her torso down past her belly button. Her body looked less like a dolphin than he remembered. He rose again to the sight.

"Go on," Chloe said, taking a step back. Her look cleaved him open like an ax, and he imagined that she could see the maggots swarming violently from side to side in his brain.

Josh had just pulled his pants down, when Miss Garner walked through the brick wall and saw them there, giving each other an eyeful. "Oh my God!" she yelled. "I cannot deal with this." She turned and walked back through the gate, and on her way she said, "Fucking South Carolina shit."

"Judgmental bitch," Chloe said. She winked at Josh. "All right then. Where were we?"

37

TA TA CONTEST

The fact that Josh's father was willing to go to Myrtle Beach, a place he abhorred, put the boys on edge. And the fact that he and Ryan's dad George had volunteered to take them to The Pavilion made Josh even more suspicious that something was amiss.

The Pavilion was an amusement park that had long been the heart of Myrtle Beach's tourist culture. These days Josh and Ryan were less interested in roller coasters and more interested in meeting girls and trying to get them to ride the Love Canal, a slow-moving log flume through a dark tunnel that played romantic oldies. Many a hickey had been given and received on the Love Canal.

As Ryan's father's Suburban careened northward this Friday night, Josh and Ryan huddled in the backseat. The radio was blasting the classic rock station, and in the front seat their fathers passed a bottle in a brown paper bag back and forth.

"Something's up," Josh whispered. "We've got to follow them."

"What about the Love Canal?" Ryan asked.

"I know, but the Love Canal will be there next time."

"Dude, I've only lost like a quarter of my virginity." Josh was all too familiar with his story about dry humping a girl named Mary.

"I know. But when's the last time we hung out with our fathers?"

"Never."

"When's the last time they did us a favor?"

"Never."

"Right. And now they're willing to drive us all the way to Myrtle Beach. This doesn't smell right."

"Fine," Ryan said. "But I know if Chloe was going to be there tonight, we wouldn't be putting on this little detective routine."

"Look. We'll follow them for a little while. If they don't go somewhere interesting, then we double back to the Love Canal. Deal?"

"Whatever."

The radio cut off and the car went silent. "What are you two whispering about?" Josh's dad said, twisting around in the passenger seat.

"Nothing," Josh and Ryan yelled back in unison.

They parked near The Pavilion, and Ryan, Josh, and their fathers walked through the main thoroughfare together. They stopped beneath the Ferris wheel, which was the central feature of the park.

"See this?" Josh's father asked, pointing up at the flashing lights of the Ferris wheel as it slowly turned in the night sky. Josh and Ryan nodded. "Meet us back here. The park closes at eleven. Be here by 10:45. Sharp."

"Yes, sir."

Their fathers opened their wallets, and each handed his son a twenty-dollar bill. With that they turned and walked away. Josh and Ryan hung back a few seconds and then took off after them. The two men made a beeline eastward. Between the park and the ocean was the boulevard—several miles of oceanfront hotels, bars, and tourist shops. The stretch of the boulevard paralleling The Pavilion was the wildest, as it was perpetually populated with drunken roisterers.

The boys followed their fathers across the street at a crowded traffic stop. They passed a store called The Gay Dolphin and then a dance club called The Magic Attic, where many of the children of Pawleys Island had come to shed their virginity.

Josh eyed The Magic Attic longingly, but then turned his gaze back, careful not to lose sight of their fathers on the teeming sidewalk.

After two blocks the men entered a bar called The Beaver Lodge. Josh and Ryan stopped at the entrance. A bald-headed bouncer sat next to the doorway. He was wearing a Mötley Crüe T-shirt that was too small for him, and his tattooed arms were each about the size of Josh's torso. His trucker hat said, "Got Beaver?"

"Shit," Ryan said. "We'll never get through there."

"Let's try around back."

They walked around the side of the building and climbed the sand dunes that rose up behind it. From the top of the dunes, they could see down into the back of The Beaver Lodge, where a large deck sprawled from the building. The deck was crowded with people who danced to the rhythmic thumping that issued from a stack of speakers on the roof. Their fathers were easy to spot, given that they were twenty years older than everyone and dressed like they were going golfing. Both held pint glasses above their heads as they navigated their way toward a group of girls. When they spoke to them, they cupped their hands to shout over the music. To Josh's and Ryan's surprise, the girls leaned in and giggled at whatever they were saying.

After a couple of minutes, two of the girls followed their fathers to a tiki bar on one end of the deck. Both were wearing short shorts and bikini tops. One had a crown made out of glow sticks, and the other had a plastic, rainbow-colored Slinky on her arm. Josh's dad slapped down a wad of cash on the tiki bar, and the bartender lined up a series of shot glasses filled with clear liquor. All four of them licked salt from their hands, downed the shots, and sucked limes. They then repeated the ritual twice more.

The song on the stereo faded, and a DJ Josh couldn't see said, "Here's everyone's favorite dance hit, 'Macarena'!"

The girls grabbed their fathers and pulled them out to the middle of the dance floor. The girl with the glowing crown put a baby's pacifier in her mouth; she ignored the dance moves of "Macarena," which everyone else was doing, and instead began grinding on Ryan's father's thigh. Josh's father seemed reluctant at first to dance, but once the other girl showed him the moves, he fell into "Macarena" with abandon. His arms went out in front of him, then behind his head, and finally to his sides; his hips turned in a circle, before he made a quarter turn and began the sequence again.

After "Macarena" ended, the DJ said, "And now what you've all been waiting for: The Beaver Lodge's Fifth Annual Ta Ta Contest!" The crowd erupted in screams and applause. A man in the crowd trumpeted from a conch shell.

Josh and Ryan stared from the dunes as a parade of women walked across a small stage on the deck, each flashing their breasts to the crowd. Both of the girls who were with their fathers joined the procession. The noise level of the crowd determined the winner, and neither of their fathers' girls received very loud cheers.

The winner wore a red wig and Union Jack dress like Ginger Spice; when she pulled it down, her breasts were large and stuck out from her chest as if at attention. The conch shell sounded a deep moan beneath the cheering of the crowd. Several people swung whirly tubes around in the air, creating an alien bleat. Josh heard the DJ say, "She's got a couple of high hard ones," and a few seconds later, "A set of pins on her too."

Someone in a full-body beaver costume walked onto the stage and gave the winner a large boob-shaped balloon and a gift card for the tiki bar.

The two girls rejoined their fathers and began to yell into their ears. For some reason, "Macarena" started playing again, and Josh's father moved away from his girl and back into the pulsing crowd. His girl looked insulted and walked over to the tiki bar alone, while Ryan's father and the girl with the glow stick crown left the deck of The Beaver Lodge and walked down a long stairway to the beach. The boys watched them until the illuminated crown disappeared into the darkness.

Josh then turned his attention back to the party deck, where his father was still dancing to "Macarena" in a frenzy. Josh wasn't sure what was sadder—Ryan's father going off into the darkness with a Myrtle Beach woman or his own looking happier than ever, without his wife, without his family.

38

WATER FOLLOWS THE MOON

Josh had nightmares about Elvis. Tonight he was riding around in a car with Elvis, and Elvis was driving hell for leather. They'd gone for hours, barreling through the Mississippi darkness.

"I'm hungry," Josh said, as the back roads and pine scrub whizzed by.

"You always will be, boy," Elvis said. He then threw his head back and laughed maniacally, a moonshadow falling across his face. When they went around a bend, a passing car wiped the shadow away. Then the light drained, and Elvis became Josh's father.

"What are you doing?" he asked, looking disgustedly over at Josh.

Even in the dark, when Josh peered down, he could see his penis cradled in both hands. For no reason it began to grow, doubling in size and then quadrupling. Josh pushed it down but it resisted, engorged and now four feet in length. It bounced against the window. Josh winced and hit the button to roll it down. His penis snaked out, wagged in the breeze, and seemed to sigh, its meatus winking open and shut.

Josh's father punched the gas pedal and sped into a curve. Another car passed, and he eyed Josh's penis, bent now almost double as it was buffeted by the rushing wind.

"You'll grow up to be a pervert," his father said. "That much is certain." He swerved the car and Josh's penis struck a light pole.

"Ouch!" He pulled at it like a cowboy bringing in a lasso. But his penis pulled harder, reaching out toward the moon.

Josh's father swerved again. A blackberry thicket was up ahead.

"Please, Dad."

"I'm not your dad, boy." Elvis, dark and dashing, was in the car again. Still laughing, Elvis's gums started to bleed, and he rubbed a red line across his high cheekbones. The blackberry thicket neared. Josh's penis reached for the thorns, and the thorns reached back.

"Please, Elvis."

"It's gotta happen," Elvis said, leaning on the wheel and shepherding the car ever closer to the thicket.

"No, Elvis," he screamed, pulling hard as the first thorn began rending his flesh. "No!"

All of a sudden he was back in bed, naked and sweating, sheets twisted, the moonlight outside filtering through the blinds. Josh felt his penis, which was hard enough to cut glass. He loosed himself of the dream and descended the bunk bed ladder to stand before the window. He pulled on a pair of purple satin panties and felt whole again.

39

BUTTERBEAN

It was Halloween, and the mothers of the eighth-grade class had banded together, confident it was a sinners' holiday and fearful that the youth of Pawleys Island had turned to hooch, which of course they had. So they organized a slumber party, hoping to corral their kids' aberrant hormones in a safe space. Although the guys and girls would be together at the party, they had devised a partition that would be erected between genders at midnight, wild with passion and yet sober as nuns.

Josh and Ryan arrived at the school's gymnasium at eight p.m., dropped off together by their mothers who offered pearls of wisdom from the front seat of the Suburban: "Have fun. But no hanky panky." "If there's dancing, keep your hands above the waist at all times." "Don't you dare drink. You'll be on school grounds and could go to jail." "Let me see your wallet. If there's a condom in there, you're dead."

Josh and Ryan entered the gym and met Spregg inside. He had recently shaved the sides of his head, so that when combed back, his long honey-colored hair on top made him look like a golden wood duck. "I got a magnum of wine and some fireworks in my backpack," Spregg said, before walking away to a dark corner of the gym. Josh and Ryan followed and set up camp, unrolling their sleeping bags next to one another and stuffing their backpacks under their pillows.

"Pretty decent camp," Spregg said. They all nodded. "We'll get fucked up good tonight."

࿎

When it got dark, their gym teacher Mr. Murphy stood in the middle of the floor and barked into a microphone connected to the gym's loudspeakers. "Gather round, chillens," he said. "It's Halloween, and the ghosts and goblins are out. For one night only, the portal between this world of the living is opened to that other one, the land of the dead!"

Mr. Murphy pressed a button on the remote control he was holding, and the gym went dark, pitch black. Everyone squealed, guys and girls alike, running around, arms flailing, smacking one another, and copping cheeky feels.

When the lights came back on, Mr. Murphy had a knife plunged into his cheek. "Who stabbed me?" he said into the mic. Mr. Murphy pulled the knife from his cheek and spit out a stream of fake blood. "Must have been one of those ghosts. Pawleys Island is lousy with them." The lights went out again, and Mr. Murphy groaned into the mic. "Alice Flagg will come for you in the night. Angry because she cannot be with her fiancé, she will kill you as soon as you fall in love." The lights came back on. Bobby Brown and a few other meek-looking boys peered around anxiously. "And when you're dead, she will ferry your soul to the deepest, darkest pit of hell."

Josh watched the girls as they ran around the gym. He found Chloe in the crowd and wanted to hug her tighter than a can hugs Spam.

"And in hell," Mr. Murphy continued. The lights went off. "And in hell you'll never know light again, never feel joy. And you'll rot there alone."

The lights came on, and Mr. Murphy said, "Sleep tight, chillens." He howled and then dropped the mic, before walking off to the equipment closet.

Ryan shrugged. "He didn't even say the part about Alice ripping off dudes' dicks."

"Jack the Ripper," Spregg said dramatically.

"What does that even mean?" Ryan asked.

"Jack the Dick Ripper," Spregg said. His pupils were huge. "Dick the Jack Ripper."

"What are you on, man?"

Josh ignored them, looking around for Chloe again. But al-

ready the girls were on one side of the gym and the guys the
other.

Mr. Murphy erected the volleyball net and draped three
sheets over it, creating a barrier and cutting the gym in half.
"Guys on this side, gals on that," he said into the mic. "Or else,
I'm calling Alice."

Later the guys stood in a tight huddle, passing between them
Spregg's bottle of wine, all beginning to feel ripe. Ryan set up
a boombox next to them and popped in a tape. "Mr. Roboto"
started playing.

"Wait, wait," Spregg said. He'd been slurping wine, and it
dribbled down his chin. "Stop it. Stop it. I love this song." Ryan
paused the tape and stared at Spregg, who held up a finger,
while taking another quick slug from the bottle. Spregg rummaged around in his backpack for a second and then ran to the
bathroom.

After a minute, Spregg duck-walked his way back to their
camp. He nodded to Ryan who started the boombox again.
Spregg began dancing like a robot, his arms pumping up and
down to the bass line, as he beat a mechanical jig on the gym
floor. His arm spun in a circle, and when it stopped, it landed
on the front of his pants. He flicked the button open and ran
his zipper down. Of their own accord, his pants dropped to the
floor. "Freeballin', y'all," he said in a robot voice. He continued
to gyrate his hips, and his penis flopped side to side, smacking
his thighs. Several more boys had gathered around, and they
erupted in peels of laughter.

With "Mr. Roboto" blaring, Spregg hopped around one hundred and eighty degrees. He bent over and spread his cheeks,
and they all saw that there was a Double A battery stuck in
his asshole. Spregg clinched, and the battery popped out and
skidded across the gym floor. He droned, "Power down," and
slowly leaned over, stopping at a forty-five degree angle. This
sent the crowd into a fresh fit of giggles.

"All right, settle down," Mr. Murphy yelled from the other side of the gym. "Time for bed."

But before moving to his sleeping bag, Josh walked to where the battery had landed. He stooped down and saw that clinging to its positive end was an undigested butterbean.

Josh looked back, and the boys had hoisted Spregg up into the air. His pants were still halfway down, but he was riding their shoulders like a prince upon a palanquin.

40

Buxom Baptism

"It's your big day, Joshy," his mother said, as his father parked the station wagon at the south end of Pawleys Island an hour before sunset. Josh smiled nervously. "Your time to get right with the Lord."

Josh was sitting in the middle of the back seat. From his right, his older sister Jennifer punched him in the arm. He pushed his younger sister Liz to the left, and she exited the car. He followed and noticed right away that the parking lot was full of people from their church. They walked in the direction of the saltmarsh that separated Pawleys Island from the mainland. The creek spooled out to the southernmost tip of the island where it met the sea. The moon had tugged the water for the last few hours, and it was nearly high tide.

The members of the flock made their way to the creek. Pastor Ben was already there, wearing black dress slacks, a white button-down shirt, and a red vest. His cheeks were freshly shaven but he sported a thick brown mustache the color of his thinning hair.

Ben was standing before a table draped with a long white cloth. A silver dish full of wafers and a carafe of grape juice sat on top of it. Ben was tuning his acoustic guitar, while the congregation set up beach chairs in front of the table.

Josh sat down on a large quilt with his family. He scanned the congregation, which was about sixty strong, for anyone he knew from middle school. He recognized several people, but none of his friends were there. He'd screwed up his nerves last week and invited Chloe, but she had said she hated "church stuff."

Ben began strumming his guitar, and the general chatter of the crowd subsided. As he strummed, Ben sang "I Have Decided to Follow Jesus," and when the song finished, he bowed his head. The congregation did the same. "Lord, we are gathered here today to baptize those who have devoted their lives to you. Some are old and some young, but they all come together with a singular purpose: to confess their sins in order to be washed clean in the blood of the Lamb. Guide us this day, Lord, and keep us forever close to You."

Ben raised his head. His hands were palm up to the heavens, the guitar swaying from a shoulder strap. "Amen," he sang.

"Amen," the congregation replied.

"Today, we come before the Lord with a sacred mission. We gather here for this." He paused and gestured to the environment surrounding the creek. The saltmarsh flowed slowly before them, and the breeze moved through the sea grass on its far bank. "This is not unlike where Jesus, our Lord and Savior, was baptized. Moreover, we do not hide away in our own sanctuary. We baptize where all can see, where the world can witness the dedication of the saved." Ben gestured to a row of people, men and women, fishing in the marsh just down the creek. As if on cue, a man holding a tall beer nodded in the direction of the congregation and flashed Ben a crooked, gold-toothed grin.

"I call forth our first member of the flock. Cheryl is not, like so many who will be saved today, in middle or high school. Rather she comes to us to be redeemed after a life of sin."

A middle-aged woman stood up. She had on short jean shorts. Josh examined her legs, tanned and slightly wrinkled like a pair of buckskin britches. Cheryl had on a white T-shirt, and Josh could see the straps of a lime-green bikini top peeking out from where they were tied at the back of her neck. Cheryl had the largest breasts that Josh had ever seen on such a skinny woman. They stood out like two cantaloupes wrenching themselves from her torso.

Ben waded into the creek, and Cheryl followed close behind

him. She paused when the water was up to her thighs, shaking with cold. Ben turned around and nodded, encouraging her onward. Soon she stood beside him. The water was up to just above her waist. Josh watched it enter and exit her belly button, visible now beneath the wet midriff of her shirt. The water went in and out like rapid ebb and flow tides in a seaside cave.

Ben said to her, "Do you renounce Satan?"

"Yes."

"Do you give yourself over wholly to the Lord?"

"Absolutely."

"I then baptize you in the name of the Father, the Son, and the Holy Ghost."

With one arm behind her back and the other holding her outstretched hands, Ben lowered Cheryl into the water. She was submerged for three counts, and then he yanked her back up. She surfaced, blowing air from her nostrils, as they had been instructed to do. As soon as she was standing again, Cheryl exclaimed, not a discernable word, but a sort of excited animal-istic yelp. Her white T-shirt had gone all but invisible, and her lime-green bikini top shone electric in the light of the setting sun.

As Cheryl trudged out of the water, Josh could see her nip-ples poking out as hard and big as marbles. She looked directly at him and winked when she took her place next to the table at the front of the congregation.

Ben called Josh next. He hobbled awkwardly to the marsh, hoping his erection would subside before anyone noticed.

Ben went through the same renouncing Satan routine. Josh nodded and said yes when it seemed necessary. Finally, Ben dunked him into the water and held him down much longer than he had Cheryl. Josh came up gasping, and his long hair hung behind his head like ropes pulling him down. Ben slapped him hard on the back and said, "His miracles never cease."

Wet and shivering, Josh joined Cheryl at the front of the congregation. She grasped his hand and gave it a squeeze. She winked again, and Josh felt his pants go tight at the same time that a quartet of maggots appeared in his mind and began humming a devilish tune.

As Josh stood at the front of the gathering, his hands clasped together in front of his shorts, the baptisms went on for another half an hour. Then the baptized were led through communion. Ben stood before each of them and said, "The body of Christ. The blood of Christ." He then fed them a wafer and gave them a small plastic thimble full of grape juice. He went down the line in the order that they had been baptized. Cheryl was first and then Josh.

After Josh had downed the body and blood, he noticed that Cheryl was still holding her juice. She leaned over to him. "Can you believe Jesus is hiding in those little crackers?" Her lips were so close Josh could feel her breath against his earlobe. She handed him her juice and whispered, "I'm an alcoholic, so I can't drink this." She paused for a second, smiled, and added, "But I wanna smell you drink it."

"I think it's only grape—"

"Temptation is temptation," she said.

Josh took the juice, and as he shot it down, he felt her hand moving on the small of his back. She leaned in close and inhaled the air around his mouth. Josh looked out into the crowd. Not a soul was watching. Most had their heads bowed, their thoughts rapturous and devoted to Him.

Cheryl held her other hand up in front of his face. Her long fake nails were painted magenta. Her index, middle, and ring fingers each had a gold cross painted on it. "When I hold 'em together," she whispered, "it forms the hill of Calvary with the crosses of Jesus and those two sinners. See? It's a cute little baptism thing I thought up."

Josh pulled away from Cheryl and stumbled from her and the crowd. The dunes separating the saltmarsh and ocean side of Pawleys Island spread forth like a rumpled quilt. He crossed two of the dune-hills, and in the gathering dark, he saw a sandy valley, in which two human forms engirthed one another. He could not tell their genders; he saw only a back moving above another back. Soft, contented moans came from the pair, undulating in and out.

Josh slipped away. *There is no evil present here,* he thought. He felt himself cast upon a beach and the sea had been all he had ever known. "The people of the sea," he said to himself, "know diddly-squat about love."

41

A Man Now

Josh awoke with a start. It was still dark outside, Friday night or Saturday morning, and his father was shaking him, standing on the futon and looking into the top bunk above it. Josh groaned and rolled over onto his side to face the wall.

"Get up," his father said.

"Why?" Josh muttered.

"Now."

"It's not even a school night."

His father jerked his shoulder, forcing him onto his back. "I've got something to show you."

He wasn't the kind of dad to awaken his son with surprises in the middle of the night. Josh drug himself upright, his long hair tangled in mats. His father was already through the bedroom door and making his way down the hall. Josh quickly put on jeans and a T-shirt from a pile in the corner of his room and followed his father downstairs.

In the kitchen Josh flicked on an overhead light, illuminating his father who was standing over the sink pouring gin through a small funnel into a silver flask. "Turn it off," his father said. "You'll wake the girls."

"No one else is coming?"

"Just you and me." He finished filling the flask and slipped it into his back pocket. He returned the bottle to a cabinet high above the sink. The clock on the stove said 2:30 a.m.

Josh and his father snuck out the back door, carefully closing it behind them to ensure all remained silent. When they were both in the truck and buckled in, Josh's father began to laugh just loud enough for Josh to hear. He then turned on the radio and tuned it away from his mother's Jesus-y station to his favorite classic rock one. His hands shook as he put the truck in gear and backed out of the driveway. Neil Diamond came on the radio, and Josh heard his father say something about the song being "campy crap." He tuned the dial again, and Bruce Springsteen's voice started blaring through the speakers. "Now that's more like it."

They drove only a short distance down the coastal highway before reaching a long line of traffic. The cars were snaking so slowly that some people were getting out and walking up to other cars to chat. Josh's father rolled down the windows and let The Boss bleed out into the night. It was April and already hot. Josh felt the humid air blast in through the windows. Other people in cars nearby had their windows down, and they were laughing and calling out to one another.

"What's going on?" Josh asked. The truck in front of them honked, and the driver whooped, while banging his hand on the side panel.

"Wings is on fire," he said slowly, his eyes glossed over. "Somebody torched it."

The Boss was still singing about dancing in the dark, and Josh had to yell over it, "How did you know about this?"

"Someone called right before I woke you up." Josh was confused. Whenever the phone rang late at night, it always woke up everyone in the house. Josh was about to inquire about this when his father inched the car forward, and he could see around a bend in the highway. The sky was aglow, and flames licked upward almost as high as the pine trees.

Wings was a large, garishly pink beachwear store that had recently been built in Pawleys Island. The architectural review board, which Josh's father was on, was split over the development. It had been voted down several times before being railroaded through by a local bigwig named Soup Kennedy. When the review board finally approved the design, an editorial in the town's newspaper suggested that there were a number of corrupt board members whose palms had been greased.

As they drew closer, the red glow of the fire mixed with

the whirling blue lights of what seemed like the entire Pawleys Island police force. A tall officer in a wide-brimmed hat walked down the middle of the road. Josh's father yanked the radio's volume knob all the way down and checked his pocket to make sure the flask was hidden. The policeman leaned down to their open window and said, "You can't stop. Move it along, or pull into the Piggly Wiggly." Josh's father nodded in an overly enthusiastic manner. The burning structure was to their right, and he turned to the left into the grocery store parking lot. There were over a hundred cars parked there, all with people sitting or standing on their hoods to watch the fire. Josh's father swerved the truck through the lot until he found an empty spot with a clear view of the blaze.

Josh and his father got out and sat high up on the hood with their backs against the windshield. As he listened to the gathering cacophony of the crowd, Josh wiped sweat from his forehead. The night was already balmy, and the hood of the truck radiated heat up through his jeans. Josh put out his hand toward the burning building, and he could actually feel the warmth of the fire moving across the dark air.

More cars poured into the parking lot, surrounding their truck so closely on all sides that it would be impossible to leave until everyone else did. Out of a small Honda hatchback poured ten teenagers like it was a clown car. Josh recognized a couple of them and thought they were seniors. Each had a tall beer stuffed into a narrow brown bag. Periodically one would yell, which would lead the rest of them to whoop madly. Two men from another car had pulled a grill out of their trunk and were lighting a pyramid of charcoal.

"It's so hot," Josh said.

"I know," his father said without looking over. "Isn't this beautiful?"

"I guess."

"You guess?" He glanced over at Josh, who was still feeling the air, measuring the heat. "Josh, that Wings was tacky. This is Pawleys Island, not Myrtle Beach."

At that moment, someone started shooting bottle rockets into the air. They screeched, and everyone present, including Josh's father, cheered and clapped. Two small children, barely even kindergarten age, ran past. They had sparklers in each hand, waving them about. Josh's father's face was flashing light and then dark, and Josh watched him sigh. "I'm glad the community's behind this."

Josh was still not sure what *this* was. "I guess."

"Is that all you have to say tonight?"

Josh shrugged. He was watching a police officer run through the parking lot, looking for the person who was shooting off bottle rockets. The officer ran to one side of the lot, and then the other exploded with bottle rockets; by the time he got to that side, the original one began to shoot them off again.

A man ambled by, wearing one of those hats with beer cans attached to either side. It had straws going out of each, and the man took turns sipping from them. He was singing, "Burn baby burn, disco inferno. Burn baby burn, burn that mother down." He sang this over and over, each time eliciting a standing ovation from those nearby.

Josh's father laughed, and as he did he took a long pull from his flask. "Are you enjoying this?" he asked Josh. "And don't say, 'I guess.'"

Josh nodded. He was trying to recall the last time he had been alone with his father. "Why did you bring me here?"

"To see this, Josh." His father gestured frantically toward the scene as if he was a deranged tour guide.

"I know," Josh said. "But why me and not mom or Jennifer or Liz?"

He lowered his flask and secured it between his legs. "To tell you the truth, I brought you because I saw you naked the other day."

Josh looked shocked. "What?"

"Remember," his father said, "last Sunday. We were late for church, and I came into your room to tell you to hurry up. You were getting dressed. I know you've gotten a lot taller lately, but

I hadn't seen you naked in a long time. Probably since you were a toddler."

"So what?"

"So you're a man now."

"Gross, Dad. Please stop." Josh wondered what his dad would say if he knew that he wore a pair of purple panties to bed each night.

His father looked around, surveying the parking lot. The fire department had arrived, and they were spraying thick arches of water into the burning building. The people in the parking lot booed.

"I guess I hadn't really thought it through," his father said. "I still tend to consider you a kid. But since you're not, I wanted you to see this. These things were connected in my mind somehow."

Josh watched a long ladder extend from the top of a fire truck. A man in a red jacket was clinging to the top. "What do you suppose he's going to do?" Josh asked.

"All I know is that Wings is a goner."

The man on the ladder directed a stream of water down into the store. Josh looked away and toward his father.

"Well, I'm glad you brought me," Josh said. "I guess."

His father smiled and handed Josh the flask. "Have yourself a little tipple."

Josh took the flask and held it before his face reverently. He had drunk beer and wine on a number of occasions, but never liquor and, of course, never in front of his parents. Closing his eyes, Josh took a long pull. He coughed, feeling its heat course down his gullet. His father took the flask back before Josh could spill any of it.

Josh leaned back against the windshield, feeling the heat from Wings growing colder, as the fire fighters went about their work. But the warmth in his belly was just beginning to bloom.

42

At the Fish Hut

The summer after eighth grade Josh's father made him get a job at a fried seafood place called the Fish Hut. Locals generally avoided the restaurant, as they had heard too many tales of rats in the dry storage, pink mold in the ice, fish from Taiwan masquerading as local. And, worst of all, Spregg had worked there and had once drunkenly puked into a large pot of she-crab soup while stirring it with a spoon the size of a boat paddle. Spregg spread word around town that when he reported the incident to Brett, the restaurant's owner, Brett asked Spregg if the crabmeat had already been added. After Spregg affirmed that it had, Brett had merely said, "Crank up the heat; then sell it."

But this knowledge stayed confined to locals, and in the summer months the restaurant was packed with inland tourists, sunburned lobster-red.

After a busy service one evening, the restaurant cleared out quickly, the tourists heading back to their hotels and beach houses to put their kids to bed. Josh and a high school girl named Hannah cleared empty Budweiser bottles, plastic cups of sweet tea, and baskets of shrimp tails from the tables. Some of the waitresses said Hannah was related to Brett. Hannah knew that Josh hung out with Spregg and seemed to hold Josh responsible for the she-crab soup story getting out.

They flipped a coin to see who would scrub down the rubber mats behind the bar and wait station and who would vacuum the restaurant. Josh called tails as Hannah flipped a dime into the air. It landed in the palm of her right hand and she then slapped it onto the back of her left. "Tails," she said.

"I'll vacuum," Josh replied.

"Fuck you." Hannah huffed and stomped away toward the back of the restaurant.

Josh got the vacuum from a closet and wheeled it to a far corner; he uncoiled the cord and stretched it out across the main dining room.

The waitresses were already sitting around the bar. All of them, except for Ava, were smoking thin cigarettes and drinking Miller Lights. Ava, long dark hair, cat-eye glasses, and a permanently pouty expression, was drinking a screwdriver. Josh thought she was the most beautiful woman his mother's age he had ever seen. In the restaurant, Ava was a "passer through" as opposed to a "lifer." She only worked there because she was struggling to set up a business as a stained-glass artist. When Josh once asked her what kind of stuff she made, she said, "Anything except for church shit. No crosses or Jesus-y windows." And with that he felt that he could love her.

As Josh dragged the cord closer to the wall and the outlet, Rosie, the restaurant's manager and a definite lifer, said, "I gotta get my baps out, ya'll. This bra is killing me." Rosie was known around town for the size of her breasts. She was three times the age of Josh, but he and his friends marveled at her. Josh and Spregg had recently spent several pleasurable evenings drinking beer and dreaming about what, fully unclothed, she would look like.

"Let those sisters loose," Kelly said. Kelly was a nurse and thus a passer through. She took a long sip of beer, swallowed, and, throwing back her head, let out a howl.

Rosie unclasped her bra and, as if by magic, withdrew it without removing her shirt. Josh pretended to fiddle with the vacuum, but Rosie sensed he was watching.

"It's okay, sugar," Rosie said from the bar. She always called Josh sugar, and he liked it so much that he had found himself daydreaming lately about discovering—perhaps on one of those dramatic daytime talk shows—that Rosie was his real mother.

Before he started bussing tables at the Fish Hut, Josh had

a growth spurt and he now stood at six feet exactly—six feet, one inch if he was wearing Doc Martens. His body appeared stretched out, long and thin as a seahorse. His hair was almost black, and he had been growing it out for nearly two years. At work he kept it pulled back in a loose ponytail.

When Josh looked up from the vacuum cleaner, all three of the waitresses were staring directly at him. He flashed red, and they laughed.

"Your interest in these old gals is flattering," Rosie said.

Kelly flashed a wicked smile. "You gotta girlfriend, Josh?"

"No?" he said like it was a question.

"Not too sure?"

"Well, kind of," he said, thinking of Chloe.

"Sounds like she's not giving you any," Kelly said. He turned red again and imagined maggots beating down a flimsy wall in his mind. "I like 'em a bit…" Kelly held up an arm and let her wrist go limp, as if it was devoid of bones. She purred, staring at Josh. "God, I want to make a man out of you."

Rosie slapped the bar and giggled. She dropped her cigarette and left it to burn out on the carpet.

Ava exhaled, something not quite a laugh. "Goddamn it, Kelly. You can't talk to him like that."

With an obscene glint in her eye, Kelly ignored Ava and looked at Josh from her high barstool. "You're so tall, Josh. I hope you don't have one of those long, narrow dicks."

"Y'all are terrible," Ava said.

"Can I get a witness?" Kelly said.

"Amen to that," Rosie said, all holy sounding. "God, I hate a pencil dick. My husband's got a big ole pecker. Sometimes it takes thirty minutes to get him off."

Josh was worried, for he had developed just such a dick, long but hopelessly narrow.

Ava raised her hands toward Rosie and waved them about. "Please stop. We all know about Gerry's dick."

Rosie smiled and returned to rolling silverware. Kelly licked the rim of her beer bottle and winked at Josh. Ava shrugged at him, as if to say she was sorry. Josh clicked on the vacuum cleaner and started going over the stained, greasy carpets. He could hardly focus, so consumed was he by the thought of Rosie and her husband going at one another with their enormous flesh. He imagined a baptism, sinners dunked in a creek and then coming out clean. That's what he hoped sex was like, a willful dismay, a total immersion of skin.

The bag on the vacuum quickly filled with the hush puppies and French fries that had been ground into the carpet. Josh unfastened the bag to dump it out. Someone had already removed the trashcans from the front of the restaurant, so he walked into the kitchen to see if one was still there. Normally Josh didn't go into the kitchen, because when he did, the kitchen staff, all older African-American women, would glare at him, giving him the distinct impression that this was their turf.

The air smelled so strong of fish in the cramped kitchen that it burned Josh's nose. He moved swiftly and found a trashcan before anyone saw him.

When he reentered the dining room and approached the bar, it was strangely silent. No one was talking and even the radio had been turned off. He looked toward the bar, and without warning, Rosie stood up out of her barstool and lifted her shirt all the way to her throat, gifting Josh an eyeful. He was still in motion but his eyes surveyed as best they could, drinking it all in. Something then happened with his feet. He found himself ass over elbow, falling and falling and finally landing on the floor. His face caught the rough carpet, and a stinging strawberry began forming there as he struggled up to a sitting position.

"Those are some powerful titties," someone said from the kitchen.

Kelly and Rosie were laughing hysterically, and even Ava was having difficulty stifling a giggle.

"Knocked clear off his feet," Kelly managed.

Rosie smiled and blew smoke at the ceiling. "Men really are simple creatures," she said. Kelly and Ava nodded as they turned back to rolling silverware.

43

FIREFLIES

The proselytizing had begun in earnest, and Pastor Ben was fired up, warning the middle schoolers in the audience of Wednesday Night Youth Group about the evils of cigarettes and beer and touching one another.

"Now the works of the flesh are manifest," Ben said before pausing. He placed a hand in the pocket of his vest and sucked on a corner of his dark moustache. "They which do such things shall not inherit the kingdom of God."

Chloe leaned over in the pew and said to Josh, "I can't handle any more of this shit. Let's get out of here." He nodded, and they both rose and slunk away as quietly and nonchalantly as possible. Ryan was sitting in the pew behind them. He put the back of his hand to his mouth and tongued it. Josh rolled his eyes and whispered, "We're just going to the bathroom."

"Together?" Ryan asked, frenching his hand again.

"Be cool," Josh said. "Please."

"Okay, fuckhead."

Josh and Chloe walked to the back of the church and were about to go outside, when they noticed that it had started to rain.

"The balcony," Chloe said, nodding toward a dark hallway, closed off with a purple velvet-covered rope.

Josh removed the barrier, and they tiptoed their way up the stairs, careful not to make a sound. The balcony was dark except for what light filtered up from the sanctuary below, where Ben was extolling the joys of waiting till marriage. The chairs in the balcony were all stacked along the walls, so Chloe and Josh sat down on the floor. They could still make out Ben's enthusiastic proclamations from the front of the church. But they both felt more at ease with this degree of remove.

"I want to try something," Chloe said. She was sitting with her back upright and her legs stretched out before her. "Here, sit like this across from me."

Josh did, his feet outstretched, almost touching hers. "No, wait," she said. "We have to remove our shoes for this to work." She quickly shook off her Birkenstocks, and Josh undid the Velcro of his Tevas before flinging them to the corner of the balcony.

"Press the soles of your feet to mine," Chloe said.

They sat with their feet together, Chloe's smaller than his and hitting them just below his toes. He suppressed a laugh as she footsied her way around his arches. "My brother's girlfriend told me about this," she explained. "She does yoga and knows all this new age-y stuff."

"Neat," Josh said.

"This is called 'the souls of our feet.' If we concentrate, with our bare feet together, we can feel each other's souls as they move around our bodies and out into the world. You have to concentrate, though."

"Okay," Josh said. His erection was threatening to tear a hole through his shorts.

"You feel it?" Chloe asked.

"I do," he managed.

Just then Ben was working his way to some sort of Jesus-inspired crescendo. His voice seemed to boom out around them. "Sex is the devil's tool. Mighty clever is he at masking an evil punishable by eternal damnation."

The fire and brimstone were doing nothing to detract from Josh's erection, but maggots were beginning to dance the Carolina shag in his mind. He felt their every tap-tap-tapping step.

Chloe muffled her ears with her hands. Her soul was finding it difficult to work through her feet. "This is fucked," she said, louder than Josh was comfortable with.

He said, "What blurt is this about virtue and about vice?"

"What does that mean?"

"It's from something I've been reading lately. Walt Whitman. Too much ducking and deprecating, he says."

"What are you talking about?"

"Sorry. Let's try the foot thing again."

"No, I hate youth group." The reason Chloe was there was because Josh had begged her. It was the only time other than school and Friday nights at the mall that they were able to see one another.

"Maybe we can go outside."

"It's raining, remember?"

Josh jumped up and ran to the window. He was thankful for the darkness, as his penis was making his pants stick out from his center like an obscene weathervane. The window was stained glass and depicted Jesus standing next to a vapid-looking quadruped that Josh assumed was a lamb. He peered through the green blob of glass that Jesus stood upon and could barely see the conditions outside. "I think it's stopped."

"Great," Chloe said. "Let's go."

They snuck back downstairs, and as they crept out the door, Josh could hear Ben calling on sinners to genuflect before the Lord.

Chloe and Josh darted down the path that led out from the church, the same path used by newlyweds as they were pelted with rice and well wishes. They ran through a small stand of trees next to the church, their hands outstretched before their faces, deflecting tree limbs and spider webs. They soon came to an empty field that was only used for overflow parking on Christmas and Easter. The two of them collapsed together on the ground, feeling the rain-drenched grass soak through their T-shirts.

They were free at last from the Bible thumpers, and as they lay in silence, the fireflies began to emerge, blinking yellow in the darkening sky. Chloe snuggled into Josh's neck. She kissed him there, and he snuck his hand up under her shirt, pulling her in close and exploring the back of her bra. Chloe sucked on Josh's earlobe until he could stand it no longer. He guided her mouth to his, and they kissed until both of their faces felt raw to the wind.

"You need to shave," she said, pulling away and laying her head back in the wet grass. The fireflies were going mad above them.

"I read about them recently," Chloe said.

"Beards?"

"No." She laughed without turning to him. "Fireflies. Do you know why they blink? Why they illuminate?"

"To let one another know where they are?"

"Well, kind of. It's a sex thing. Every time one of them is blinking away up there, it's trying to get laid." Chloe pointed up at one blinking quickly and then another pulsing much slower. "See. Some are fast and some slow. The fast ones are young, and the slow ones are old. They try to find a partner that has a similar speed. They want to link up their flashes before they do it."

Josh followed Chloe's finger across the sky as she pointed. "That one's so fast," Chloe said.

"Yeah, that one's way too young for such a sexy ritual."

"And see that one?" Chloe asked. "It's really slow."

"That one is lucky he could even get his fat old gonads off the ground this evening."

Chloe rolled toward him, laughing into his neck and fingering his long dark hair. They were quiet again for a time, hugging one another against the unexpected chilliness of this summer night.

"Do you think we'll ever?" Josh asked.

"Ever what?"

"You know."

"You can say it, Josh. You're such a prude."

"Flash for one another."

"Don't say it like that. Don't make it a joke," she said.

"Okay. Fine. Do you think we'll ever have sex?"

Chloe thought about it for a second. She was no longer smiling. "If you ever grow up."

The fireflies were beginning to go dim overhead, and with them this moment of Josh's yellow youth began to blink and fade. Shuddering lusciously, he clung to Chloe with the desperation of a barnacle, but she had shut up like a clam.

44

A Bulgarian Furry Saves the Day

Josh and Ryan sometimes tried to avoid Spregg. Since his father had recently been imprisoned for trafficking exotic pets, and his mother had taken to church with a fervor that rivaled even Josh's mom, Spregg's behavior had become more erratic than ever. But Spregg was in possession of four pints of vodka, so when he called Josh to tell him about this cache, Josh said that he should come hang out with them for the day.

The summer was creeping along, and Josh and Ryan had begun going to the Pawleys Island Inn, where they would sneak into the private beachside pool.

They waited at Josh's house for Spregg, backpacks packed, their bikes ready. A wild desire gnawed at them but they could not name it. At 12:30 Spregg finally arrived, driven by his mother. She rolled down the window and waved at Josh and Ryan. "Hi, boys," she said, smiling like a maniac. "Thanks so much for inviting my Gregg."

"Sure thing," Josh said through the car window.

"You boys be good. And have a blessed day." Josh cringed but waved and feigned a smile.

When Spregg's mother drove away, Josh and Ryan looked at Spregg expectantly. He hefted his backpack, and they could hear bottles clink inside.

"Wait. Where's your bike?" Ryan asked.

"I rode with Mom," Spregg said.

Ryan rolled his eyes. "I fucking know you rode with her. We just saw you get out of her car."

"So what?" Spregg asked.

"So how the fuck are we supposed to get to the beach. We specifically said for you to bring your bike."

"I forgot. Who cares?"

"We care," Ryan said.

"Don't blow a gasket, man," Spregg said. "Your face is all red."

"I'm going to—"

Josh stepped between them, putting up his hands. "All right, Jesus Christ. Cool it, guys." Ryan turned from Spregg to Josh and nodded. "I'm ready to go to the beach," Josh continued. "Let's figure this out." Josh was thinking about Chloe, whom he hoped would be meeting them there. "Spregg needs to ride on one of our handlebars."

Ryan shook his head. "You," he said. "You're the one so desperate to go and see Chloe. You carry his dumb ass around."

"Fine. Fuck it," Josh said. He mounted his bike and nodded toward the handlebars. Spregg pulled himself halfway up but then slumped over and fell, the bottles rattling in his backpack as he hit the driveway. He tried again and fell even quicker this time, laughing on the ground and waving up at Josh.

"Good lord," Josh said. "Are you already drunk?"

Squirming on the driveway, Spregg gave a thumbs-up. Josh reached down and pulled Spregg upright. With Josh's hands clutching each of Spregg's hips, Spregg settled onto the handlebars and finally got his balance. They took off through the neighborhood and toward the beach. Spregg fell off several times on the way to the inn, once hitting his head on the pavement. A bright red goose egg formed above his left eyebrow. He seemed not to notice.

One side of the pool opened to the beach, and the inn surrounded the other three sides. Josh and Ryan ditched their bikes in the dunes just outside of the inn's property, and they snuck into the pool area from the beach. The deck was teeming with people, and the pool itself seemed to boil with splashing children. Trying to look nonchalant, Josh and Ryan began setting their stuff up on two lounge chairs. They were about to grab a third when they turned around to look for Spregg. He was running across the deck, fully clothed, his backpack bouncing up and down like a jockey on a horse. He yelled, "Watermelon!" and jumped through the air, tucking his legs and plunging head-first into the pool in a sort of upside-down cannonball. Several men, who were standing around the pool deck talking and nursing beers, clapped and whooped. An older couple shook their heads disapprovingly, and a mother tucked her small daughter under her protective arm.

"Shit," Ryan said.

"I know," Josh replied. "Why did we agree to this?"

"Booze, I guess. Not sure it's worth it."

Spregg swam a lap around the pool before coming back toward them. Josh pulled him out, using his backpack to drag him up from the water and over the ledge of the pool. Holding him firmly by the shoulder, Josh led Spregg to the area where they had set up camp. He helped Spregg off with his backpack and shirt, his body going limp as a ragdoll. Whatever he had drunk or taken had fully set in since they left the house. With his shirt off, Spregg was painfully skinny. "He could use some meat on his bones," Josh's mother had recently said. Josh was a string bean himself, but Spregg looked sick. His body brought to mind images Josh had seen in school of imprisoned people, starving, eating their own shoes and toenails and hair.

After Spregg passed out on a lounge chair, Josh and Ryan pilfered his bag. Sure enough, they found the four pint-sized bottles of vodka. One of them was empty. They both bought Cokes from the inn's cabana, and while Josh held up a towel, Ryan poured generous glugs of vodka into their cups. Leaving Spregg asleep in his chair, Josh and Ryan slipped into the shallow end of the pool. They stood in the water leaning against the concrete side, their drinks held in front of them just above the surface. Both took a series of hard pulls, and they started feeling pleasantly jingled. The water was cool, and the sun was hot on their shoulders. The vodka worked its way through their bloodstreams, limbering their minds and bodies.

Every couple of minutes, Josh looked around, surveying the pool deck.

"You've got to fucking relax," Ryan said.

"I know, I know. I was just hoping she would be here."

"You looking around like some kind of asshole pelican isn't going to make her get here any faster."

"You're right," Josh said. He took a drink and leaned back, his eyes closed to the sun. Ryan did the same. They had both almost fallen asleep in this position when Josh felt someone tapping on his shoulder. Thinking it was Chloe, he swiveled around. Spregg was crouched behind him on the pool deck. He held a clutched hand close to Josh's face and then unfurled his fingers one by one. He was holding a silver key with a green diamond-shaped keychain. The number 213 was embossed on it.

"What is that?" Josh asked.

"Found it," Spregg said.

"Found it where?"

"Over there." He pointed vaguely around the pool deck behind them.

Ryan was looking on now. "Did you steal someone's fucking room key?"

"No," Spregg said, shrugging his shoulders. "Found it. Honest."

"Well, don't let anyone see it, you idiot," Ryan said.

"Why?" Josh asked. "Just take it to the cabana."

"No," Ryan said. "Let's go check out the room."

"My thoughts exactly," Spregg said.

Josh shook his head and looked at Ryan. "Nope. I expect this shit from him, but not you."

"I'm bored," Ryan said. "All you do is worry about whether Chloe is going to show up."

"Wait, you don't think she's coming?"

"See," Ryan said. "All you do is worry, and all he does is..." Spregg stared at the two of them, his eyes glassy, the goose egg shining red on his forehead. "We could all use a distraction."

"If you don't do it," Spregg said, "I'm going to go piss on that old man asleep over there." Josh and Ryan followed

Spregg's line of vision to the sleeping man. They looked back at Spregg and knew he was serious.

"Ice machine," Josh said. The three of them trudged off to an isolated nook of the pool deck where there was an ice machine tucked under a flight of metal stairs. They huddled there, discussing how to enter the room most inconspicuously. Spregg thought that they should wear masks of some sort. Ryan recommended that they try to find outfits like the ones worn by the hotel staff. "No," Josh said. "We need to do this now, if we're going to do it. Otherwise someone will figure out their key is missing. We'll canvas the second floor, and if the coast is clear, we'll all slip into the room quickly and quietly. Quietly, Spregg. Hear that?" Spregg nodded, and the three of them took off up the stairs.

Room 213 was on a deserted hall. Ryan knocked on the door. When no one answered, he used the key to open it. Ryan and Spregg ran in. Josh looked down both sides of the hallway to make sure it was still empty. When he slipped into the room, Ryan and Spregg were staring dumbly down at what lay before them on the bed. The room was dark, only a single beam of light cutting through the parted curtains and falling across the bed. Two costumes were there, one mouse and one elephant, both quite large.

"What the—" Josh said, pausing and looking down. "Are these Disney?"

Ryan and Spregg laughed. "Not hardly," Ryan said.

"What then?"

"I've seen this before," Ryan said. "About a year ago I found this magazine in my dad's truck."

Just then there was a knock at the door. They all froze. The knock came again, harder this time.

"Shit," Ryan said.

"Fuck," Spregg said.

"We're shit-fucked," Josh said.

The knock sounded again, even louder. "Police. Open up."

"How'd they get here so fast?" Josh whispered.

He and Ryan looked at Spregg who shrugged and said, "I may have mentioned the key to a girl at the pool." Ryan slugged Spregg in the shoulder. "What! She was cute."

Josh moved to the door and cracked it open. The officer pushed hard, slamming it into Josh's torso. Wheezing and holding his chest, he stared up at the man, who was so tall he had to stoop to get through the doorway.

"What's going on in here?" the officer demanded.

Josh was struggling to breathe. Spregg ambled forth. "This is our room," he said.

Josh stepped forward and held Spregg back. "No, it's not." His breathing was slowly becoming easier. "We just found a key and were—"

"Come with me," the officer said. He led them out of the room, down the stairs, through the lobby, and out the front entrance. "Sit down," he said sternly, indicating a bench with a nod of his head.

Spirits flagging, the boys sat down, heads lowered, hands between their legs. The officer called into the receiver attached to his shoulder, indicating a code number and then saying something about juvenile delinquents needing to be picked up. The officer put on a pair of sunglasses and stood before the boys. The lenses were like mirrors, and Josh could see his own sad reflection in them.

"You boys realize you've broken the law. Trespassing. Breaking and entering."

They remained silent. Josh was rummaging through his mind for a response, when he saw Georgi walk around the corner of the inn. Ryan looked up and saw him too. Georgi was dressed in a garish Hawaiian shirt and Bermuda shorts, a Bulgarian dandy who used to work for Ryan's father.

"Georgi!" Ryan yelled.

Georgi approached them, taking off his straw hat and assessing the situation. "What seems to be the problem here, officer?"

The officer looked Georgi up and down. "I'm arresting these boys for trespassing. Move along please."

"Hey now," Georgi said. "I know these boys. Where are their parents?"

"How should I know?" the officer said. "Certainly not here keeping them in line."

"These are good boys, officer."

"That may be, but they've trespassed, and we're taking them in."

Georgi approached the officer, put a hand on his shoulder. The officer started and withdrew. Georgi whispered something into his ear that the boys could not hear. The officer laughed knowingly. Georgi laughed, too, and said, "Let me call their parents. They'll punish these boys more severely than you ever could."

The officer nodded and said, "Well, I am getting off soon. Don't want to do the paperwork if I don't have to."

Georgi ran inside the inn, and within five minutes Ryan's father George arrived in his truck. He got out and yelled, "Goddammit, Ryan. I'm gonna cut your butt."

The officer nodded to Georgi and walked away toward his cruiser.

George shook Georgi's hand and said that he appreciated the call. "Get in the fucking truck," he said to Ryan. "You, too, Josh."

Spregg locked eyes with George for a second. "Are you that kid Spregg?" George asked.

Spregg shot him a look and then ran from the front of the inn toward the beach. He yelled, "You'll never get me in the pokey." He made it to the dunes and tripped in the soft sand. He righted himself, and the last they saw was him hightailing it up and over the dunes, his legs scissoring through the sand. With each dune that he crested, he seemed smaller and smaller, until at last he was gone.

45

First Flare

Chloe and Josh ran through the sand dunes, their skinny bare legs cutting their way through the sea oats. The wind badgered the dunes and stung their ankles until they dipped into a valley, where they fell on their backs and hunkered down. As they looked up at the night sky, their shoulders were just barely touching. Josh felt a flare go through his body, starting at his shoulder and moving out.

Voices were all around them, friends screaming in a large game of Capture the Flag that they were supposed to be playing. The Wednesday Night Youth Group did this occasionally, getting kids together in a last-ditch effort to save their souls before they entered high school and were lost forever.

Chloe and Josh were hiding from the world, peers and all, sprawled in a labyrinthine series of sand dunes that stretched out on the southernmost tip of Pawleys Island. Hurricane Hugo had barreled through the land a few years ago, ripping deep trenches through the dunes.

Chloe turned to Josh. "What'll we do if they find us?"

"We'll get lost again," he said.

Chloe smiled. "Good."

"I only came here in the hopes of seeing you."

"Not for God?" Chloe asked sarcastically.

"If there's a God, my only request is that no one find us here."

Chloe put her head onto Josh's shoulder and whispered, "My dad left. For good this time."

Josh had only recently begun seeing his parent's marriage for what it was, the chinks in the armor they presented to the church and the community. "Both our parents' relationships are shit," he said, not knowing what else to say.

"When I left the house," Chloe said, "my mom was crying in the kitchen. She was standing over the sink drinking vodka straight from a bottle."

"I'm sorry."

"I told her I was leaving, and all she said was that I should find a ride home."

"My mom can probably give you a ride."

"I know. I'm not worried about that. It's just—" She stopped. "I don't know."

"You can say it."

"We're fourteen years old."

Josh waited for more, but Chloe had gone silent. "We're fourteen *and?*"

"And we're already skeptical."

"Oh…yeah, I guess."

"Our parents did that. Did that to us."

Josh had never considered this. "I'm skeptical of them, but not of myself. And not of us."

"Josh, we're already ruined."

He grabbed Chloe's hand and felt the same flare as before. They were quiet and stared up at the sky. Everything was still now, not even a breeze stirred in the dunes.

Someone ran by them, up and down the dune nearby. "I spy with my little eye," a voice said. Josh sat up, sand falling out of his long hair. He was still holding Chloe's hand. Although it was dark, he could make out the face of a shrimpy guy the age of his little sister. "Hey, Stewart," Josh said.

Chloe sat up now too. "Get the fuck out of here."

Stewart looked hurt. "I'm telling Pastor Ben you're here and that you used the f-word."

"If you tell anyone where we are," Chloe said, "I swear to god, I'll beat the shit out of you."

Stewart shook his head and ran off over the dunes, his legs skinny as croquet mallets.

Chloe and Josh lay back on the sand. Her fingers danced over his. Each time her pinky wrapped around his, he felt the need to stifle a laugh. As they gazed up at the stars wheeling across the heavens, Josh wished he had some command of astronomy and could impress Chloe by pointing out the constellations. They both felt the weight that had settled between them.

A whistle blew loud and sharp from the other end of the dunes. "That's the end of the game," Josh said. "Wanna go back?"

Chloe laughed. "No. I hate this part. The come-to-Jesus part."

Josh still found himself riding the fence, hating church and yet fearing to repudiate it. "Yeah."

"How Capture the Flag leads to people feeling their souls are vile and in need of salvation I'll never understand."

Josh considered this for a second, and it made sense. He thought of Whitman, saying, "And nothing, not God, is greater to one than one's self is." But mostly he was not ready to let go of Chloe's hand.

They could hear everyone congregating on the beach beyond the dunes. Pastor Ben had a bullhorn, and it was hard to ignore his calls to repent.

Josh tried to tune it out, to focus on how good it felt to lay here with Chloe staring up into the sky. At one point he heard Ben shout, "Hallelujah," apparently ushering another one of the damned into the camp of the saved. But Josh imagined the "Hallelujah" to be a proclamation for him and Chloe, some stirring toward revelation.

"Your dad's an asshole," he said.

"He is. No doubt about that."

"Do you really think we're already ruined?"

"I don't think it. I know it."

"But why?"

"You only ask that question because you're less ruined than I am."

Josh sat up. He gestured to her and then back to himself.

"But we have this. This is our place. Right now. Hurricane Hugo destroyed this whole area, but look at us. We're lying here and having a special moment."

"A special moment? You sound like a fucking Hallmark movie?"

"It's not…" he began, but faltered to find the point he wanted to make. "We could be like explorers. Pretend no one has ever been here. Pretend that our parents aren't fucked up, haven't fucked us up. We're here on this spot that was carved out by the hurricane. Maybe no one has ever been here, exactly here. The hurricane created this just for us. We're on new ground."

Chloe eyed him skeptically. "That's not true. You know that, right?"

"But let's pretend right now that it is."

"Well, what will you call this new land?"

Josh heard an "Amen" from the bullhorn. He cringed, thinking of those sad souls. "I don't know. What do you want to call it?"

Chloe thought for a second. "Shit, I don't know. Let's call it The Hideaway."

"Perfect," Josh said and lay back, squeezing her hand.

The next fall another hurricane would barrel through the area, destroying much of Pawleys Island as it pressed its way into the state. The Hideaway would be lifted from the south end of the island, its sands taken far inland and far out to sea, parts of it ending up in many places, none of which Chloe and Josh would ever inhabit together.

NINTH GRADE

46

BROWN MULLET

Shortly after the start of ninth grade, Josh and Ryan went surfing after school on a Friday. It was late in the afternoon, and they were next to the pier, bobbing on their boards, the sun setting behind them as they looked east in the hope of a wave that would never come. The water appeared gilded as the sun went down and spread the last of its rays over the surface.

"God, the waves suck today," Ryan said.

"Yep. They usually do."

"I've gotta shit." Ryan paddled twenty feet away from Josh. He then hopped off his board and treaded water next to it as he worked down his bathing suit.

A few seconds later, Josh heard him yell, "Brown mullet."

Josh saw a turd float by in the sea-drift. "Goddammit, man," he said. "You know the rule. Go down current to shit."

Ryan paddled back and sat his board like it was an anxious pony. He was soaking wet now and his red hair looked dark brown. He sported the same bowl cut he'd had since first grade; he shook it partially dry. "No," he said. "The rule is you yell, 'Brown mullet,' to warn those down current that a turd is coming their way."

Josh shook his head.

Ryan said, "Don't give me that look."

"What look?"

"That I'm-sad-so-don't-mess-with-me look."

"Fine. Whatever."

"Also, don't 'whatever' me. You sound like my sister."

Josh sat silently, putting both hands up to his face to shield them from the dying sunlight. He looked out over the water like a pilgrim seeking fresh green land.

"So you're not going to talk to me about it?" Ryan asked.

"There's nothing to talk about. I've already told you that."

"And yet you just continue sitting there like you're ready to take a knife to your wrists."

"Fuck you, Ryan."

"Fuck me? Fuck me? You lost her, Josh. *You* did. Not me. Not because of me. Blame Tommy; blame her. I didn't do shit."

"You did plenty. You were there. Tommy is your brother's best friend."

"So I'm to blame because you got dumped? Because my brother and her brother and Tommy are at my house all the goddamn time?"

"You introduced them."

"They were all there. We were all there. Hell, she was there because she thought you were going to be there. And doesn't Tommy live at her house now. It would have happened at some point."

"That was way later. Every story has a starting point. And you were it." Josh slapped the water next to his board and splashed Ryan.

"You need to level out, fuckhead."

"Chode."

"Don't call me a chode, pencil dick."

Out of the corner of his eye, Josh saw a jellyfish float by in the water.

Ryan continued, "You've got to take responsibility for your own shit. You've been a mopey piss-ass for weeks."

Josh grabbed the jellyfish from the water, careful to grip its translucent skull-like orb and avoid the tentacles. He hurled the jellyfish at Ryan. It splashed in the water next to his board. Ryan grabbed it and duck-paddled his legs closer to Josh. He swung the jellyfish and swiped Josh across the face with it. The tentacles burned red slashes across his cheek just below his eye.

Josh continued to sit on his board stoically, never turning to see Ryan as he paddled to shore. After the sun had set and he could no longer see the coming waves in the expanse of black, Josh too paddled in. Stalking the beach back to the boardwalk, Josh thought himself entirely isolated from the clank of the world. But ahead in the gathering darkness, he saw the figure of a young woman. In sharp relief against the westering sun, she was dancing, throwing svelte legs to the wind, arms akimbo. She twirled, tattooing small circles in the tight sand.

Josh approached slowly, watching her routine, thinking that he had never seen anyone so uninhibited, so unconcerned with the world, as she performed this twilight ballet.

He paused a few feet from her, marveling as she continued to twirl. Then mid kick, she stopped, seeing his silhouette against the lights of the pier that were just beginning to twinkle on behind him. Josh raised a hand in a sort of salute and salutation. She turned and ran to the boardwalk, leaving him there on the beach, his arm still in the air. He imagined himself forever being a maggot-minded lover of women, whom women would love to leave.

47

SOUTH TOWARD HOME

This morning, like most, Pastor Ben was set to meet a member of his flock for a prayer meeting. He parked in the lot closest to the Pawleys Island Pier, removed the long board from the rack on top of his car, and walked with it onto the beach. He placed his board in the sand and looked out over the ocean. The day was cool, although it was early September. A light breeze was blowing, and Ben, who was wearing board shorts and no shirt, stiffened against the cold. The beach was deserted except for the seagulls that flew overhead and cawed frantically at the sun as it rose over the sea.

Ben surveyed the waves. There was a small swell, and the sea was glassy despite the wind. A hundred yards down the beach the pier jutted out into the ocean, five stories tall and stretching far over the water. Even the fishermen were not yet out.

With his eyes squinted against the rising sun, Ben followed a wave that peeled off the pier, barreling for a few seconds before crumbling, white and foamy, into the shallow surf.

"Hello, Ben," someone behind him said softly.

Fixed as he had been in this ocean reverie, Ben was surprised to see Peter standing so close behind him. Peter was a full head shorter than Ben, but he had fifty pounds on him; he had the body of box turtle, stout, rectangular, and powerful. Peter was wearing board shorts and a baggy white T-shirt.

Ben reached out his hand and the two men shook. "I didn't even hear you there."

"The sound of the surf, it blocks all else out."

"Precisely," Ben said. "That's one of the reasons that I like to have prayer meetings here. I do my best thinking on the water."

"Well, you'll soon see that I'm not much of a surfer."

"No matter. We'll bob and chat."

"All right then. I'll grab my board."

Ben nodded and watched Peter take a surfboard from the bed of a blue truck and tuck his car keys up under the wheel well. He then took off his shirt and tossed it in the bed. Ben was surprised at how hairy Peter was. His entire chest and upper back were covered with hair so thick and dark he still seemed to be wearing a shirt.

The two men walked down the beach. Neither said a word until they reached the pier. Ben nodded toward the waves on the north side. "It's best here. Probably the best break on the island."

The water was bracing when they walked out. "Good Lord," Peter said as it reached his waist. He smiled at Ben uneasily.

"I recommend plunging in as quickly as possible." Ben pushed his board forward in the surf and dove into the water. He surfaced and was once again perpendicular with the board. "Try it," he said, looking back at Peter. Ben sucked on his wet moustache.

Peter pushed his board forward between waves and dove into the water. When he came up, he was flushed. "Refreshing," he said, trying to keep his teeth from chattering. Ben laughed, and the two lay on their boards and paddled out past the break line. There they sat their boards like cowboys on horses and looked out over the water. The ocean stretched like a bulging belly given shape by the belt of the equator.

"Beautiful," Ben whispered. "It's so beautiful here."

"It really is."

Ben bowed his head. "Thank you, Jesus, for giving us this place to live. We are grateful to have nature as a restorative force, as a corrective to the stresses and worries of our culture."

Peter had not bowed his head. He watched Ben who continued to move his lips in silent prayer. After a few moments, Ben said, "Amen," and lifted his head.

The two were quiet, until Peter said, "You seem different here. More serene. Less fire and brimstone."

Ben laughed. "There's a time and a place for that."

"It's not really my speed."

"I guess I feel like I have to be dramatic sometimes to turn people away from sin."

"Well, I don't go in for all that sanctimonious prayermongering. I like you better like this."

"So what brings you here today? Why did you ask to meet?"

"My wife, Kim. She wanted me to talk with you."

"Ah," Ben said. "Sometimes I think my own wife knows me better than I know myself." He glanced over the water and continued, "So you don't actually want to be here?"

"To be honest, no. I don't want to be here. I don't see the point."

"All right, what does she think the issue is?"

"Look, I don't want to beat around the bush. I came here because I respect my wife. I figure I at least owe her this."

"And the issue is?"

Peter looked him in the eyes. "I suspect you have some idea."

"No. I don't."

"I'm gay, Ben."

Ben appeared bewildered for a second, until he could regain his composure. "This is normal," he stammered. "Just because you have certain thoughts on—"

"No, Ben, I'm gay. I've always known. I think even Kim has always known. The lie has gotten to be too much to bear."

"There are things that can be done. Special seminars designed to combat these desires."

"Ben, this is me. There is no changing what we are."

Ben looked nervous. He sucked at his moustache and stared out toward the horizon. "Can I pray?"

"You can do whatever you want."

"Lord, I pray for Peter, that he can learn in time to dismiss that which defiles him, body or soul."

"I'm leaving if you're incapable of having an honest conversation."

"We can pray about this. We can change."

"Ben, I see you. I know you."

Peter lay down on his board and paddled in to shore. Ben bobbed alone and looked out over the horizon. Something told him to pray, but he couldn't. His mind had gone blank. It had become a sort of free-ranging eyeball, and it was following Peter as he paddled shoreward. Soon the eyeball saw Peter, leaning against one of the pilings of the pier and looking at him.

Out of the calm, glassy sea, a large wave arose. Ben lay on the board and paddled with the wave's momentum. It overtook him and cupped him like a loving hand. Ben stood up and rode the wave all the way to shore.

When Ben looked up at him from the surf, Peter was still leaning against the pier. He was smiling and gave Ben a little clap. "Best wave of the day."

Ben and Peter abandoned their boards in the sand near the surf. They walked under the pier, away from the sea. Where the pier met the sand dunes, there was a sort of dark room hidden from view of the beach. The wood of the pier came together there like the rafters of a cathedral.

The maws of waves beat against the pilings below them; their roar, like distant lions, deafened Ben and Peter to all but the chirping dalliance of sea birds. Ben shifted his mind, focusing on the flesh before him. Hidden beneath the pier, they kissed. Ben tasted the salt that had crusted on Peter's lips; it burned his tongue like holy fire.

Peter's bathing suit dropped to the sand. All feather-legged, Ben's need to pray and prattle stemmed. He moved south down the man's body toward a place that felt like home.

Later they lay under the pier side by side, the breeze drying their bodies. Ben dozed, waking only to find Peter licking the salt crusted between his rib bones. It was then that some sort of beast lurched in his mind, beginning to come into hideous focus. But Ben knew now that this beast was him and was no beast at all. He realized the work of priests was done.

48

Mosquito Bites

"Hey, sugar," Rosie said as Josh walked into the Fish Hut. She and the other waitresses loved when Josh was there. Desperate to buy a car now that he had started high school, Josh worked harder than any of the other bussers. The interior of the Fish Hut was dark as he came in from the bright afternoon sun. Because she was the manager, Rosie was the only person in the restaurant at this time of day, between late lunch and early dinner. As usual, all the other employees were late.

"Hey, Rosie," Josh said. "How's it going?"

Rosie grinned at him. "I'm hung as hell."

"Late night last night?"

"Left here around midnight and went home. But my husband is off on a three-day toot. So I drank twelve beers and smoked a pack of cigarettes. Woke up on the living room floor about hour ago." It was four o'clock.

Josh shook his head. He'd been hearing about Rosie's husband's misadventures for a long time. Last summer he had gotten drunk and fallen out of a boat while flounder gigging. He tore his back to shreds on an oyster bed; after the doctor fixed him up, Rosie said the black stitches made his back look like an Appalachian mountainscape.

As he did most days, Josh glanced at the schedule on the wall behind the bar to see who he'd be working with that night. How well his shift would go and how much money he would make was entirely dependent upon who else was working. He and his fellow bussers got a cut of the waitresses' tips. The calculation for determining this percentage was mysterious and changed from night to night.

Josh examined the schedule: Kelsey, Ava, and Kelly were waiting tables, and under "Bussers" he saw his own name and then Chloe. "What the fuck?" he said.

Rosie looked over at him from the other side of the bar where she was slicing lemons. "New busser," she said.

"And her name's Chloe?"

"Yeah, and she's cuter than a basket full of puppies." Rosie gave a high-pitched wolf whistle.

Josh walked to the bar and leaned over it, as if giving himself the Heimlich. "What's her last name?"

"You okay?"

"What's her name, Rosie?"

Rosie reached her hand across the bar and settled it on Josh's forehead. "What's got you all hot and bothered, sugar?" Josh unleaned himself from the bar and asked the question again with only his eyes. "I don't know her last name, Josh. You think you know her?"

"Well," he said, "I know a Chloe."

"Know in a good way or a bad way?"

Josh thought about this for a second. He'd never considered his relationship with Chloe in such black and white terms. "I guess," he said, "it started good and then turned bad."

Rosie crossed her arms. "Isn't that the story of all relationships?"

"I guess."

"Cheer up, sugar," Rosie said. "You're too young to be this beat up by the world."

Josh nodded and began setting up for dinner service. He filled salt and pepper shakers, checked on ketchup bottles, swept the floor where the lunch staff had left French fries and shrimp tails all over the place. A few minutes later the rest of the crew began to trickle in: Kelsey who was always angry because she had a baby at home and her husband had abandoned her; Ava who was saving up for a stained-glass studio; and Kelly, a nurse who only waited tables on Friday and Saturday nights for "pocket money," which Josh was convinced meant cocaine money.

Chloe came in last, tall, gangly, and sun-freckled with her black hair pulled up in a messy bun. She looked older somehow, and her suntan made her appear almost Mediterranean. Chloe squinted in the dark interior of the restaurant. Josh saw her from behind the wait station where he was filling up a basin with ice. He hurried from her field of vision.

Moments later Josh was in the back of the restaurant scooping a five-gallon bucket into the belly of a wheezing ice machine, when Chloe walked up and stopped just behind him.

"I should have told you," she said.

Josh laughed, shaking his head, and continued filling the bucket.

"It's just that my mom knows the owner," Chloe said. "And my dad's gone, you know, so we need the money."

"It's fine," he said, hefting the bucket and heading back to the front of the restaurant.

It didn't take long for word to circulate that Josh and Chloe had dated and recently broken up. Knowledge of this spread through the women who worked in the front of the house and then to the women who worked in the kitchen. Just before service began, Joyce, a woman with long gray dreadlocks who had cooked at the Fish Hut for twenty-five years, motioned to Josh. Poking his head through a small cutout in the wall used to pass food from the kitchen to the dining room, Josh looked at Joyce. She smiled sympathetically. "Love's the shit for everybody sometimes." She reached through the window and patted him on the shoulder. "Chin up, sweetie."

"Thanks," Josh said. He turned back to the dining room and walked to the wait station. Kelly was standing there. Like everyone, she was wearing a T-shirt with the restaurant's logo on it. She had bleached blond hair and had knotted her shirt so that her belly button was visible, a small pierced jewel perched atop it. Kelly got more tips than any of the other waitresses, and they all hated her for it.

Kelly grinned at Josh. "That Chloe's a cutey," she said. "I can see it." She winked at him.

"See what?" he asked.

Just then Chloe walked up. Kelly smiled at her too. "So what happened between y'all?"

Josh squirmed, looking down at his feet. Chloe stood up straighter and stared at Kelly. "That's none of your business," she said.

Kelly popped a piece of gum in her mouth. "Okay. Not intending any offense. I'm just saying that Josh here is getting to be a looker. So tall and dark. He's shot up like a bean since the first time I met him. And I love that long hair." Kelly put her hand on Josh's shoulder and let it linger there. "So tall," she said again. "Makes one wonder." She flashed a quick look down at his crotch and then eyed Chloe, raising her brows in mock surprise.

"Wow," Chloe said. "That's sexual harassment. You could probably be fired for that."

Kelly smirked at Chloe and said, "It's impossible to sexually harass a man."

"Of course, you can," Chloe replied.

"Well, I don't give a shit. They usually love it, and if not, they deserve it. Women have taken it for long enough. Men these days can take whatever I dish out. And they can like it, or they can shut the fuck up about it."

"I hadn't thought about it in quite those terms."

"Think about it, sister."

That night the restaurant was busy enough that Josh didn't have time to worry about Chloe. After the last of the tourists had teetered away into the night, Josh and Chloe carried the heavy rubber mats from the bar and wait station outside. There they laid them out on a concrete landing behind the restaurant. Josh showed Chloe how to fill a mop bucket with soap and hot water, and how to use a wire brush to scrub the mats.

Chloe grabbed the brush and began to move it gently over a mat. Josh shook his head. "You're not even cleaning it."

"Well, how do you do it then?"

"You just scrub it. There's no fucking secret. Just get it clean."

"Are you mad at me?"

"No," Josh said, taking the brush from her and scrubbing the mat violently.

"Do you not want me to work here? I know it's a bit weird, but we haven't seen each other in a while. I thought it would be okay."

"I don't care," Josh said, still scrubbing. Sweat was beading off his forehead and trickling down his temples. His long hair was becoming wet, and he wished he had a rubber band to hold it back from his face. "We're not dating, so do whatever you want."

Just inside the door, the telephone rang. After a few rings, Rosie answered it; she tucked the phone between her shoulder and face, as she had a cigarette in one hand and a Miller Lite in the other. She listened but soon hung up. The phone immediately began ringing again. She answered, and after a few seconds, she came out to where Chloe and Josh were cleaning the mats.

"A guy's on the line," Rosie said, "who's asking for someone named Mosquito Bites. I thought it was a prank, but he keeps insisting."

Chloe exhaled. "It's for me." She left, following Rosie inside, and was back within a minute.

"Friend of yours?" Josh asked. Chloe looked uncomfortable, but Josh wouldn't let the issue drop. "Are you Mosquito Bites?"

"It was Tommy. He's my brother's friend."

"I know who he is. He used to tie tree frogs to bottle rockets. My sister told me all about it." Josh paused for a second. "You're still hanging out with that guy?"

"He lives with us," Chloe said. "His dad beat the shit out of

his mom, so she left. Then his dad got a job working construction somewhere in North Carolina, so he left too."

"And he calls you Mosquito Bites?"

"Whatever."

"Why? Tell me."

"Because my boobs are so small, okay?"

"What?"

"Anyway, I don't even take off my shirt when we—"

Josh bent over like someone had gut-punched him. "You're
having sex with that guy?"

Chloe stared at the rubber mats on the ground between
them. "Keep your voice down."

He stood up straight and said, "That guy is such an asshole.
I can't believe you would sleep with him." He lowered his voice
now. "I mean, we never even had sex."

"Whose fault was that, Josh?"

He turned red and started walking back into the restaurant,
but Chloe stepped forward and grabbed his shoulder. "Josh.
Wait, please."

Lingering, he picked up a hose and sprayed suds from the
rubber mats. His eyes were lowered. "I chickened out, all right.
That night, I mean. What else can I say?"

"Then I freaked the fuck out," she said. "I'm not even sure
why. I thought you didn't find me attractive or something. We
never talked about it. Afterward." Josh could think of nothing to say, and he pretended to concentrate on the hose. Chloe
continued, "Plus, you were still going to church. That stuff is
lodged in your brain. It's like a disease you can't ever fully get
rid of."

"You think that's what came between us?"

"I know it. You can't live with a foot in each world. Either
go with the fanatics and be a fanatic, or join the rest of us in
the real world. It's sad and hopeless out here, but at least we're
not slaves to fantasy."

"But still," Josh said, "why be with Tommy? He may be real
in that sense, but he's also a genuine asshole."

"He was just there, I guess."

"So you just let him use you like that?"

Chloe slapped the hose from his hand. "Let's get one thing straight, Josh."

"Fine."

"I use him. No one uses me."

49

DICKS OF GRASS

Spregg had to deal not only with the fact that his father had recently been in jail, but also that he loved snakes more than Spregg. And poisonous snakes at that. One of Spregg's first memories was visiting his father in Florida when he was four. His father had asked nothing about his hot-blooded son; rather, he said, "Seen any good snakes this year?"

Other than snakes, Spregg's father loved practical jokes. For most of Spregg's childhood, he had believed that the neighborhood ice cream truck only played music when it was out of ice cream.

His father was missing half of his left index finger, an old injury he'd gotten from a copperhead bite as a child. Whenever he came around, his father would do that trick that dads do when they pretend to pull off their own fingers; except in the case of Spregg's father, he would pull off a prosthetic finger and Spregg would be left looking at a raw red-tipped nubbin. When Spregg became old enough to realize it was a prosthetic, his father would lie to him about how he lost it. Something or someone usually bit it off: a rabid dog, a shark, a prostitute in Tijuana.

Now that Spregg's father was out of jail and traveling around the South again doing his Okefenokee Job routine, Spregg was anxious that he might come and visit. Spregg felt no need to impress his mother, though he loved her far more than he ever could his father. He had a recurring dream that his father was a hermit crab, and this dream, as well as everything else, made him want to keep his distance. And yet he also wanted to make his father laugh, to share with him a lark he would appreciate.

In the fall of ninth grade, Spregg figured out what this prank would be. He had filched a can of orange spray paint from the local hardware store and had pilfered Roundup from the maintenance shed at a nearby golf course. Then one Saturday night at nearly midnight, he put two gallons of Roundup at a time in his backpack, shouldered it, and rode his bike to the football field behind the high school. Spregg made six trips.

Standing at the center of the field, Spregg turned on a headlamp. This illuminated the grass before him, and he worked quickly to avoid getting caught. Within five minutes, Spregg finished spray painting and turned out the headlamp. He walked up to the top of the bleachers overlooking the field. From there he beheld his work. Even now in this dim, moon-dappled light, one could clearly see an orange penis as large as a blue whale's at centerfield. "Eureka," Spregg whispered, thinking of his father.

He then left the bleachers and set to dousing the grass inside the orange outline of the penis with all twelve gallons of Roundup.

The next day in school, news of the orange whale dick on the football field spread. During first period, students tittered and giggled about it, and in the break between first and second periods, several students, including Josh and Ryan, snuck out to the field. The fence surrounding the field was locked, so they climbed the hill outside the south end zone. This hill was known as Hand Job Knob. From that vantage point they could see the full painted penis on the grass. "Spregg," Josh said.

"Fucking Spregg," Ryan agreed.

In second period, Spregg was lavished with attention. "Just wait," he kept telling everyone.

With the torrential rains that fall, the orange penis soon faded and everyone forgot the prank. Spregg still bit his tongue, saying nothing. In the coming days, though, the penis reappeared on the field, the enormous shaft and balls emerging as the grass died. Talk rekindled, and Spregg was once again a hero. The school principal, Dr. Hughes, got wind that it was Spregg but could never pin it on him.

Spregg's father had come back to town and told Dr. Hughes that Spregg had been with him the weekend the penis appeared. He said they'd been searching for snakes out on the Black River.

A week later Friday night's football game was played atop this khaki cock, and the day following that the local paper ran a story about it; the paper even featured a picture on the front page showing the opening coin toss, the two teams' captains facing off on the wide shaft. Several state papers picked up the story.

Dr. Hughes ordered the school groundskeeper to dig up the dead grass and reseed it. By the time the next home game came around, a bright green, grassy penis had filled in the shape of the old brown dead one. A TV crew from a news station out of Myrtle Beach came and filmed the game. All those boys capering about on this leviathan-sized penis apparently made the people of Myrtle Beach feel better about the fact that they had to live in Myrtle Beach.

Thus Spregg became a legend and was thereafter spoken about in the school's hallways with reverential voices. In the yearbook at the end of the year, he would be voted *Most Likely to Be the Next Carrot Top*.

50

POWDERPUFF

Josh had always envied them the freedom that seemed to come with womanhood. He and his sister Jennifer had fought once, nearly coming to blows, when she found him in her room wearing her jelly bracelets and shoes.

Today, though, was the annual Powderpuff, when the high school boys dressed up like cheerleaders and the girls like football players. It was the one day of the year when the repressed people of Pawleys Island celebrated that which scared them, without scrutiny, without scorn, when a more complex knit of identity could be sung.

Josh was in the locker room. He put on a short cheerleading skirt and was surprised by how well it fit. His hips were slender and his legs long. He pulled the top on over his head. It left his entire midsection exposed. Josh looked at himself in the mirror, considering whether he should give his legs and belly a quick shave. Jennifer had done his makeup at home; the mascara was dark and his lips ruby red. His hair was long enough that she was able to crimp it and give him a side ponytail. Josh squatted up and down before the mirror, doing what he imagined to be a good warm-up callisthenic. He worried about how much he liked the way he moved in the skirt. His mind seemed split in two. One side, so full of maggots, was a fright to behold. The other was thinking, *No one's gonna sing "U-G-L-Y, you ain't got no alibi" at this beautiful lady. Not today. No siree!*

Two older high school guys walked by and saw Josh standing before the mirror. "Looking good," one of them said. He was blond and muscular, and Josh recognized him from the football team. Josh was surprised he was not in costume, too, and, dressed as he was, Josh felt uncomfortable.

"Thanks," he managed.

The other guy, dark, short, and wide in the shoulders, snickered. "You need some tits, though." He punched the blond guy in the arm. "Let's go talk to the girls. You stay," he said to Josh. He nodded as they left him standing there before the mirror.

A few minutes later, when the guys returned, Josh was in a bathroom stall. They didn't see him, and before Josh could say anything to indicate he was there, he heard one of them say, "Where is that little sissy britches?"

"Don't know," the other replied. "Hey, do you think he's... you know?"

"I don't think so, but you never can tell these days. If not, he missed a good opportunity to be."

"My dad calls it having sugar in your blood."

"If that's the case, Josh is a bit sweet. He's a pretty good-looking girl, though."

Josh flushed the toilet and exited the stall. The guys looked surprised to see him there, but the blond just shrugged, and the short guy stepped up to Josh and handed him a white, lacy bra. "Try this."

Josh took the bra reluctantly, not sure if they were playing some sort of trick on him. He'd been concerned all week that Powderpuff would, as it had in years past, devolve into a game of Smear the Queer.

"Try it on," he said again. Josh had a hard time reading him, as he seemed both serious and overly enthusiastic. Josh went back into the stall, feeling suddenly modest. He put on the bra and then walked back out into the locker room with his shirt off.

"Hot," the short guy said and seemed to mean it.

"Yeah, but..." The blond ran a finger lightly over the bra. He went into the stall that Josh had just vacated, and when he came out, he was holding large wads of toilet paper. Without asking, the blond stuffed the toilet paper into Josh's bra. When he finished, Josh had roughly the proportions of Barbie.

"Hot," the short guy said again.

"Too cha-cha for words," the blond said. "Knock 'em dead out there."

In the center of the football field, there was an enormous green, grassy penis, nearly twenty yards in length. The wind blew into Pawleys Island from the south and with it the rotten egg smell of Georgetown's paper mill. Several people in the crowd fanned with their hands in front of their noises. The bleachers were fuller for Powderpuff than for any of the regular football games. Josh's parents were there alongside Ryan's parents and Spregg's mother, sitting together in the same row. They were all smiling, although Josh's parents looked worried and shifted in their seats uncomfortably.

Okefenokee Job was there too; he'd come to see Spregg's giant grassy penis, although he'd refused to pay the five-dollar admission fee, and now sat atop his truck, which he'd parked on Hand Job Knob beyond the south end zone. Georgi was there with his wife Anna. They held hands and cheered despite not having kids themselves in the game. Jaybird and Birthdaysuit were also in the bleachers. Jaybird winked at Josh. She had on a homemade T-shirt that said, WWWD, which Josh assumed meant, *What would Whitman do?*

Next to them were Pastor Ben and Peter. They met each other at the beach most mornings these days.

The surprising thing about Powderpuff, especially in a community such as this, was that the students took their roles seriously, the guys and girls alike. The two all-girl football teams had strategized for weeks, formulating plays well into the night following their afternoon practices. When they donned the shoulder pads and helmets today, they did so to wage war. Josh had seen them practicing, running drills over and over after school in their full gear. It was a marvelous sight, these broad-shouldered, bulbous-headed women. Josh had joined the cheerleading squad because he had wanted to feel that beautiful.

The all-boy cheerleading squad had also planned for the day, memorizing more than a dozen of the cheers the regular squad used during football and basketball season.

The overall academic focus of the high schoolers dropped significantly during the weeks leading up to Powderpuff, and grades slipped all around.

As Josh walked onto the field, the marching band began playing the school's fight song. The blast of the brass and roar of the drums seemed to somehow highlight the fact that the entire town had focused its attention on the verdant god-like penis on the field.

Along with Josh, Ryan and Spregg were also dressed as cheerleaders. With his long red wig and fair skin, Ryan looked a bit like Ginger from *Gilligan's Island*. Spregg, for some reason, had tried to dress like Cher, but his dark makeup was so smeared from sweating that he looked more like Robert Smith of The Cure.

Before the players took the field, the cheerleaders began their routine, launching into "Hot To Go." For Josh, the bra, the skirt, the ponytail, they all felt right. He left the herd and, slightly out front, did his best Axl Rose imitation, crab-walking side to side and shaking his pom-poms, as the cheerleaders all sang, "H-O-T-T-O-G-O."

"Shake it, baby," someone said from the bleachers.

"These girls are hot to go," the cheerleaders sang.

With abandon, Josh did the can-can, kicking his legs high in front of him. Everyone was laughing, and he turned and bent over, revealing his purple satin panties. He bent so low his side ponytail touched the ground. "Awhoop, hot to go. Awhoop, hot to go."

"Show us that good shit," someone else yelled.

"Whoop, whoop," the cheerleaders cried.

Josh stood up and turned back to the raucous crowd. He lifted his shirt to reveal his stuffed bra. The volume of cheering increased, and he strutted his stuff left to right, back to center. "Awhoop, hot to go. Awhoop, hot to go." Josh bounced his breasts one final time, and the cheers became frantic. Birthdaysuit and Jaybird jumped up in the bleachers and others followed, whooping and hollering and giving Josh a standing ovation.

For a brief moment, it seemed the people of Pawleys Island whooped their way out of a collective repression decades in the making.

℔

At halftime, Josh was flushed, and he exited the field. He was guzzling water beside the bleachers, when Chloe walked up to him, seemingly out of nowhere. "You make a better-looking girl than guy," she said. For a second, he barely recognized her. She had gotten a haircut, and it was short and spiky.

"Why, thank you, sweetheart," he began in his best Dolly Parton voice, southern and falsetto. "You're a doll. And I love your Sid Vicious hairdo." Chloe laughed and then just stood there, awkward and silent. The only thing he could think to say was, "It's been a while. You know you didn't have to quit working at the Fish Hut." He had dropped the Dolly voice and for some reason now wanted desperately to hurt her. "You and Tommy still a thing?"

Her face grew red, and Josh could tell that she was contemplating walking away. "Tommy and I are not a *thing*. Never were. I don't know how many fucking times I have to tell you that."

"Right. I got the letters you put in my locker."

"Anyway, I was wondering if you're going to that party out on the island tonight."

"Are you into me now just 'cause of these titties?" Josh did a little shimmy until she smiled.

"I sort of am," she said, her voice more earnest than he had expected.

"Does that mean we're a thing now?"

"You really are a fuckhead, you know that?"

"I know."

"If I didn't miss you so much, I'd tell you to go fuck yourself."

"So I'll see you at party?"

"I hope so."

The band concluded its last number and left the field. The other cheerleaders started to congregate again on the sideline, ready to pep the crowd up before the second half. "I need to go back out there," Josh said. As he turned, Chloe slapped him hard on the ass. Josh went so weak in the knees he had to put a hand on her shoulder to steady himself. She gave him a little push in the direction of the field.

"You better shake it for me, fuckhead," she said. "I'll be watching."

51

COLORED LIGHTS

The night of the Powderpuff was hideous with desire. The youth of Pawleys Island, most still virgins or at least partial virgins, were wild to canoodle. The house where the party was taking place was next to the pier on the oceanfront. With its long wooden pilings, the house perched on the edge of the sea like a blue heron.

Josh arrived alone on this mad naked summer night and walked into the house. People flooded every square foot, and music blared, different from one room to the next. He grabbed a red cup from a long table and pumped beer into it from a keg that sat in a trashcan full of ice in the kitchen. Josh took the beer down in a single gulp and felt right away like he was all lit up from the inside.

He refilled his cup and from the kitchen entered the living room. The lads and lassies whipped one another around on the dance floor. The music was so loud that Josh could not even name the song. It was loose and frantic, and everyone except him was fastened to someone else, pulsing to the beat. When the song ended, the room was immediately subdued. People turned left and right in search of another partner or another drink. The crowd parted and through an inlet in it he saw Chloe. She was dressed all in black, and the makeup around her eyes was like smeared charcoal. Her dark, short hair was soaked through with sweat and looked like a hobnail crown.

This night was the fag end of something Josh and Chloe had begun long ago.

Chloe's face, once contracted, seemed to open when she saw Josh, and she moved to him through the parted crowd. The music started back, a slow song. Josh took her hand in a way that seemed too formal. She pulled his right arm around her back, and he spread his left around her other side. As they danced, Josh moved his hands up and down her ribs. He played them like a xylophone and relished the hot sweat soaking through her shirt. Even despite the musk of so much young flesh in the room, Chloe smelled to him like Play Dough—sweet and salty and nearly edible.

Their parents used to exhort them, when dancing, to leave room for the Holy Ghost. There was no room now, though. The thinnest of spirits would have been ground out between their pressing torsos.

When the slow song ended, Josh and Chloe left the soiree and moved into the night, past where the party spilled into the yard and out toward the colored lights that shone from the pier. They stumbled onto the beach, holding hands and bracing one another as their feet caught on sea oats and driftwood. Two hawks have never been more wild, more free, descending in the air in a love-embrace.

Like all children of Pawleys Island, they were drawn to the ocean. Half of the babies around here had been conceived on one body of water or another.

Fully clothed, Josh and Chloe waded out into the surf, the waves crashing against their bodies. Chloe pointed down. All around them the water sparkled with bioluminescence like diminutive, fallen stars.

"So beautiful," she said.

"Beautiful," Josh whispered. He was looking at her, oblivious to the lights that shone up from the sea.

The sounds from the party floated across the beach. The music thumped, and the people whooped idiotically into the night. Josh thought of these people and this land; he hoped that they would know it and love it for a time before the sea rose and reclaimed it all.

Chloe left the water and scurried over the dunes like a ghost crab. Josh followed close behind her as if in glory. His body was aquiver, all love-flesh, and he indexed himself from top to toe.

She stopped in the dunes and they collided. She handed him a small plastic package and said, "Nobody's putting a trout in my well." His heart said, *Holy!*, but his head seethed with scores of maggots thrashing about.

Her hands were a flight of birds moving down the length of his body, fluttering just right. His knees nearly buckled but he steeled his nerves, concentrating on the action before him, exultant and lawless. She was a force discorrupting, and his body was electric and pure.

Chloe took off her shirt. Her torso was goose-pimpled and skinny, all sparkle and dash. Her belly button looked like a tiny black hole cut into the fabric of space. She giggled and removed her bra. Her small breasts made her look boyish and titillating. Staring at her there, splashed in moonshadows, Josh connected the freckles on her chest with her nipples, forming new constellations. He removed his shirt. They looked at one another for a moment before Chloe laid hers across the sand and pointed to it. Josh shucked off his jeans and then his satin panties. Seeing them, Chloe grinned and said, "Lie down."

The moon rose as she straddled him, her silver face bobbing up and down, in sharp relief, each time causing, from his perspective, a full eclipse.

Later they lay side by side in the sand, each moonblanched, their hearts still beating like mad. Of his own fond flesh, he grew fonder still, and of hers there were no words. Language was incapable of distilling this moment, to call it sin or celebration. His dreams were buoyed now by the maggots of his mind, joining hands and for the first time singing a hallelujah chorus.

52

ONWARD, PARADE

A span of youth complete.
The day ends, the runaway sun before the promenade.
The baton of the maestro ceases beating time.
The routine long danced, the one-two-three, one-two-three, rock-
step of the crowd slows to a halt.

Colored party lights twinkle out of the darkness from rented
rooms.
Glasses are filled to cheer and to forget lovers lost.

For now this phallic procession has ended, the boy must learn to
turn out the maggots of his mind,
To make for them no quarter.
He finds the land a tonic for a time, but his end the same as any
rough beast unhoused.
The words of the old graybeard itch at his ears, this boy, lover of
wickedness, lover of virtue.
Topsy-turvy marionette to the desire of his flesh, he must unlearn
his own ruin.

Tomorrow the marchers will lay the chuff of hands on the hips
of those before them,
The drum-taps will throb, the fifes a bravuras of birds sounding
off,
Jacks of all colors wild-flapping in the wind, and buntings high.

America cannot now be lost, for there will be holy scores moving

hand in hand in the wake of the old courage-teacher.
The frantic singing of the festival dervish will commence, and an
    air antique will fill the boy, pulsing his heart to chant anew.
And onwards they will tramp, another day to yawp ecstatic in the
    clanking, spanking crowd of the parade electric.